Berkley Prime Crime titles by Jenn McKinlay

Cupcake Bakery Mysteries

SPRINKLE WITH MURDER
BUTTERCREAM BUMP OFF
DEATH BY THE DOZEN
RED VELVET REVENGE
GOING, GOING, GANACHE
SUGAR AND ICED
DARK CHOCOLATE DEMISE

Library Lover's Mysteries

BOOKS CAN BE DECEIVING
DUE OR DIE
BOOK, LINE, AND SINKER
READ IT AND WEEP
ON BORROWED TIME
A LIKELY STORY

Hat Shop Mysteries

CLOCHE AND DAGGER
DEATH OF A MAD HATTER
AT THE DROP OF A HAT
COPY CAP MURDER

COPY
CAP
MURDER

Jenn McKinlay

BERKLEY PRIME CRIME, NEW YORK

**BERKLEY
PRIME
CRIME**

An imprint of Penguin Random House LLC
375 Hudson Street, New York, New York 10014

COPY CAP MURDER

A Berkley Prime Crime Book / published by arrangement with the author

ISBN: 978-0-425-27958-8

PUBLISHING HISTORY
Berkley Prime Crime mass-market edition / January 2016

PRINTED IN THE UNITED STATES OF AMERICA

10 9 8 7 6 5 4 3 2 1

Cover illustration by Robert Steele.
Interior text design by Laura K. Corless.

Penguin
Random
House

For my son, Beckett Orf.
With your quick wit and compassionate heart,
you are one of my very favorite people. I am so proud
of the fine man you are becoming and I look forward to
watching you pursue your own happiness as you
go forth in life. Love you forever.

Acknowledgments

Setting a mystery series in a London hat shop was such a leap of faith for me. I didn't know if I could write a book in a foreign setting, about a business of which I know nothing and in first person no less. I have come to love this series, and I am so tickled by all of the readers who have told me that they love it as well. Thank you all so much!

I want to thank my editor, Kate Seaver, for never doubting me and Katherine Pelz for keeping track of the details. Special kudos to the art department for the amazing watercolor covers that capture the setting so well.

I also want to raise a glass to my travel buddies Beckett and Wyatt Orf and Susan McKinlay for hiking all over London to help me with my research. Lastly, special thanks to the Hub, Chris Hansen Orf, for encouraging me to go wherever the stories take me. I love you all.

Chapter 1

There was a sneaky draft taunting me while I worked the front counter at Mim's Whims, the hat shop I co-own with my cousin Vivian Tremont. It slipped through the cracks of our old building and snuck up on me; sliding beneath the collar of my shirt with its cold fingers and making me shiver.

Well, two could play this game. I had stopped by the Tool Shop in Marylebone over by Regents Park and picked myself up a caulking gun and the junk you put in it. I felt like one of Charlie's Angels with my caulk gun on my hip, filling in any gap that allowed November to blow its wintery breath across my skin.

I had already filled four cracks when I felt another gust of chilly air. I pulled my caulk gun out of my tool belt and whirled around, ready to fire goop into the offending orifice.

"Blimey, don't shoot, Scarlett. I just had this suit pressed." The handsome man who entered the shop slowly raised his hands in the air as if this would make me less likely to blast him.

"Give me one good reason why I shouldn't," I said. I did not lower the gun; instead I squinted at Harrison Wentworth over the top of it as if I were adjusting my aim while I tried to ignore the ridiculous fluttery feeling that filled my chest at the sight of him.

"Rough day, Ginger?" he asked. His voice was kind when he used my nickname but his eyes were laughing at me and it looked like his lips weren't far behind as he pressed them together as if to keep the guffaws in.

"Yuck it up, Harry," I said. I liked to use his nickname, too, the one he'd gone by when we were kids. The one he didn't care for now. I holstered the caulk shooter. "You're not the one freezing to death in this drafty old building."

"It's Harrison," he corrected me. "And I think it's actually quite toasty in here."

He shrugged off his overcoat and draped it over his arm. "Maybe you should wear more layers."

I glanced down at my outfit. I had on a cashmere heather gray turtleneck, a black wool cardigan and a black corduroy miniskirt over thick gray tights paired with my favorite black riding boots.

"I'm pretty sure the only people wearing more clothes than me this early in November live in the polar regions," I said.

This time he did laugh. "Scarlett Parker, your Florida is showing."

"It is, isn't it?" I asked. "What I wouldn't give for a martini on the beach right now."

"I can't offer you that, but I can give you a mulled wine and a bonfire in Kensington," he said.

"No palm trees?" I asked.

"No, 'fraid not."

"No sand between my toes?"

"No."

"No bikini?"

"No, damn shame," he said.

"Actually, that's a high point," I said. "With this ghostly complexion I've got going I'd scare even the sharks away."

"I don't think anyone in their right mind would notice your complexion if you went trotting by them in a swimsuit," he said. The look he gave me scorched.

And that right there was the trouble with Harry. He gets me so flustered I can't even think. Yes, it could be his charming British accent or his wavy brown hair, his broad shoulders and his bright green eyes, but I think it was more than that. Honestly, I liked Harry for more than the swanky packaging. I liked him for himself.

I liked the way he was unfailingly polite to everyone from waiters to bus drivers to elderly ladies in the street. I loved the sound of his laugh and how he always seemed delighted to find himself laughing and it made him laugh even harder. I enjoyed the way he whistled when he made tea, even though he was not the most gifted person in the whistling arts. And I loved how gentle he was with the young children and pets we frequently ran into on walks in Hyde Park. Even his own particular scent, a manly bay rum sort of smell, had worked its way into my head and I found any man who didn't smell like Harry was lacking.

"Well, what do you say?" he asked.

"I don't know," I hesitated.

First, I needed to be clear that this was not a date. Yeah, I know he was the perfect male but that didn't mean I was ready to date. My mother, bless her heart, had convinced me to go one whole year without dating anyone at all. This may not sound significant but I had never gone more than two weeks between boyfriends before, so yeah, kind of a big deal.

Why did I agree to my mother's crazy suggestion? Good question. True story, funny story, okay, it isn't funny to me yet, but I've been assured that it will be someday. In a nut, my last boyfriend and I had a breakup of epic proportions, the kind that found a video of me, aka the party crasher, throwing fistfuls of wedding anniversary cake at him.

Yes, you read that right. My boyfriend was married, not to me, and I didn't take the news very well. It went viral on the Internet and I pretty much had to flee the state of Florida and, well, the continent of North America to save face. Talk about your walk of shame.

Needless to say when my cousin Viv sent me a one-way ticket to London encouraging me to take up my half of the millinery business we had inherited from our grandmother Mim, I was all in. It's been eight months now and it's almost begun to feel like home.

I love my cousin and our friends, dearly, but as the holiday season approached, and the cold air took up permanent residence in our abode, I was surprised to find I was feeling more homesick than I had expected. And I did not want to throw myself at Harrison in a weak moment of pitiful loneliness, so I needed to be very clear on the boundaries of his suggested mulled wine and bonfire.

"How does one dress for a bonfire?" I asked.

Yes, this was my pitiful attempt to get more information. Harry knew I wasn't dating and he'd said he was willing to wait, which I hadn't believed, but it had been months and as far as I knew he wasn't dating anyone else. Another point in his favor, unless this was his sly way of getting me to go on a date without actually asking me on a date; boys can be sneaky like that, you know.

"Bonfire?" Viv asked as she entered the store front from the workroom in back. "Who's dressing for a bonfire?"

"We all are," Harrison said. "My company is having a huge Guy Fawkes party and you're all invited."

"Me, too, yeah?" Fiona Felton, Viv's apprentice, asked as she followed Viv into the room.

"Absolutely," Harrison said.

Now I was irritated that it had not been a covert way to ask me out. I'm impossible to please, yes, I know.

"Who is Guy Fawkes?" I asked.

All three of them turned to look at me. This was another one of those moments where I just felt utterly, boorishly, ignorantly American.

"Ginger, really?" Harrison asked.

"Do you know who Bigfoot Wallace is?" I countered.

"Basketball player," he guessed.

"No." I laughed. "He's an American folk hero, so don't be judgy just because I don't know who Guy Fawkes is."

"Was," Fee said. She blew an orange corkscrew curl out of her eyes and smiled. "He failed to blow up Parliament in 1605."

"Oh, he does have Bigfoot Wallace beat then," I said. "Wallace was a Texas Ranger, one of the good guys actually."

"Guy Fawkes night is bonfire night," Viv said. She looked delighted as she looped her arm through mine. "You've never been here for bonfire night before, this will be so much fun."

For Viv alone I would freeze my tail feathers off and go to the bonfire. Things had been strained between us for the past several weeks. You see, Viv is the eccentric artist in our business while I am more the people person. She and Fee create amazing hats for people and I charm them into buying them. It's a system that works for us.

Unfortunately, Viv takes after our grandmother in more than just her creativity. She is impulsive, rash, scatterbrained, impetuous and reckless, especially when chasing down some crazy artistic whim or another. Most recently, she had leveled me with the news that she is married. Yes, married.

Shocking, right? It wouldn't be so bad but so far she has refused to give me any details. I don't know his name, where he's from, how they met, how long they've been married, or where he is right now. I badgered, cajoled, begged, pleaded, whined, stomped my feet and bellowed, but Viv could not be moved. She has refused to tell me absolutely anything about her husband. Not one darn thing. It has sort of festered between us like a hot boil because, yeah, we can be like that sometimes.

What's worse is the fact that Harry knew about her marriage and he never, not once, even hinted to me about it. I was still sore at him for that, which was another reason I had been keeping him at arm's length. I was still a bit miffed at him, even though he had assured me that he knew no particulars about the marriage, just that it had happened.

"Where's the party?" Viv asked.

"My boss's house in Kensington," Harrison said. "He's hoping to make a splash in the society pages."

"We can wear some hats from the shop," Fee said. "It'll be a nice opportunity to advertise our creations amongst Harrison's posh clients."

"I thought *we* were his posh clients," I teased.

"Well, there's certainly no one quite like you . . . three," Harrison said.

His gaze moved away from me to include the others and again I was charmed stupid by his ability to make me feel that I alone had his attention while I admired his sensitivity in including the others, who were actually much more attractive than me.

I glanced at Viv, with her long blond curls, big blue eyes and curvy figure; she was a woman who turned heads everywhere she went. And then Fee, with her West Indies heritage, boasted a lovely dark brown complexion and a model's figure, tall and thin, that she topped off with her amazing hair, which she wore in a curly bob that she liked to streak with unusual colors; currently it was orange. I'd seen men literally walk into walls when she passed by. Then there was me, medium height, average figure, too many freckles to count and shoulder-length auburn hair that was on the thin side. I most definitely got by on my personality.

Still, Harrison was right. We made a threesome that was hard to ignore, mostly because Viv made us wear her most outrageous hats whenever we went anywhere together. I wondered if that was why he had invited us.

"Aren't we a bit small scale to be invited to your boss's shindig?" I asked.

"Ginger, you're overthinking it," Harry said. "It's a bonfire with music, mulled wine and a view of the city's fireworks."

Both Fee and Viv nodded in agreement as if I was being silly for thinking that a bunch of milliners at an investment broker's party was weird. But they didn't see what I saw, which was that Harry wasn't meeting my eyes.

Perhaps because I hadn't dated him and gotten bored with him just yet, I spent an inordinate amount of time thinking about Harrison Wentworth and covertly studying the man who took up entirely too much of my head space. In any case, I knew him and I knew he was hiding something. I was sure of it. And now, no matter what crazy creation Viv wanted to slap onto my head, nothing could keep me from attending the party.

Chapter 2

"I refuse to wear that," I said to Viv. "There is nothing you can say or do that will change my mind."

"Oh, don't be difficult, Scarlett," Viv said. "You'll look adorable in it."

I frowned at the felt concoction she was holding out at me. It was a bright yellow cap like something a paperboy in the nineteen twenties would wear. It was lumpy on top and saggy at the back and the narrow brim would sit just over my eyes, destroying my visibility.

"I'll look like a flattened banana," I argued. "I'm not wearing it, unless . . ."

"Unless what?" Viv looked wary. Smart girl.

"Tell me about your husband," I said. "Name. Birthplace. Occupation. Anything."

"No." She blanched. "I can't."

"Why?" I asked. Yes, I was trying to give her time but every now and again I felt the need to poke the bear with the stick to see if I could get her to bite or at least offer up some details.

"It's too . . ." Her voice trailed off and she shook her head.

I stared at her. What was the big secret?

"Oh, my god, he lives with his mother, doesn't he?" I asked. "And you can't get him to leave her."

She looked as if she was going to let me believe that for just a moment and then her chin dropped to her chest in defeat. "I wish the problem was his mother."

"What do you mean?"

"Never mind, I'm not discussing this anymore." Viv looked at the hat and then at me. She had a very determined look in her eyes and I had a feeling she was transferring her conflicted feelings about her marriage to my head and a hat. "You have to wear a hat."

"Fine," I said. I realized it was time to put my stick down before the bear mauled me. "But not that one."

"Which would you prefer?" Viv asked.

"That one," I said. I pointed to the hat on her head.

"But . . ." Viv puffed out her lower lip.

I snatched the bright blue cashmere ribbed beanie off of her head and moved over to a mirror, where I could try it on. It was a perfect fit, very hip and cool without the nerd quotient of the hat she'd been trying to get me to wear. Plus, she had hand stitched seed pearls all over it, giving it a solid wow factor.

"This will do," I said.

"Oh, that looks terrific on you, Scarlett," Fee said. She

entered the shop from the workroom, wearing an adorable bright red bucket hat fashioned out of a quilted flannel material and trimmed with a wide black ribbon.

Viv twirled the yellow felted hat on her finger. "I really thought Scarlett would look adorable in this one."

Fee looked at the hat and then at Viv. It was clear to see she was struggling with what to say. I gave her the hairy eyeball to make sure she didn't gang up on me with Viv and try to force me into the hat. There are very few times that I don't love Viv's designs but this was one of them and I was not going to wear it.

"Fine, I'll wear it," Viv said. "But it's not nearly as eye-catching with my hair color as it would be with yours."

"Maybe," I said. I pointed to my head. "But this one looks amazing on me and I'm keeping it."

Viv opened her mouth to argue but the front door opened and in swaggered our neighbors Nick Carroll and Andre Eisel. They were a couple who owned a photography gallery/studio a few shops down Portobello Road from us. Although Nick was a dentist by day and his partner Andre was the photographer of their twosome, they ran the gallery together.

They lived above their shop just like we lived above ours, and the five of us had become fast friends after, well, after Andre and I had stumbled across a dead body together. What can I say, that sort of thing bonds people.

"Good evening, ladies," Nick said. He was using a walking stick with a silver knob at the top. By the way he was twirling it and admiring his reflection in the window glass, I got the feeling it was a new toy for him.

Andre was dressed all in black, as always, and looked

at his partner with amusement. As we exchanged greetings, Andre hugged me close and said, "I just don't have the heart to tell him it looks pretentious."

"Let's not," I agreed. "He looks so happy."

The doors opened again and this time it was Harrison arriving to escort us all to the party. Per usual, my treacherous insides clutched at the sight of him, a fact that was not missed by Andre.

"Why don't you just date the poor man already?" he asked.

"You know very well why," I said.

"Scarlett, you can't punish yourself just because your last boyfriend was a heartless git," Andre said.

"Quite right," Nick agreed as he joined us. "Did you ever get the tally of women the blighter cheated on his wife with?"

I made a face like I had a bad taste in my mouth. "I stopped counting at five."

"Five?" Harrison asked from behind me. "I can't even manage one girlfriend never mind five and a wife."

I glared at him. "Do not sound impressed. He is a horrible person."

"Agreed," Nick said. "But still, juggling six women is . . ."

"Morally reprehensible, socially repugnant, blatantly misogynistic and utterly unforgivable!" Viv snapped.

I patted Viv on the back. "Well said, cousin."

"Brilliant," Fee agreed.

"All right, now that's sorted," Harrison said. "Is everyone ready to go?"

Viv straightened the cap on her head. With her long

curly blond hair flowing out from under it, it really did look so much better on her than it would have on me. Yes, that's my story and I'm sticking to it.

We locked up Mim's Whims behind us and set out into the early evening. I love Portobello Road not just because I spent all of my school holidays here with Mim and Viv, although that is a lot of it, but I love that it has its own village sort of charm, where everyone knows everyone else and we all keep an eye out for each other.

The lower level of the buildings on our street are done in vibrant shades of red, blue and green while the upper resident stories are white or exposed brick. There is even a side street of buildings painted a glorious rainbow of pastel colors in a stubborn show of cheerfulness that I've always admired. Mim's Whims is white with a royal blue trim. I once suggested a color change but both Mim and Viv were horrified, probably because I was going through a hot pink phase at the time. Either way, I'm glad it has stayed white with a blue trim. It had been one of the constants in my life and now that Mim is gone, I can't imagine it any other way.

Another thing I love about Notting Hill is that travelers from all over the world come to the Saturday market, which stretches for over two miles. You can find anything from antique clocks and cameras to T-shirts with animal faces painted on them, there's even a booth with all things Beatles, and of course, we sell our hats.

Portobello Road has such a frantic friendly atmosphere that I really couldn't imagine living anywhere else in London. I traveled all over the world as a hospitality major, yes, I convinced myself it was research, and London is by far my favorite city.

Still, with the winter cold creeping in, I was longing for some beach time. As a redhead, I am the person with SPF 50 slathered on every bit of my exposed skin and I have a sun hat the width of my own personal beach umbrella, still, there is something about the feeling of powdery sand between my toes, the briny smell of the sea and the sound of the waves crashing on the shore that soothes me like nothing else. Or maybe I just wanted some space between me and the man who had come to dominate my thoughts.

"Nice lid, Ginger," Harrison said.

See? It's like just thinking about him conjured him to my side. He looked ridiculously attractive in his black suit jacket with a matching cashmere sweater underneath framing his crisp white dress shirt and dark gray silk tie with a fancy embroidered design. Truly, I needed to put three thousand miles of ocean between us for a bit for my own mental health.

He fell into step beside me and I noted that we had paired off on the narrow walkway with Harrison and I in the lead, Fee and Viv behind us and Nick and Andre bringing up the rear.

"Lid? Is that your attempt at American slang?" I asked.

"Yes, how did I do?" he asked.

"Not quite as bad as your Southern accent," I said. "If I remember right your 'y'all' still needs work."

He grinned and I glanced away. How could a man's smile make me dizzy? That had never happened to me before. I was pretty sure it was a bad thing. Maybe I was allergic to him.

"I'll keep working on it," he said.

"So tell me more about Guy Fawkes," I said. "Give me

the four-one-one on why it's still celebrated over four hundred years later."

"Honestly?" he asked. "I think it's because we like to burn things."

I glanced at him in surprise and he laughed.

"Just teasing, although . . ." His words trailed off and I thought maybe there was a kernel of truth to what he said. Bonfires are fun, after all.

"Let's see what I remember from my school days," he said. "From what I recall, in 1605, Guy Fawkes and his coconspirators planned to blow up the House of Lords using kegs of gunpowder hidden beneath the building. They failed. To celebrate King James I surviving the dastardly plot, people lit bonfires all over the city. It had much more political and religious overtones for the first two hundred and fifty years, but now it's more of a social event for bonfires and fireworks, although people do still like to burn a Guy Fawkes effigy."

"I can see where that would be therapeutic," I said. "Any chance we could make it look like my ex?"

"Still feel the need to burn him at the stake?" Harrison asked.

I sensed he was watching me closely while trying to appear not to be, and I realized my answer was important. I tried not to blow it, but I figured honesty was best.

"Not as much as I used to," I said.

Again, he grinned and I felt it all the way down to my toes.

"Well, I'd say that's good, no, great progress," he said.

We continued walking. Occasionally, his arm brushed

mine and I felt the urge to link my arm through his, but we weren't there yet and that was okay.

"What exactly is it that you do at Carson and Evers?" I asked.

"Money stuff," he said. "Basically, I make a lot of money for people by telling them what to buy and when to buy and conversely what to sell and when to sell it."

"Is that what you always wanted to do?" I asked. I found I was curious about what the boy I had once known had wanted out of life and if it mirrored what the man had become. So many people our age had settled into careers they loathed just for the money; I wondered if he was one of them.

Clearly, I was since I had always dreamed of managing a grand hotel with hundreds of staff but was now managing a hat shop with no staff except an intern, who really worked for my cousin.

"Uh, no, not exactly," he said with a self-deprecating laugh.

"Interesting," I said. I gave him a sidelong look, wondering if I could get him to confess. "Tell me, what would you be doing with your life if not 'money stuff'?"

"Ugh, this is embarrassing," he said. "I have to be clear that I think I landed exactly where I am supposed to be, but when I was younger, in my teens, I had thought I would be something much more daring like a spy."

"A spy?" I goggled at him. "Like 007? A womanizer?"

"With the babes but without the misogyny," he clarified. "Yes. In my defense, I was a teenager."

I laughed, enjoying his look of chagrin.

"What stopped you?" I asked.

"The family needed me to take up my uncle's clients, and I wasn't sure I was cut out for a life of espionage," he said. "I still love a good thriller, though."

"Me, too," I said. I grinned at him. I couldn't help it. Never in a million years would I have pegged Harry as a wannabe spy. I found it thoroughly charming.

"Oy, Harrison! Scarlett! You missed the turn, yeah?"

I glanced over my shoulder at our party, who were all clustered around Notting Hill Gate. Caught up in our conversation, we'd missed the entrance to the underground.

"Oh, sorry!" Harrison shouted back. He took my elbow and guided me back to our group.

"We were discussing the history of Guy Fawkes, fascinating stuff," I said. "My fault."

"No, it was me," Harrison said. "I was distracted."

"That's one word for it," Nick said and gave us a broad wink. "Come along, loves, we're off to the Boltons, second wealthiest street in all of London according to the *Daily Mail.*"

"Nick, how can you stand that rag?" Fee asked.

"Are you kidding?" he asked. "It's the highlight of my day. Now come along, I don't want to miss a moment of our time living like the other half or the upper tenth, more accurately."

He brandished his walking stick like a drum major's baton and led the way down the steps. As everyone fell in behind him, I glanced at Harrison and found him looking at me. It made me too aware of him, of us, of whatever was happening between us, so I did what I always do, I made a joke of it.

I forced a laugh and rolled my eyes and said, "I wonder

how far we would have walked before we realized we'd missed our gate."

Harrison reached between us and straightened my beanie although it didn't need it.

"I have a feeling, Ginger, that I could have walked all the way across Merry Old England with you by my side and never have realized we'd left the city."

The man charmed me stupid. There was no other explanation for why I suddenly couldn't remember how to make my legs move in an alternating motion that would propel me forward, you know, that thing called walking.

"Come on," he said and grabbed my hand. "We're going to miss the train."

I let the man lead me to the platform to meet our friends with the sneaky suspicion that I would pretty much let this guy drag me anywhere. Uh-oh.

Chapter 3

When we arrived at Harrison's boss's house, Nick's comment about the other half hit me like a frying pan upside the head.

Viv and I do pretty well in the hat shop. We're on one of the main tourist thoroughfares in London; Mim bought the building outright forty years ago, so we're not mortgaged up to our eyeballs. Viv is brilliant and has a lot of high-society clients, who are more than happy to pay four to eight hundred pounds for a hat. Yeah, chew on that conversion for a bit. So we're doing well, better than most, in fact, especially since Harrison is in charge of the money and is much more fiscally responsible than we are.

But there's doing well and then there's doing spec-freaking-tacular. As we stood on the sidewalk looking up at the glowing white monstrous colossus that loomed over us, I felt small, like ant under boot small. It occurred to me that the ant's perspective on things stinks.

Harrison led the way into the courtyard. It was festively decorated with twinkling lights and glass lanterns, which made the entire front of the house glow. Large dried corn-stalks stood on either side of the massive front door with pumpkins of all sizes scattered about. It reminded me of Thanksgiving in the States and I felt a sharp pang of homesickness.

Although I had most recently lived and worked in Florida, I had always traveled north to spend the holiday with my parents. They resided in New England, where my father was employed as a research scientist. I loved going back to enjoy the cold crisp air, the snuggly feeling of impending winter, and my mother's apple pie. I realized this would be the first Thanksgiving that I hadn't shared with them.

"All right, Scarlett?" Andre asked me.

"Yes, I'm fine," I said with a forced smile. Then the front door opened and my eyes went wide. "I'm just taking it all in."

"I know what you mean," he said. "I wish I'd brought my camera."

A stern-looking man in a crisp black suit, white shirt and narrow tie stood in the doorway. His face was impassive as he took in our party. Then his eyes lit on Harrison and he lowered his head in greeting.

"Good evening, Mr. Wentworth," the man said. "Please come in."

"Thank you, Price," Harrison said. "And how are you this evening?"

"Very well, sir," the man said. He stepped aside and Harrison led the way into the house. "I hope the evening finds you the same."

"It does," Harrison said.

"The party is in the back garden," Price said. "If you'll follow me."

"I feel like I'm in an episode of *Downton Abbey*, yeah?" Fee whispered.

"I call the part of the good-looking footman," Nick whispered in return.

I snorted. I couldn't help it. Viv giggled and Andre guffawed. Harrison looked back at us as if we were a pack of unruly children he'd discovered on his way here and hadn't been able to ditch us.

A golden chandelier hung over our heads, sparkling its jubilant light all over the foyer. I gawked. I can admit it. I was pretty sure the thing was made of real gold. Holy bananas!

We entered a great room that was bare except for several giant paintings that decorated the walls and a lone glass table in the center that upon second glance was probably a pricey sculpture of some sort. Andre froze. I slammed into his back with a very unladylike oomph.

"Andre, love, what are you staring at?" Nick asked.

"He's looking at the Rothko."

I turned at the sound of the voice and saw a woman stride into the room, watching Andre with a knowing look as if the two of them shared a secret.

I glanced back at the painting. My knowledge base of art is pretty rudimentary, but even I knew who Mark Rothko was, an abstract expressionist who came into popularity in postwar America with Jackson Pollack and William de Kooning. Of course, my first thought was to wonder whether the piece was an original and then I did a mental face palm. In this palatial estate of course it was an original, just like the chandelier was made of real gold.

"Ava, it's good to see you," Harrison said.

The woman was a tall, willowy blonde with pouty red lips and large eyes that were accentuated by an amazing amount of black eyeliner. She was dressed all in lavender cashmere with dark purple leather boots and a matching belt. The sparklers on her fingers were bigger than my knuckles and the perfume she wore was the sort of fragrance that is one of a kind, made especially for the person wearing it. I'd like to say it was tacky and noxious but no. It was a light scent that brought to mind fields of wildflowers and warm summer breezes.

"Harrison, it's been too long," she said. Her voice was a low-slung sultry growl as she enveloped him in a hug I found to be entirely too chummy, and I wondered at Harrison's relationship with her.

"It has," he said. "But you look as if time stands still around you. You never change a bit."

The way Ava preened under the compliment I gathered that vanity was her weakness.

"Be sure to tell Tyler that," she said. "I don't think my husband appreciates me nearly as much as he should."

Ah, she was the boss's wife. I felt myself stand down.

"It will be the very first thing I say to him tonight," Harrison said.

"Be sure that you do." Ava slipped her arm through Harrison's and turned to study us. "Are these your friends?"

"Yes, friends and clients," Harrison said. He introduced each of us by name. "This is Ava Carson, our hostess for the evening."

She looked at each of us in turn as if trying to memorize our faces. Then she clapped her hands together in a gesture that reminded me more of a little girl than a grown woman.

"How lovely it must be to have friends," she said. She looked at me. "You're from the States. My father loves your country-western music. He fancies himself quite the singer."

Her gaze seemed to go fuzzy as if her mind had just wandered off leaving no forwarding address.

"Awkward," Nick whispered in my ear. Andre gave him a quelling look and approached Ava with his usual Andre Eisel charm.

"Tell me, Mrs. Carson, is the Rothko your favorite?"

She stared at Andre for a moment and then her eyes cleared and she smiled. "Yes, it is. How did you guess?"

"Because it is as breathtaking as you are," he said and flashed a smile at her. She beamed. "Also, it's the first thing you see when you walk into the room and I assumed you hung it there to give it preferential treatment."

Fee made a bit of a gagging sound behind me but Ava looked entranced.

"Quite right, Mr. Eisel," she said. "How very clever you are."

"Please call me Andre," he said. Oh, he was a charmer, our Andre. With his sculpted physique, dark complexion and close-shaved head, he could have been in front of the camera instead of behind it, and very few people, men or women, were immune to his flattery.

"Ava," she returned. "Are you an artist, Andre?"

23

"I dabble." Andre ran a hand over his smoothly shaved head as if he were embarrassed. His diamond earring winked in the light as he looked down to study his shoes.

"Oh, dear, I'd best rein him in. He just doesn't understand the effect he has on people, it's like a superpower," Nick said to me. He stepped forward and spoke to Ava, "He is a brilliant photographer. Don't let his modesty fool you."

Ava smiled at the couple. "I like you two. Come with me, I'll give you an art tour of the house."

Andre looked as if he'd hit the lottery while Nick gave us a tiny finger wave as they disappeared behind Ava.

"She seems nice," Viv said.

Harrison sent a rueful glance in the direction the three of them had taken. "Sometimes."

He and Price shared a glance that was rich with understanding, and I got the feeling there was more to Ava Carson than I had just seen. I also got the feeling that both Price and Harrison were very relieved that she was nice at the moment, which I found interesting.

Price led us down a long corridor that opened up into several great rooms on each side and ended in a gorgeous solarium. Stone statuary, plants and several water features filled the glassed-in space, which had the rich smell of earth and the spicy musky scent of things growing.

Several groups of people were scattered among the labyrinth of plants and trees, sitting on stone benches or on groupings of padded iron furniture. Three sets of French doors were wide open on the far end of the sunroom and Price led us toward them.

The sound of music grew louder as we approached the outdoors. Voices in conversation and laughter mingled with the music and I could feel the party atmosphere kick into high gear as we strode through the doors.

"Here you are, sir," Price said as he gestured to the party unfolding before us.

"Thank you, Price," Harrison said.

Price went back to his post as we turned to take in the sight before us. More twinkling lights lit up the entire terrace as well as the backyard, which looked to be the size of a modest football field, meticulously landscaped with flower beds, hedgerows and enormous trees. Even in the dark, it was a slice of wilderness paradise in the heart of the city.

More cornstalks and pumpkins decorated the terrace and lawn, as well as hanging glass lanterns in red and orange. A huge bonfire was roaring in a large concrete basin in the middle of the backyard while clusters of people filled the terrace and the yard, most of which were dressed just like us in hats and scarves and warm coats.

There were several bars serving mulled wine and hot toddies as well as multiple food stands, offering roasted chestnuts and warm pasties. Despite my bout of homesickness earlier, I felt my spirits lift at the festive atmosphere.

"Vivian Tremont!"

As one, the four of us turned to see who was calling for Viv.

It was a beautiful brunette, Elise Stanford, who was easily recognizable not just because of her trademark thick glossy brown tresses but also because she greeted us every morning on the television, where she delivered the day's news with a side of tea and gossip.

"Hello, Elise," Viv said. They exchanged an air kiss.

"I love the hat. I simply love it," Elise gushed. "Is that the new fashion? I simply have to have one."

Viv glanced over her shoulder at me with a very clear I-told-you-so look on her face. I just smiled. Obviously, there was no accounting for taste.

"They are becoming all the rage," Viv said. "My assistant, Fee, and I simply can't keep up with the demand."

Fiona looked as if she might swoon when Elise glanced her way.

"Do you have a moment?" Elise asked. "I want to introduce the two of you to my producer, Sam Kerry. I think we could do a brilliant segment on winter hats in the next few days. What do you think?"

Viv and Fee disappeared into the crowd, and I found myself standing alone with Harrison. I wasn't sure what to say or do because while we're friends, we're rarely alone. I decided now was as good a time as any to discover a bit more about the man who had the uncanny ability to make my heart go pitter pat.

"So, Harry, looks like you're stuck with me," I said as I slipped my arm through his and pulled him toward the bonfire. "Tell me, who does a gal have to kill to own a place like this?"

"Why, the person who already owns it. Right, Harrison, old boy?" It was not Harry who answered me.

A distinguished-looking man, with perfectly cut silver hair, a clean shaven face and an impeccable navy suit under a matching overcoat, was standing on the other side of Harrison smiling at me in amusement. I knew without being told that this had to be Harry's boss. Oh, gees!

Chapter 4

"Scarlett Parker, this is Tyler Carson," Harrison said. He, too, was looking at me with a smile tucked into his cheek. I dropped his arm and ignored him.

"It's nice to meet you," I said. Tyler Carson took my hand in his and patted it as if to reassure me that my social gaffe was just fine.

"Likewise," he said. "And this is Reese Evers, my partner in crime."

"More accurately your late partner's wife, but I do appreciate you keeping me around," Reese teased. She was short and sturdy with stylishly cut and colored dark hair and a rose-colored sweater dress under a perfectly tailored black winter coat that I was sure cost the equivalent of my parents' new car.

"A pleasure," Reese said when she shook my hand.

The two of them glanced between me and Harrison as if trying to figure out our relationship. I felt like saying "good luck" since I had no idea what our relationship was myself, but I didn't. Remarkable restraint, I know.

"You really pulled out all the stops," Harrison said. "It's incredible."

"It was all Ava," Tyler said. An expression of sadness passed over his face. "She has her moments."

I wasn't sure what to say to that and clearly neither did Harrison or Reese. Tyler stared out across the throng of people and then visibly shook himself loose from whatever was on his mind.

"Yes, well, make sure you get some of the mulled wine," he said. "Reese, I do believe I see Jeremy Hinton across the way. We should probably go butter up the old goat."

"Ah, yes, duty calls." Reese sighed as she followed in Tyler's wake, giving us a small wave.

I glanced at Harrison and saw worry lines form in between his brows.

"Everything okay?" I asked.

"Hard to say," he said. "I think it is one of those things that only time will—"

"Harrison Wentworth, I have been looking all over for you!"

A woman about my age, wearing ridiculously high heels, a tiny skirt and a puffy jacket, tripped across the patio toward us. She had black hair cut in a severe bob, overly plucked arching eyebrows and the reddest pillow lips I'd ever seen.

"Tuesday," Harrison greeted her.

He looked uneasy, and I felt my left eyebrow arch

inquisitively. Upon closer inspection, I realized Harry looked downright nervous. I had a feeling I was about to find out what I had suspected he was hiding when he'd invited all of us as his guests. Another woman!

"Scarlett, this is Tuesday Blount," he said. "We work at Carson and Evers together."

"Nice to meet you," I said. I held out my hand but she shook her head.

"Sorry," she said. "I forgot my gloves."

What the heck was that supposed to mean? I had to give her a ten on the rudeness scale for that one, but then I thought maybe she was a germaphobe and I should let it slide. She licked her red lips and looked at Harrison like he was a snack. Okay, so I was not going to let her slide on the rudeness.

"Harry, be a love and get us some wine," she ordered.

"It's Harrison," he and I said together.

He looked at me and I looked at him. He grinned and I shrugged as if it were no big deal. Of course, it was a very big deal. No one is supposed to call him Harry except for me.

"Harrison, then," Tuesday said. She rolled her eyes. "Please go get us some wine. I'm simply dying of thirst."

I had a hard time figuring why that was a bad thing. Okay, that was mean, but I really, really, really did not like this woman.

"I'll be right back," Harrison said. Then he leaned close to me and whispered, "Behave."

I would have protested, but I didn't want to give Miss Bats for Eyebrows any reason to think I had just been reined in. I had a feeling she would enjoy that entirely too much.

"Of course I will," I said. I gave him my brightest and falsest smile.

He frowned at me, and I noticed when he left he was moving at a speedy pace, so the man was not a complete idiot.

As soon as he was gone, Tuesday looked me over as if she were considering a purchase. I returned the scrutiny, and I'm pleased to report that she had knobby knees.

"So, you and Harrison, eh?" she asked.

"I'm sorry," I said. "I'm not sure what you mean."

"You two are a couple?" she asked. "I've been wondering how long it would take him to move on after our breakup."

Despite myself, I made a sputtering noise. Yes, that's the sound I make when I'm trying not to swallow my tongue.

"Oh, he didn't tell you about me?" she asked. "It's not too surprising. He took our breakup very hard."

"Oh, no," I lied. "He's mentioned you." Judging by Tuesday's style, I figured she was the sort who liked attention, *all* the attention. In a nanosecond, I knew exactly how to shut her down. "In fact, I think he said something about the boredom getting to him, but I couldn't really say because he seemed to think it wasn't even worth talking about."

BA-BAM. Direct hit. Tuesday's face became a mottled shade of maroon, clashing quite horribly with her lipstick, and now she made a sputtering noise. Her turn to swallow her tongue, I imagined. Too bad it couldn't be a permanent condition.

"You . . . he . . . it . . ." she stammered.

I gave her my most benign expression. "Yes?"

"Harrison and I belong together," she said. "We work together, we enjoy the same things, and we are intellectual equals." She paused as if I were slow-witted and she needed to give me a moment to let that sink in. I don't think I have ever wanted to kick anyone quite so much as I wanted to kick her at that moment.

"He and I will get back together," she continued. "We're soul mates. Whatever it is you think the two of you have, it won't last. Mark my words."

"*Tsk, tsk, tsk*, always so dramatic, Tuesday." A man crashed our party of two and Tuesday turned toward him as he continued. "What's the matter? Afraid your affair with the boss ruined your chances with Wentworth?"

"Shut up, Dashavoy! You don't know anything," she snapped. She spun on her heel and stormed off into the crowd.

I turned to the newcomer. He was handsome in a squeaky-clean, pressed pocket square sort of way. Of course, the smell of alcohol on his breath diminished that image, but still, I was pretty grateful for the rescue.

"Winthrop Dashavoy, at your service," he said. He put his hand on his chest and gave me a half bow. He staggered a bit on rising but he managed to fight off the lure of gravity.

"Scarlett Parker," I said. "You have excellent timing, Mr.—"

"Call me Win," he interrupted. "Everyone does and it fits, because I always win."

"At what?" I asked.

His gaze was bleary when it met mine, and I got the feeling he wasn't really seeing me or maybe it was more that he was seeing four of me and having a hard time picking the right one to talk to.

"Why, at whatever I choose," he said. He took my arm

and led me down the steps out into the yard toward the fire pit.

I glanced over my shoulder, wondering where Harrison was and whether he'd be able to find me if I moved. I almost protested but Win had saved me from the horrible Tuesday so I didn't want to be impolite.

"Excuse us," he said as he propelled me through the crowd. "Pardon us. Make way."

We stopped in a clearing away from the fire. I could feel the cold creep in under my clothes without the warmth of the fire or the gas heaters that were scattered all over the back terrace.

I glanced back at the house, hoping to see Harrison or Viv and Fee or Nick and Andre, but no. In the crush of hats, coats and scarves, I didn't see anyone I recognized.

"You're quite lovely," Win said. "I can see why Harrison is smitten. That's old Wentworth for you, though, biggest office, prettiest girls, largest salary. Yes, it must be bloody awful being Harrison Wentworth."

"I'm pretty sure it's not all unicorns and glitter," I said. I knew for a fact that just managing Viv and me caused Harrison more than a little heartburn.

Win made an impatient gesture. "You don't get it. Nothing bad ever happens to that bloke. It's like he was born under a charmed star. You probably fell out of the sky and right into his lap. Am I right?"

He reached out to touch my hair, I think. I dodged to the left, so I really have no idea what his intention was. I knew mine, however, was to get out of there.

"Harrison and I are just friends," I said. I wasn't sure why I said it, but I got the impression Win was jealous of Harrison and I didn't think it would do me any good for Win to suspect that we were more than we were at present.

"Bollocks! I saw the way you two were looking at each other," he said. "It's clear that his intentions toward you, my dear, are sordid to say the least."

I tried to walk around him and get back to the party. He blocked me. For a drunk, he was surprisingly agile.

"Whatever is between me and Harrison is our business," I said as I stepped back. "I don't know what your issue is, but you can leave me out of it."

I wanted to kick myself as my voice wobbled, making me sound either close to shouting angry words or on the verge of fearful tears when I was really just frustrated that I couldn't politely get away from him.

"Don't back away from me," he snarled. "You're just like her. She thinks she can end things and just walk away from me, but she can't and neither can you."

"What are you talking about?" I snapped. I don't have much patience for drunken ramblings. I'd had too many celebrity guests trash too many hotel rooms in artistic bouts of drunken stupidity during my years in the hotel industry. Frankly, I was tired of cleaning up messes and I damn well wasn't going to clean up after this guy even if he had saved me from Tuesday.

"Rich, beautiful 'it' girls who use a man for his fortune and his connections and think they can tell him how to act, how to behave and to smile pretty for the camera, then they bin him like yesterday's rubbish," he said. "I won't let her get away with it."

He made a grab for me, but I ducked to the side. I glanced around to see if anyone was aware of my predicament, but no, they were all gathered around the fire with their backs to us.

"Aw, don't be like that, love," Win said. Gone was his previous rage and now he was oozing a sloppy sort of charm, or at least, I'm sure he thought he was being charming. Me? Not so much.

He hiccupped and then made a staggering lunge at me that ended up with the two of us grappling like basketball players over a loose ball.

My face was mashed against his throat and I had to force myself to mouth breathe so as not to take in too much of his aftershave, which might have been pleasant if he hadn't bathed in it, probably to cover up the stench of the booze. I felt the shirt button on his open collar press hard against my cheek as he tried to pull my body up against his. Oh, hell no!

I reared back and he clipped me on the chin with his elbow as I planted my heel on his instep. We both reeled back. Thankfully, a strong pair of arms grabbed me before I did a butt plant in the grass. When I glanced back to thank my rescuer, my eyes went wide. It was Harrison and I had never seen him look so angry before.

"All right, Ginger?" he asked. His voice was clipped, hitting like bullet points on a résumé of really pissed off.

"Yes, I'm fine," I said. "Honestly, it's not what you think."

"Yes, it is," Win slurred and grinned. "Me and the little bit were having an amorous tussle. Why don't you go away so we can finish it up?"

Harrison shrugged off his jacket and thrust it at me.

"Harry, don't," I said. I could feel the eyes of the crowd behind us turning to take in the scene.

"Don't what?" he asked. "Defend you? Sorry, I'm not made that way."

Win grinned at him, and I realized from the malice that sparkled in his gaze that this was what he'd been hoping for all along. He wanted a fight with Harrison, which was why he'd led me to the edge of the crowd and behaved so horribly.

"You're giving him exactly what he wants," I said. I clutched Harrison's arm. "Please don't do this."

Harrison met my gaze for a moment and his eyes softened with affection. I thought I had gotten through to him, but before I could even register his movement, he spun around and blocked an incoming punch from Win, who had taken a swing at him while his back was turned. Then Harry walloped the drunk with an uppercut that made Win's teeth clack.

I heard shouts of dismay or approval coming from the people behind us, but I couldn't take my eyes off the two men in front of me. I felt adrenaline surge through my body as Win lowered his head and charged Harrison, looking to do some damage.

Harrison took the hit by wrapping his arms around Win. The two of them crashed to the ground. Harrison twisted so that Win landed on the bottom. The huff of air he emitted made me think he'd had the wind knocked out of him. Harrison pulled back his fist and plowed it into Win's eye.

I yelped, so helpful I know, and Harrison glanced up at me. Our eyes met and I said, "Please stop."

Harry looked reluctant. His nostrils were flared and his fists were still clenched. I had a feeling he was nowhere near done.

"Please, Harry," I said. I couldn't stand the thought of him getting hurt, and I really loathed being a part of an ugly scene. I've had my fill of those, thank you very much.

Harry let go of Win and rolled off him. As he staggered to his feet and began to walk toward me, Win rose up from the ground with a brick in his hand. I had no doubt he was going for Harrison's head.

"Look out!" I cried.

A body dove out of the crowd and tackled Win to the ground. When Harrison would have jumped back in, I grabbed his arm and held him back.

"No!" I said.

The man sitting on Win grabbed the brick from his hand and tossed it aside. Then he leaned forward and shouted in his face, "Enough, Dashavoy!"

Win slumped back onto the ground, clearly done. The man sitting on him turned and grinned at me.

"So, Scarlett, is Viv here tonight?"

Chapter 5

Alistair Turner hadn't even muddied his coat in his takedown of Winthrop Dashavoy. He and Harrison were longtime rugby mates and I knew he carried a small flickering torch for Viv, even though he was aware that she was married.

"She's here somewhere," I said.

"Excellent," he said. "I'll just get this git some ice for his eye and see if I can track her down."

"She'll be happy to see you, Alistair," I said.

"Is she still married?" he asked.

"As far as I know," I said with a shrug. With Viv, these things were fuzzy.

He looked momentarily disappointed but then brightened. "Well, if he's not here, then I say her dance card is all mine."

He left us, dragging Winthrop Dashavoy behind him as if he were no more significant than a bag of trash.

I turned to face Harrison with a look on my face that felt positively matronly in its disapproval.

"What?" he asked.

"That was a ridiculous display," I said.

"I know." He shook out his right hand. "Whatever was he thinking?"

"I meant both of you," I said. "Disgraceful behavior and over me, I just can't approve of that sort of thing."

"It wasn't completely over you," Harrison said. He took his jacket out of my arms and shrugged back into it.

"Well, that's deflating," I said.

He laughed and I felt it all the way to my squishy center. See? I must be allergic to him. He draped his arm over my shoulders and pulled me close as we strolled over to the bonfire. The people who had witnessed the scuffle moved aside to let us through and I heard a few of them shout out encouragement to Harrison. Barbarians.

"So what happened to our wine?" I asked.

"When I saw you rucking with Win, I left it at the bar," he said. He indicated the temporary bar on the other side of the yard. "I'll just go fetch it."

"Wait," I said. "What does 'rucking' mean? Because just so you know, it does not sound polite at all."

He made a face as if he got where I was going. "Nothing like that! It means fighting."

"Okay, then," I said. I could live with that since it was true. Harrison left, and as I watched him, I stretched my left arm out. I'd only grappled with the drunkard for a few minutes, but it felt as if I'd gone three rounds in a prizefight.

As the adrenaline eased, my hands began to shake. Wine might not be a bad idea. Under the cover of the darkness, I watched Harrison retrieve our mulled wine. I enjoyed watching him. I felt as if it gave me a glimpse into who he really was to see him interact with his other business associates.

I saw him stop to talk to people who I assumed were his clients. He seemed comfortable, despite the recent scene, and he even threw his head back with a laugh, which was surprised out of him by an older gentleman in a bright green coat. Even from across the yard, I could feel a mutual affection between Harrison and the man. I couldn't even imagine Winthrop Dashavoy pausing to laugh at an older man's joke.

I glanced into the fire thinking about the world of high finance and how it turned some people into really horrible human beings. If you asked me, Win and that Tuesday woman made a perfect pair; maybe more should be done to bring those two awfuls together.

I spun a variety of scenarios in my head, not limited to getting them both drunk and locking them in a room together to more subtle maneuvers like sending them flowers or candy from each other. No, I wouldn't really do any of those things but it was amusing to think about.

When I glanced up, Harrison appeared beside me with two thick glass mugs full of a steaming burgundy liquid garnished with a cinnamon stick and a spiraled orange peel. He handed one to me, and I took it gratefully.

"It occurs to me that I should clarify what I said earlier," he said.

"In what way?" I asked.

"The fight between Win and me was about you in that seeing him touch you made me feel the need to punch him repeatedly, but the enmity between us goes way back," Harrison said. "All the way back to boarding school, in fact."

"You went to boarding school? How did I not know that?"

I took a sip of my wine. The spicy cinnamon and tart orange made the pungent wine taste divine and it heated me up from the inside out.

"I went to Eton when I was thirteen," he said.

"And the last time I saw you when we were kids, you were twelve," I said.

"Yes, you stood me up on our ice cream date to chase some dodgy football player," he said.

"You're never going to forgive me, are you?" I asked.

"I might," he said. "Assuming, of course, that when you start dating again, it involves ice cream and me."

I burst out laughing. "Well, that brings some tawdry images to mind."

His cheeks darkened with embarrassment and then he laughed, too. "You absolutely wreck me, you know that, right?"

I wasn't sure that he meant it as a compliment, but I took it as one.

"So you wore Eton blue? Did you meet anyone famous there?" I asked. Yes, I was angling for any gossip about the royals. How could I help it?

"A fair few," he said. He did not name names. Darn it.

"Mostly, I realized no matter the status of your birth, you're just a teenager living with a bunch of other teenagers, trying to survive puberty and homesickness as best you can," he said.

I felt my heart squinch up a bit at that. I didn't like the idea of Harrison feeling lonely at school or anywhere for that matter. I took another sip of wine to stop myself from impulsively giving him a hug.

"But then there were students like Win," he said.

"Was he a bully?" I asked.

"The worst sort," Harrison said with a shake of his head. "Every school has them but Win singled out the scholarship kids, like me, for the brunt of his wrath. That's actually where Alistair and I met, too. He had my back then and clearly he still does."

"He's a good man," I said. Alistair was an attorney who had helped a client of ours when she was pinched for a crime she didn't commit. That told me more than enough about his character but it was nice to hear that he had always been there for Harrison.

"You can imagine how thrilled I was when both Win and I ended up at Carson and Evers," Harrison said. "I had thought university might have helped Win to mature but no. He's still just as vile as he was when we were first years."

"But he can't bully you on the job, can he?" I asked.

"No, but that's mostly because Tyler Carson is my mentor whereas Jason Evers was Win's. Jason passed on two years ago and Tyler refused to take on Win as a protégé," Harrison said. "Reese, Jason's widow, took him on but it's not the same and Tyler's snub grates on Win, but it's justified. Win is a terrible analyst and an even worse advisor.

Be glad I'm your business manager and he isn't, otherwise, I'm quite sure you'd be broke."

"His personal history makes it seem as if he has only a passing familiarity with ethics," I said. "Does Tyler know this?"

"He might suspect," Harrison said. "As do I, but I haven't been able to prove anything. Win's family is loaded, and if ever there is even a hint of wrongdoing, the injured party is compensated and the inquiry dropped."

"Does Win know you're watching him?" I asked.

"Oh, yes," Harrison said. He took a long sip of his wine and then smiled. "And he hates me for it, so I consider that a plus."

"So, most likely, luring me out into the dark and groping me was Win's idea of revenge against you?" I asked.

"I think so," he said.

"What a jerk!" I squawked.

"In Win's defense, if one can be made, you are immensely gropable," Harrison said.

I blinked at him and then I started to laugh. Probably, it was the wine going to my head but his words struck me so funny, I couldn't help but chuckle.

"Why Harry, I think that's the nicest thing you've ever said to me," I said and patted his arm.

He smiled and there was something in his gaze that made the laughter stall on my lips. It was a look ripe with intent, and I knew exactly what his intention was and I didn't mind a bit.

Harrison and I had kissed before. It had been months ago when he was concussed and I was watching over him, because it was sort of my fault. Really, it was the bad guy's fault but why quibble. In any event, I had never forgotten the kiss or the way it had made me feel, which was loopy in the best possible sense of the word.

"Ginger, I know you're not dating—" he began but I cut him off by taking his glass and mine and putting them down on a nearby table; then I grabbed the front of his jacket and hauled him close.

"But what?" I asked.

Desperation was probably wafting off me like a bad smell. I didn't care. As a serial dater, I was feeling desperate. Up until now, the longest I'd ever gone without dinner and a movie was two weeks. The past eight months of nada on the man front was making me a little squirrelly.

"I think I need to kiss—" he began but was interrupted before he could finish.

"There they are! I told you they'd be by the fire."

"You did not."

"You said they'd be on the terrace, yeah?"

"No, he said upstairs."

"I did not."

Unbelievable! Our friends arrived *now*, not five minutes from now, not one minute from now, no, they had to find us right now.

I let go of Harrison's jacket and smoothed the lapel with my hands. When I turned around, Nick, Andre, Viv, Fee and Alistair were all looking at us expectantly.

"Timing, as they say, is everything," Harrison said from behind me.

I was pretty sure I heard the same disappointment I was feeling in his voice. Then I reminded myself that this was the Universe keeping me true to my word. I had four months to go to make it to one year man free. I would make it, even if it killed me, which seemed more and more likely the more time I spent with Harrison.

"I was just dusting Harrison off from his brawl," I said. I looked at Alistair. "Did Win get some ice for his eye?"

"I left him in the very capable hands of the caterer," he said. "Nasty swelling on his cheekbone. Nice punch, mate."

Alistair gave Harrison an approving look and I frowned. "Don't encourage him."

"Thanks," Harrison said. When I let out an impatient huff, he added, "For intercepting him."

"The pleasure was all mine," Alistair said. He looked at Viv and flexed his upper arm in a show of strength that was well hidden beneath the layers of his coat. "I saved your business manager from a thrashing."

"Hey!" Harrison protested.

"What?" Nick asked. He ran a hand through his thinning blond hair. "There was a fight and we missed it!"

"Not a fight," I said. "More like a shoving match."

Harrison gave me a chagrined look.

"Who is Win?" Fee asked.

"Harrison's office rival," Viv said. "A real pain in the ar—"

"She knows about Win?" I asked Harrison.

"She's visited me at the office," he said. "They've met."

"Was he as charming to her as he was to me?" I asked.

"No," Harrison said, leaning close so only I could hear him. "I suspect he's figured out that you're something special."

And just like that, all was forgiven, the brawling, the fact that Viv had been to his office and I hadn't, and that we missed our chance to kiss. Yes, I am hopelessly easy when it comes to flattery. But you have to admit that being called "something special" can go to a girl's head.

Several spotlights snapped on, illuminating the back terrace, and there stood Tyler Carson. On one side of him was his partner, Reese Evers, and on the other his wife, Ava Carson.

Maybe it was my non-monarchist upbringing but I found the way they stood over the crowd a bit off-putting. Then again, it was their company that made vast sums of money for all of the people in attendance, so I supposed there was a bit of the overlord to them.

"Good evening," Tyler called out to the crowd. "Welcome to the Carson and Evers bonfire night party."

Cheers sounded and I took a moment to study the crowd while Tyler droned on about the business and customer loyalty, blah, blah, blah. He seemed nice enough but mixing in a joke would have helped. I noted that Ava looked to be holding in a yawn and judging by the buzz of conversation in the crowd he wasn't holding everyone's attention.

"He's a lovely host, truly, but I think he needs some new material," Nick said.

"Tyler's gift is economics not public speaking," Harrison agreed.

"And now, before the fireworks start, we will add our Guy Fawkes to the fire. Together let us burn this effigy to represent all of the distrust and misplaced loyalty in our lives and like a mythical phoenix let us rise out of the ashes and forge a new and stronger relationship out of the old."

"Whoa, that's a heavy request for a straw man on a bonfire, don't you think?" Fee asked.

I glanced at Harrison and noted that he was frowning at Tyler.

"You don't think he heard about your scuffle with Win, do you?" I asked.

"I can't imagine he would devote a speech just to that," Harrison said. "No, I think there must be something more going on, but I have no idea what; probably he's trying to win over a new client or fluff up an old one."

Tyler gestured to two men in service uniforms. They wheeled a handcart out from the side of the terrace. It had a big black cloth draped over it.

Tyler followed the men as they awkwardly moved the handcart down the stone steps to the fire pit. He shook hands and clapped some of the guests on the shoulder, smiling as he went with Reese doing the same and Ava looking as if she'd rather be anywhere but here.

The crowd began to ripple with excitement. The energy was almost palpable. I supposed Tyler was right about the symbolism of burning up distrust and discord and forging a new beginning. It reminded me of how I felt on New Year's Eve when I made my resolution for the coming year. I stood on my toes to get a better look over the heads of the others as the draped effigy passed.

On the last step, one of the men tripped and dropped his side of the handcart. It wobbled precariously for a moment and then tipped over. The draped cargo on the cart lurched to the side and then fell to the ground. I heard Ava yell, "No!"

But it was too late. The effigy rolled onto the ground and the black cloth covering it fell away. Instead of the anticipated straw man wearing a creepy Guy Fawkes mask with the standard pencil mustache, large nose and pointy chin, however, this effigy was an actual man whose Guy Fawkes mask was dangling by a thread around his neck. With a shock of blond hair and an eye that had recently been punched, I recognized Winthrop Dashavoy in an instant.

Chapter 6

Reese Evers was the first to react. She screamed and ran down the steps to Win. She knelt beside him and grabbed his shirtfront.

"Win, darling, are you all right?" she asked.

He didn't respond. The crowd stood frozen in place, waiting to see if he was hurt.

"Let me through, I'm a surgeon." A man pushed his way through the people. He was short and stout with an abrupt manner and a forceful look that had everyone stepping out of his way. He knelt down beside Reese and began to examine Win.

He checked his pulse, his heartbeat, the rise and fall of his chest. He ran his hands over him, pausing at his eye and then he moved Win's head to the side and examined his neck. The doctor sat back on his heels.

He glanced up at Tyler. I could see Tyler's jaw was tight and he'd gone a pasty shade of gray even in the warm firelight.

"I'm sorry, Tyler, he's dead," the doctor said.

Reese emitted a scream that made the marrow in my bones shiver. It was the most mournful sound I'd ever heard as if Win had been forcefully ripped away from her, but then, I suppose he had.

Harrison went to step forward but Alistair grabbed him by the arm, stopping him. "I don't think that's a good idea, mate, for either of us."

"I don't care," Harrison said. Bright red splotches appeared on his cheeks and I could see the rapid rise and fall of his chest. "If I did this—"

"No!" Alistair said. "Absolutely not. He was fine when I turned him over to the girls in the kitchen for some ice, I swear. He was still pissed from too much drink and angry that I'd halted the fight, but that's it. I promise you he was fine."

"Still, he was my colleague," Harrison said. "I have to help however I can."

He turned and pushed his way through the crowd. I didn't want him to face this alone, so I hurried after him.

Tyler was on his phone to the police. Price, the butler, and more uniformed house staff were keeping the crowd back. Reese was sobbing on Win's still form, while Ava stared off into space as if mentally removing herself from the chaos around her.

"Price, let me through," Harrison ordered.

The butler looked at him and Harrison gave him a look that said he would pick up the smaller man and bodily move him if necessary. He gave Harrison a curt nod and Harrison strode forward. I was about to follow when I was hip checked from the side and sent sprawling into the crowd.

"Oh, I'm so sorry," I said.

I pushed myself off the poor old man in the bright green jacket that I'd crashed into, and he gave me a bolstering smile that told me I hadn't harmed any vital parts.

"Not at all, my dear," he said. "That was the most fun I've had in years."

"Uncle Alvie!" The middle-aged woman beside him shook her head at me as if to say he was incorrigible.

I gave them a weak smile and turned back to join Harrison. It was then that I realized who exactly had bumped me into the crowd. Standing beside Harrison with her arm around him while she sobbed into his handkerchief was Tuesday Blount.

Normally, I am a very even-tempered sort of girl, but if you cross me, I can be very grumpy and a little mean. At the moment, the desire to shove my way into their little group and stomp Tuesday's skinny little behind was fierce and almost impossible to resist.

"No," a voice whispered in my ear. "Not now."

I turned and found Viv beside me. She looped her arm through mine and dragged me through the crowd and back to our cluster of friends.

Andre, who never handles the sight of a corpse well, was doubled over with his head in his hands while Nick had an arm around him whispering soothing words in his ear.

Fee and Alistair were standing up on a concrete garden bench trying to see what was happening.

"Harrison is talking to Tyler," Alistair reported.

"A woman with dark hair is standing beside him," Fee said. "She looks upset, very very upset."

Tuesday. I had no idea what her current relationship with Win was, but I knew exactly what her plans for Harrison's future were and, boy, didn't a fallen colleague give her a lot of wiggle room to get back into his life?

"Reese Evers is refusing to get up," Alistair said. His tone sounded grim. "She's clutching Win's jacket. Oh, she just took a swing at the butler when he tried to pull her off."

"Harrison is helping with her now," Fee said. "Oh, that's not good."

Fee didn't need to say any more. Reese's voice carried across the now silent crowd of people.

"This is your fault!" she wailed.

I rose up on my tiptoes and saw her shrieking at Harrison. He was holding her by the arms but I couldn't tell if it was to hold her up or to keep her from hitting him.

"You always had to be better than him, always had to be smarter, faster, more successful, it was killing him!" Reese cried. "Couldn't you see that? Didn't you care? It's your fault he's dead. Your fault!" Harrison opened his mouth to speak but she wrenched herself away from him, clearly not wanting to hear what he had to say. I could just see over the heads in front of me enough to see that Tuesday was right there wrapping an arm around Harrison and whispering to him in a speech that I was sure was designed to comfort.

I supposed I should be glad that she was there for him, but I wasn't. I didn't trust Tuesday and I didn't like her and I really didn't want her to be his source of solace. We were his friends, he needed us not her. Okay, more accurately, he needed me.

"The ambulance has arrived," Fee announced.

Sure enough, two men and one woman were jogging down the steps toward Win's body. As they began to work, the crowd was pushed even farther back toward the warmth of the bonfire.

A whistling sound pierced the air and it took me a moment to realize that fireworks were going off. I turned around and looked over the roofs of the neighboring houses and saw a burst of red spark up the sky.

I was torn between thinking it was Winthrop Dashavoy's essence bursting up into the heavens, melodramatic I suppose but I was stressed, and thinking it was in very poor taste to be looking at fireworks when a man lay dead just fifty feet away.

Several booms sounded and the rest of the crowd turned to watch the fireworks. It was surreal to say the least. I glanced back at Harrison. All of the outside terrace lights had been switched on, illuminating the scene, and I could see that he looked haggard in a way I had never seen before.

The instinct to be with him overrode all common sense. I left my friends and pushed through the crowd. I dodged an old lady and knocked against a young man. I was bullish in my need to get through the crowd. Finally, I broke into the inner circle around Win's body.

My momentum was such that I couldn't slow myself down and I fell into the middle of things with a lurch and a groan. A strong arm plucked me up before I hit the ground and I grabbed at it. The sleeve was navy blue wool, scratchy but warm.

When I was set onto my feet, I turned to thank my

rescuer and found myself staring into the direct gaze of Detective Inspector Simms.

"Ms. Parker, Scarlett," he said. "Why am I not surprised to see you here?"

"Uh," I began but ran out of gas before forming a single coherent word.

"She's my guest," Harrison said as he joined us. "It's a party for our clients, so it's not at all surprising that she'd be here since she is a client."

Simms looked at Harrison with a considering look. Even I could see that Harrison's demeanor was defensive when there was no need for it to be.

"Sorry," I said. I put my arm around Harrison and hugged him hard. I was relieved when he put his arm on my shoulders and did the same. A united front is always better to present, don't you think?

"I'm sorry, too," Harrison said. He extended his free hand to Inspector Simms, who shook it. "It's good to see you, Inspector. We're all a bit rattled by the events."

"Understandable," Simms said.

I glanced at the other safety officers who had arrived and asked, "Is DI Franks with you?"

"No, he's on vacation up in York," Simms said. "He goes this time of year every year. I'll be taking the lead on this investigation."

"Investigation?" I asked.

Simms nodded. "It doesn't take a medical examiner to see that this man was murdered."

"But he was terribly drunk," I said. "And he fell down those steps hard. Couldn't that have killed him?"

Simms shook his head. "The marks on his face and neck indicate otherwise. Clearly, he was in an altercation."

Harrison and I exchanged a glance. I knew we were both thinking that it was best to get this over with now.

"Actually," Harrison said on an exhale. "I put those marks on his face, but I never touched his neck."

Chapter 7

From there the night became increasingly awful. The police interviewed everyone. Most were let go but not us. Harrison and I were questioned and then they asked Harrison to come to the station to make a formal statement. I volunteered to go with him, but he wouldn't hear of it and neither would Inspector Simms.

Alistair insisted on going with Harrison so that made me feel somewhat better. It was a somber affair when the crime scene people had documented the area and the remaining guests were finally allowed to leave, including us.

Nick and Andre escorted Viv, Fee, and me home. On the way, I told them all about Harrison's history with Win. By the time we arrived at Notting Hill Gate, we were a grim-looking party for certain.

"You don't think they'll arrest Harrison, do you?" I asked Nick as we straggled at the back of the pack.

He gave me a worried glance, which I took to mean that he didn't want to give me false hope. I should have told him that was okay. I was fine with someone lying to me right now if it would make me feel better about the situation.

Nick was about to answer when we were bumped from behind. I staggered forward but he caught me about the waist and then turned around to glare at the people at our back.

"Oy, watch yourself," he snapped.

The woman was a big-haired blonde in a tiny jacket, UGG boots and a miniskirt. She was puffing on a cigarette and I could tell by the way she wobbled that she was a little worse for the wear in the alcohol department.

"Who are you talking to, you mangy clot?" she asked.

"You, you daft cow," Nick snapped.

The woman staggered forward, waving her cigarette at Nick like it was a weapon. I swiftly stepped between them.

"Sorry!" I cried. "He didn't mean it. He's just had a bit of a shock is all."

"I don't care if he just buried his mum. Danny!" the woman cried. "Come here and defend me!"

I glanced over her shoulder to see the male version of her coming at us, except he was a big hulking mass of muscle, who looked like he power-lifted cars just for fun.

"Nick," I hissed his name.

"What?" he asked.

"Run!" I ordered.

Together we turned and started to run. I could hear shouts behind us but I didn't slow down and neither did

Nick. When we passed the others, I shouted, "Knees to chest, people, knees to chest!"

Andre looked over our shoulders and let out a yip. He grabbed Viv's and Fee's hands in his and dragged them along with him. We didn't stop running until we were sure Danny had been left in the dust.

"What was that all about?" Andre asked as he gasped for breath.

"I inadvertently called a chavette a big cow," Nick wheezed. "Her boyfriend took offense."

"Oh, my god, that thug chasing us was her boyfriend?" Fee asked. "If he'd caught us, he'd have knotted us up like pretzels, yeah?"

We leaned against a nearby building as we caught our breath. When I could speak, I asked Andre, "What's a chavette?"

"Oh, how to explain," he said. He panted while he mulled it over.

"They're bottle blondes with enormous earrings and no brains," Fee said.

"They like short skirts and designer or faux designer tops," Viv added.

"They smoke," Nick said with a disgusted face.

"And they usually have a baby or five," Andre said.

"Oh, and they like to wave with their middle finger at you and it isn't to point you in the right direction," Nick said.

"Trashy mean girls," Viv said. "I think that would be the American equivalent."

"Ah," I said. "Got it."

We began walking again. During the chase, I had

managed to forget about Harrison for a few seconds but now the worry crept back in and I found myself thinking about what he had told me about Winthrop Dashavoy.

"Do any of you know the Dashavoy family?" I asked.

I didn't think it was my imagination when it seemed like everyone was avoiding making eye contact with me.

"Well . . ." Nick began but then seemed to run out of words, which for Nick is cause for concern.

"They're a bunch of toffs," Fee said.

My American brain did a quick translation. So the Dashavoys were rich. Okay, that pretty much fell in with what Harrison had told me about their private school education and always bailing Win out of trouble.

"Rich isn't necessarily bad, though, is it?" I asked.

"Well, there's nice rich and there's not so nice rich," Nick said.

"I take it they're not so nice," I said with a sigh.

"Let's put it this way, if the police arrest Harrison for killing Winthrop, it will take everything Alistair has and then some to get him off," Andre said.

"But why?" I asked. I could feel my heart pound in my chest as my panic ratcheted up.

"Because Winthrop Dashavoy Senior owns everyone in this town and he won't hesitate to call in every marker he's got to see Harrison put behind bars for life," Nick said.

Viv unlocked the front door and switched off the alarm. We all trooped into the back workroom, where we had a small kitchenette full of tea and snacks. You know, what the Brits call crisps and cakes, the sort of stuff that gets you through the workday and does a nice job on stressed-out moments like right now as well.

"We all know it wasn't Harrison," I said.

Fee plated some Hoppers Jam Tarts and Cadbury Chocolate Mini Rolls. I knew I'd be walking it off tomorrow, but for now the comfort food was welcome. I kept my eye on the black currant tart, since that's my favorite, but passed around plates for everyone else first.

"Of course it wasn't," Andre said. "He was with you the entire time, wasn't he?"

"Yes, absolutely," I lied.

Thankfully, the electric kettle began to whistle and everyone's attention was diverted. What I didn't say was that Harrison had left me by the fire to go retrieve our wine. Now I knew he hadn't done anything but get the wine, and I had kept my eye on him most of the time, but I hadn't told Simms that. I had told Simms that Harrison was with me the entire time, which I'm pretty sure put me in the category of big-nosed Pinocchio liar and quite possibly impeding an investigation. I didn't tell my friends this, because I didn't want them to worry. Yeah, and I didn't want to be lectured either.

"Winthrop Dashavoy was not well regarded," Nick said. "That much is clear from the mutterings I heard after his body was revealed."

"Given his *winning* personality, I'm sure there were plenty of people at the party who wished him dead," I said. They all turned to look at me. "What? Too soon?"

"Well, you're not going to win any friends with that clumsy wordplay," Andre chided me.

"I don't know, winners never quit," Nick said. "And quitters never win and Scarlett certainly never knows when to quit."

I stuck my tongue out at him.

"Clearly, it's a no-win situation," Viv said.

"And it's Viv for the win," Fee cheered.

We were all laughing now. I think it was equal parts post-trauma nerves and exhaustion; either way the puns from a dead man's name did not speak very well of us.

"We are horrible people," I said.

"Agreed," they all said.

Somehow acknowledging how awful we were made us seem not as awful. It reminded me of my first few years living in the Southern region of the United States. You could pretty much say anything bad about anyone so long as you added, "bless his/her heart," like that made it okay. Nice to know a variation of it worked across the ocean as well.

"Reese Evers certainly seemed to take his death very hard," Viv said. "She was quite distraught."

"She never had children," Nick said. "Perhaps she had maternal feelings for him. He was her husband's protégé and all."

"How did you know that?" I asked.

"Ava told us," Andre said. He and Nick exchanged a look and I could tell that Ava had told them quite a lot.

"Ava was pretty odd about the whole thing, don't you think?" I asked.

"She's very fragile," Andre said.

"She has a nervous condition," Nick said.

Viv poured the tea for everyone and we all fussed with our cups until we had them loaded just right. I tend to go heavy on the milk at night, thinking it helps me sleep.

"You like Ava," I said to Nick and Andre.

As one, they nodded in agreement.

"She was very gracious about showing her art collection to us," Andre said.

"But she looked utterly unsurprised when Win's body rolled out from under the tarp," I said. "Don't you find that odd?"

I snagged the black currant tart and bit into it. Tarts always make things better. It's a fact.

"I thought it was odd," Fee said. "She looked as stiff as a mannequin, yeah?"

"It's her medication," Nick said. Andre hushed him but Nick shook him off. "We may as well tell them—if they think she had something to do with it, others will, too, and the police are bound to make it public."

"Fine," Andre said. He took a long sip of his tea but he was clearly unhappy about sharing what they knew.

"Ava has a prescription pill problem," Nick said.

"And you know this how?" I asked.

"She told us in confidence," Andre said. "Note that I am stressing *in confidence*."

"Noted," Viv said. "Do you think the medication could make her dangerous?"

"No," Nick said. "She's taking an opioid analgesic. It tends to blank emotions, not cause mood swings or violence."

"Why did she confide in you two?" I asked. They gave me a hurt look and I added, "I only meant that she just met you and that's pretty personal stuff."

"When she found out I was in the medical profession—" Nick began but Fee interrupted.

"You're a dentist," she said. "Did she know you were a dentist?"

Nick heaved a sigh and shoved chocolate roll in his mouth. Andre patted his arm.

"It's okay," he said. "You are a very good dentist. It was all a misunderstanding. I called him 'Doc' and she assumed, well, it was just too embarrassing to correct her especially after she assumed Nick could give her a prescription."

"Oh, that would be awkward," Viv said.

"We merely prevaricated so as to avoid any social unpleasantness," Nick said.

"Meaning you let her think you were a doctor but one who didn't write prescriptions," I said. "Surgeon?"

"Neuro," Nick said. "I figured it's still the head. I told her I'd refer her to one of my colleagues."

Nick looked so sheepish, I had to smile. "You know I love you just the way you are, don't you?"

He actually blushed a deeper shade of pink and looked a little choked up. Viv and Fee added their praise on top of mine and Nick lost it. He blew his nose into a napkin and waved at us to stop. I glanced at Andre, who was grinning at his mate.

"He's adorable when he's flustered, isn't he?" he asked me.

I nodded and then snagged the last black currant tart while no one was looking.

It was clear that Nick and Andre didn't think Ava had anything to do with Win's death. I could let it go then, although I still found her demeanor at the sight of Win's body very odd.

"What about Tuesday Blount?" I asked.

It was as if I'd hit them all with a freeze ray. Nick

paused with his cup halfway to his lips, Fee stopped chewing her chocolate roll, Viv wrapped her hands around the cozy on the teapot as if to warm them, and Andre hugged his middle as if trying to self-soothe.

Nick spoke first. "We have never met her. Right, Andre?"

"Nope never," he said.

I looked at the two of them. "But you have heard of her."

They looked at each other with mild expressions of panic. "Maybe once or twice in passing," Andre said.

"Passing what?" I asked.

"Harrison might have mentioned her on one of our boys' nights out," Nick said. He was studying the inside of his cup as if reading the tea leaves.

"Oh, really?" I asked.

"Harrison was bevvied," Andre said. "So we didn't take what he said too seriously."

"What did he say?" I asked.

"Nothing much," Nick said. "Just that he really thought hewasgoingtomarryher."

I stared at him for a full minute. It took me that long to untangle his word jumble. "Marry her?" I whipped around to look at Viv. "Is that true?"

She gave me the sympathetic look a person gives when they're about to tell you something you don't want to hear like your dog died, you lost your job, or the man you're crushing on almost married the vilest woman in existence. I am not exaggerating.

"He was smitten with her," Viv said. She sighed. She looked like she didn't want to say any more but was forcing herself because she knew I would keep badgering her. "He did tell me he was going to ask her to marry him, but a few days later she moved out of their flat and he never mentioned her again."

"They lived together?" I asked. There was no other way to interpret Viv's words, but I was still trying to find a different angle. I'm tenacious like that.

"Yes," Viv said. "It seemed quite serious at the time."

I was reeling. It was one thing for Tuesday to announce that they had been a thing and that she planned to get him back. I had assumed they had just dated. But they had lived together, cohabited, shared a bathroom, and Harrison had almost proposed to her! I felt like I was going to have a seizure.

"He never said," I stammered.

"That's a male heartbreak for you, they don't talk about it," Fee said. I scowled at her and she shrugged. "Sorry but I've seen it with my older brothers. It's not pretty."

"On that happy note, I think it's time for us to go," Nick said to Andre. "I have an early morning."

They both finished their tea and I walked them to the front door while Viv and Fee headed upstairs. We exchanged hugs and I promised to let them know as soon as I heard anything from Harrison or Alistair.

They stepped out into the cold night, but before I closed the door, Andre grabbed my hand and said, "He's going to be all right."

"Oh, I know," I lied.

He gave me a look that told me he knew I was bluffing and then he said, "This might be a good time to let him know you care about him, a fellow facing an arrest for murder could probably use the lift."

"But I don't—" I began but Nick interrupted me.

"Oh, please, Scarlett," he said. "This is us, your first mates upon arriving in Notting Hill. We know you, pet, and you fancy the pants off Harrison Wentworth."

"It just seems that way because I haven't been dating anyone," I said. "Really, we're just friends."

Nick and Andre exchanged a look and then shook their heads.

"Deny, deny, deny," Nick said. "It still won't make it not so."

"Ugh." I banged my head on the door frame, yes, intentionally. "Good night, you two, I'll call you tomorrow if there's any news."

Andre blew me an air kiss and the two of them walked down the street to the flat above their studio.

I watched them walk arm in arm and I envied their relationship. The love and affection that they shared were certainly inspiring. It made me long for, well, that special sort of closeness. That feeling of coming home just because I'd found my soul mate.

Naturally, my thoughts flitted back to Harrison. What was happening to him right now? Was he okay? Why hadn't he or Alistair texted us to let us know what was going on? And how did I feel about Tuesday? Okay, that part was easy. I hadn't liked her before and now I was quite sure I loathed her.

I locked the door and checked the downstairs before heading up. Fee was spending the night at our place in our guest bedroom since she had a fitting with a client early in the morning. I found them sitting at the counter in the kitchen of our flat.

"I'm knackered," Fee said. She paused to let out a jaw-popping yawn. "G'night, girls."

She waved to us as she headed upstairs to the room across from mine. Viv stayed seated, eating salted caramel gelato right out of the carton. She handed me a spoon.

"On top of tea and tarts?" I asked.

"Extreme circumstances," she said.

I tucked into the frozen treat. I thought about Harry and wondered if he was still at the station. Then I remembered his desire to be a spy. I'll bet he wouldn't have ended up in this mess if he had become a spy. I wished I could call him and tell him that. I had the feeling it would make him laugh.

I glanced at Viv. It hit me, like it does sometimes, that she was married. She had a husband somewhere out there in the great big world. Why wouldn't she tell me about him? It was maddening. Then I had a crazy thought. Maybe she couldn't talk about him, maybe she was sworn to secrecy.

"He's a spy, isn't he?" I asked. "Like MI5 or MI6 or CIA or one of those top secret things."

"Who are you talking about?" she asked. She looked at me like I was mental, not as unusual a look as you would think coming from her.

I stared at her and she heaved a huge sigh and said, "The husband thing again?"

"Just tell me who he is," I pleaded.

"No," she said. Just like that. Who gets away with that? Viv, that's who, I could never get away with a one-word answer. Maybe that says something bad about me, I'm not sure.

"Fine." I nodded in resignation and tucked my spoon into the creamy dessert. We were silent for a moment.

"I don't think I'm going to sleep tonight until I know what's happening to Harry," I said.

"I know, but Alistair is the best," she said. "Harrison couldn't be in better care."

"You're right," I agreed but still I worried.

It took everything I had in me not to question her about her feelings for Alistair, but there were bigger issues at large, namely Harrison's freedom, so I resisted.

"Ava Carson," Viv said. She spooned some gelato into her mouth and let the name perch in the air between us like a bird on a wire.

"Are you going anywhere with that?" I asked after a while.

"I know that Nick and Andre like her, but she's odd and it's more than the drugs," Viv said.

"Agreed." I thought back to the events of the night. "Even if she was heavily medicated, it's still weird that she didn't look surprised when Win was found dead."

Viv met my gaze. "I think so, too."

"She is quite a bit younger than Tyler," I said.

"And they have no children," Viv said. "I don't think she's done much of anything since her modeling career dried up."

"I can see her as a model. She's all sharp angles and straight edges," I said. "And she likes art."

"I think she fancied herself an artist at one time," Viv said with a sniff. Having gone to an art school, Viv was sometimes snobby about the subject.

"Doped up or not, her face when Win fell out of the tarp showed no surprise, nothing," I said.

"So either she was loopy beyond reaction . . ." Viv said.

"Or she knew who killed him, maybe she even saw them kill him, and she wasn't surprised," I concluded.

We both reached into the tub of gelato at the same time. We worked our spoons around each other and then mulled over the situation while we ate.

"Or she was more than a witness," Viv said. "Maybe she is the killer and that's why there was no surprise when Dashavoy was revealed."

The thought of Ava being so calculating made me shiver, but there was no denying the look in her eyes when Win had tumbled across the steps to the ground. It had been a look of cold satisfaction.

Chapter 8

Viv and I packed up the gelato and called it a night. She gave me a hug and told me not to worry but I knew I would. I suspected she would, too.

Viv's room is on the same floor as our kitchen and living room. She moved into it after Mim passed away. My room and the guest room are on the floor above. I had recently painted my room. Previously, it had been a shade of heart attack pink but now it was a soothing pale green color with a creamy white trim. Don't tell anyone but I sort of miss the pink.

Okay, maybe I don't miss the pink so much as I miss the free spirit who painted her room such an eye-watering color. I suppose maturity gives a person better taste but I really hoped it didn't mean I was becoming bland.

After I was scrubbed clean and jammified, I picked up

my phone just to see if there was any word from Harrison. There was not. He was much more polite than me and it occurred to me that he wouldn't text so late, whereas I had no trouble with it.

That being decided, I fired off a text asking him if things were all right.

I picked up the novel I was currently reading while I waited for him to answer. Here's a little-known fact, it's very difficult to read a novel when you keep one eye on your phone at all times. I figured evolution would take care of this problem when we evolve into creatures with tiny fingers for texting and eyes that can go in two directions at once so we can see what's happening around us and read our texts at the same time. It was one of those wee hour ideas that horrified as much as it fascinated.

Finally, after ten whole minutes, my phone buzzed. I snatched it up relieved to see that it was Harrison.

"Hello?"

"Ginger, I just got your text. Why are you still up?" he asked.

Harrison has a nice deep voice and his British accent only makes it all the more charming. I realized that I always enjoyed talking to him on the phone but even more so right now, probably because there was a certain intimacy to having a man speak right into your ear while you're lying in bed in your pajamas.

"I've been waiting to hear what happened," I said.

"We got it sorted," he said.

I could tell he was giving me the brush-off.

"What does that mean exactly?" I asked. "Are you a person of interest?"

He was quiet for a moment, too long of a moment, and I gasped.

"Oh, no, you are, aren't you?" I asked. "It's because of the fight, isn't it?"

"Well, it certainly didn't help matters and when several people came forward as witnesses to the fight . . ."

"But I was there and I told them exactly what happened," I protested.

"I know," he said. "But there are some issues."

"What issues?" I asked. "I was with you the entire time. I'll go and see DI Simms tomorrow and tell him that you were with me. I'm your alibi."

"Ah, see, that's the problem," Harrison said. "You weren't with me the entire time."

"Yes, I was," I argued as if being bullheaded could make it so.

"Scarlett." He said my name quietly, my real name, which is how I knew he was taking this very seriously. "You know I left you for a few minutes after the fight."

"Seconds," I said. "At most, it was seconds."

He chuckled and then he sighed.

"I appreciate the support," he began but I interrupted.

"It's not support, you're innocent," I said. "And I'm not going to let a bunch of drunken toffs railroad you for something you could never do."

"Did you just say 'toffs'?" he asked.

"Yes," I said. "How did it sound?"

"Awkward," he said. "Like me saying 'dude.'"

I laughed and when he spoke again his voice was warm and teasing. "You like me."

"That's beside the point," I mumbled. I could feel my

face heating up. I wasn't sure I was ready to have this conversation, especially since he had no idea that I had been watching him pretty much the entire time he had gone to retrieve the wine at the party after the kerfuffle with Win. When I said he hadn't been out of my sight, I wasn't kidding but I wasn't sure I was ready for him to know that.

"I would do the same for anyone I knew to be innocent," I said. I tried to make my voice sound matter of fact.

"No, you really like me," he teased. "You more than like me."

"Are you being difficult on purpose?" I asked. I was beginning to get flustered. "Because it's not attractive."

"Oh, so you think I'm att—" he began but I interrupted.

"Do not read into that," I said. "Seriously, Harry, this situation is bad, very bad."

He sighed. I felt like a bit of a buzz kill but I was relieved to steer the conversation back to a safer port. Whatever feelings were happening between me and Harry, I was not yet ready to discuss them.

"Alistair assures me that it will be all right," he said. "And I trust him."

"I'm still going to tell Simms that you were only gone from my side for a few moments at most," I said. "And that's only if he asks me. I am volunteering nothing."

"You're something, Scarlett Parker, you know that?" he asked.

The affection in his voice gave me the warm fuzzies, which I promptly tamped down with serious talk.

"Who do you think did it?" I asked.

"No idea," he said. "Win was difficult. He didn't have

many friends and the ones he did have were more like hostages, beholden to him for a debt or a favor."

"So there are a lot of people who aren't grief struck to see him gone," I said.

"Yes," he agreed. "Sad, isn't it?"

"Terribly," I said.

"Listen, Alistair is signaling me that he requires my attention," Harrison said. "Thanks for checking on me. That means quite a lot."

"No problem," I said. "We'll talk tomorrow."

"Definitely," he agreed. "Night, Ginger."

"Night, Harry."

I ended the call and fell back on my bed. I felt better knowing that he was safe at home, but I couldn't shake the feeling that his time in the hot seat was far from over.

"Enid Griswold is the most demanding woman ever," Viv huffed. "First she wants a fedora then she wants a cloche and why do I have to charge her twice and can't I just bend the fedora into a cloche?"

I said nothing as I watched her cut the ribbon she planned to use on the freshly formed cloche with a pair of very sharp scissors.

"Next she'll change the bloody ribbon from red to blue and I'll go mad, absolutely mad," Viv said.

"Then you'll officially be a mad hatter," I said.

"Argh, I can't even go mad without it being redundant," she said.

"Go batty instead," I suggested. "The batty hatter sounds much more hip anyway."

Viv gave me a look that indicated I should stop talking. I am nothing if not receptive to this sort of thing.

"I'll just go open the front," I said. I gathered up the morning paper and my cup of coffee and left the workroom to Viv and her tantrum.

I switched on the lights, did a check of our stock and then went and opened the window shades and unlocked the door. It was a clear, sunny day on Portobello Road and I found it hard to be pessimistic in the face of such glorious weather.

It was still quiet on the street. We rarely had customers this early in the morning unless they were coming for an appointment for a bespoke hat, you know, one measured and created to their exact specifications.

I unfolded the paper and spread it out on the counter. I assumed there would be an article about Win and, frankly, I'd been gearing up for it all morning. The news media and I are not friends. After my very scandalous public breakup, I've never looked at reporters the same way again.

Sure enough, a professional portrait of Win was on the front cover above the fold. He was smirking and his blond bangs hung roguishly over his forehead. Even his picture gave me a bad feeling in the pit of my stomach. The headline shouted in bold letters: *Win Dashavoy Murdered at Guy Fawkes Party.*

I heaved a sigh and then began the article. It talked about Win's position at Carson and Evers and how he'd been considered a star on the rise in the financial world. I wondered who they'd gotten that bit from since as far as I could tell his star had been a dim sparkle at best.

Finally, toward the middle there was a bit about the altercation between Win and Harrison. I leaned over the paper as if getting closer to the words would make me closer to the story. It stated that several witnesses reported punches being exchanged between Harrison and Win over a plain-faced ginger.

I stopped reading. My eyes read the previous sentence again. I felt my brow furrow. Plain-faced ginger? Were they referring to me? I punched the article with my fist right in the kisser.

"So I take it you got to the part where you're mentioned?"

My head snapped up and there was Harrison, smiling at me as if I was the brightest spot in his day.

"What makes you think that?" I asked. "Do you have a shredder? I think this deserves a good shredding."

He laughed. "Not on me, sadly, but you know you have to feel sorry for whoever gave them that description of you."

"Sorry for them. How do you figure?"

"Well, quite clearly, they are blind," he said.

"Oh." The word came out of me on a soft sigh. Yeah, it took everything I had to keep from leaping over the counter and putting him in a stranglehold, you know, the good kind where you use your lips. Instead, I just said, "Thanks, Harry."

I noticed that he didn't correct my use of his nickname, and I wondered if he was just preoccupied or if there had been a subtle shift in our relationship.

"How are Tyler and Reese managing this?" I asked. "I can't imagine that Win's clients are very happy right now."

"I don't know," Harrison said. "I tried calling Tyler this morning but he didn't answer. I received a text this morning that the office was to remain closed."

"They must be taking Win's death pretty hard," I said.

"Reese is," Harrison said. "Tyler and Win were not particularly close, or so I assumed but maybe I was wrong."

Harrison's phone chimed and he checked the display. "It's Reese, excuse me."

I nodded. Then I did what anyone else in my situation would do, I eavesdropped, trying to hear what was being said without appearing to do so. Harrison did not make it easy as he paced back and forth and around the displays. I picked up the occasional grunt, which sounded unhappy, but not much else.

Finally, he pocketed his phone and came back over. "Well, I guess they are figuring things out."

"Is the office open again?" I asked.

"It will be tomorrow, but not to me," he said.

"What do you mean?" I asked.

"It seems I've been suspended from my position without pay until further notice," Harrison said.

"Oh, no!"

"Oh, yes," he said. "It looks as though they've made up their mind about who is guilty of killing Winthrop Dasha-voy. Me."

Chapter 9

"But that's ridiculous!" I said. "They have absolutely no right to do that to you."

"According to Reese, my altercation with Win proves that I had ill will toward my colleague, that I took advantage of his drunken state to thrash him, and they suspect that I got too carried away and strangled him with his necktie," he said. "I think they find it particularly distasteful that it was the company tie I used to kill him."

"That is absurd. I was there and you didn't strangle him, you socked him in the eye. You were most definitely not apart from me long enough to choke someone and then hide their body," I said. I reached for my cell phone.

"What are you doing, Ginger?"

"I'm calling DI Simms," I said. "He needs to know that

you were with me, that I am vouching for you, and that there is absolutely no way you could have done such a horrible thing."

Harrison put his hand on mine, keeping me from searching for Simms's number.

"I really appreciate the support," he said. "But having you call on my behalf like a worried mum is not going to help me. In fact, I fear it will just make me look more guilty."

I gave him a flat stare. "Is that even possible?"

"Ouch," he said.

"Listen, I'm not saying you are guilty, but if I was on the outside looking in, it would look bad for you," I said. "You and Win have been rivals since childhood; there is an ugly history there that you told me about yourself. It's not going to be difficult for the police to find the same information."

Harrison rubbed a hand over his eyes. I knew I was badgering but he needed to get a grasp of how serious the situation was and he needed to let me help him. Damn it.

"You got into a fistfight with Win in front of witnesses, just minutes before someone strangled him and now you've been suspended from your job. Harry, it doesn't look good. You have to let me advocate on your behalf," I said.

He shook his head. "No, I won't let you get dragged into this any more than you already have." He tapped the article in the newspaper to emphasize his point.

I would have argued but he started to pace around the shop, so I knew he was working through something. He was muttering to himself, another indicator of processing, so I waited.

"Suspended. How can they suspend me?" he asked no

one. "I am their best analyst. I bring in millions in revenue. They've known me for years. How could they even think that I would do anything so vile, so horrible, so evil?"

He paused by the front window and stared out onto the street. I felt for him. I knew what it was like to have the entire world watching you, judging you, thinking things about you that were unflattering and untrue. In my case, I packed up and moved to another country. I didn't think he had that option.

The Metropolitan Police might not have arrested him yet but they definitely did not want him to leave the country either. DI Simms would listen to me. I knew he would and it was imperative that they not waste time trying to prove that it was Harrison, because the real killer was out there, and whether I liked Win or not, *not*, his killer must be brought to justice.

Harrison resumed pacing and muttering again. He was working his way back to the counter when his phone rang again.

Our gazes met. I felt my heart sink into my shoes. Would this be the police calling him in for questioning? I didn't care what he said; I was going with him.

He looked at the display and then at me. His eyebrows rose and he said, "Tyler."

"Take it!" I cried. If anyone knew what the heck was going on, it would be Tyler. I leaned across the counter to listen when he answered.

"Hello, Tyler," he said. There was a pause and he added, "Yes, it was a bit of a shock."

It was obvious he was talking about his suspension and understating its napalm-like quality in his usual British fashion. As if my unwavering stare was beginning to burn him with its intensity, he turned slightly away.

"All right then," he said. "I'm glad it's been sorted. I'll see you tomorrow."

He ended the call and put his phone back in his pocket. He looked thoughtful, and as much as I didn't want to interrupt any great insights he was having, I needed to know what was going on.

"Well?" I demanded.

"Tyler lifted my suspension," he said. "He claims that Reese is quite distraught, and that she acted prematurely and all on her own. The offices will be open tomorrow and he would like me to be there."

"How do you feel about that?" I asked.

"Relieved," Harrison said. "It's bad enough the papers are looking at me, but my own people, too? It's a bitter pill."

"Maybe you should stop answering your phone now," I said.

"Good idea." He took his phone out of his pocket and shut it off. He ran his hands through his hair. "I feel as if the whole world has gone mad."

"Did Tyler say anything more about Reese?" I asked. "I mean don't you think it's odd that she suspended you without telling Tyler?"

"Reese has always been very protective of Win," Harrison said. "He was like the son she never had."

I thought about how she had flung herself across his body at the bonfire. She had definitely been wracked with grief, but I wasn't so sure I would have called it maternal, which made my thoughts dart to the other woman in Harrison's office, who was also not very maternal.

"What about Tuesday Blount?" I asked. "What was her relationship with Win?"

Harrison looked distinctly uncomfortable.

"What's the matter?" I heckled. "Don't you want to talk about your ex-girlfriend?"

"I'd rather have a tooth extraction," he said.

"Hang on, I'll call Nick," I offered.

He gave me a lopsided smile. "Why do you want to know about Tuesday?"

"Because she could be a suspect," I said.

"No," he said. "Strangling a man with his own tie is not her style."

"What is her style, bludgeoning, stabbing or zapping the poor bastard with a toaster in his bubble bath?"

He laughed. "No, she's more the sort to henpeck a bloke to death."

This should not have made me as happy as it did. Harrison leaned on the counter and picked up my coffee cup. He raised his eyebrows in silent question and I nodded. I watched him take a sip out of my mug and marveled at the intimacy of such a small casual thing.

Yes, I'd let friends drink out of my cups before. But Harrison was more than a friend and watching his lips on the mug that had just been at mine was a connection that felt deeper than friendship; it felt like something a couple would do.

"You take it just the way I like it," he said.

Our gazes met and I felt that treacherous little thrill flutter in my chest like a bird's wings against its cage, longing to get out if only I would let it.

"Did you love her very much?" I asked.

"Yes," he said.

My little bird clutched his feathered chest with his wings and keeled over dead.

"Well, I should say I thought I did," he said.

My little bird gave a hopeful chirp.

"Thought?" I asked.

His gaze met mine and he gave me a rueful smile. "I don't think I really knew what love was back then. I was ready to spend my life with someone, but she would have been the wrong someone. I have discovered since then that some people can make you preposterously happy just by walking into the room and smiling at you. She never had that effect on me."

My little bird was now flying loop-the-loops and wing-overs, but I refused to lose my head. I had the horrible thought that if Harrison had been that ga-ga over Tuesday, I could be the dreaded transition woman. Oh, horror!

Then again, if he was railroaded for Win's murder and sentenced to prison, it really wouldn't matter if I was his transition woman or not.

The bells on the front door jangled and in strode Tuesday Blount. I wondered if talking about her had conjured her, sort of like a witch, which was an unnerving thought to say the least because I thought it was entirely too accurate.

"Harrison!" She strode briskly, brandishing her phone like a weapon. "I've been calling and calling. Why haven't you answered?"

Harrison tipped his head to the side. "Didn't you hear? The office is closed. We have the day off."

She waved her hand in the air like she was karate chopping his words. "There are no days off for us. You know that." She gave me a disgruntled look as if his lack of a work ethic were my fault. "Besides, I need to talk to you about other matters."

"Can it wait?" Harrison asked. "I've got some things to do here."

To my credit, I didn't even flicker an eyelash at his bald-faced lie.

"No, it can't," she said. "It's about the unfortunate incident."

"You mean where someone strangled our colleague with his own tie?" Harrison asked. He seemed to be enjoying goading her.

"Shh," she hissed as she looked around the empty shop. "There are ears everywhere."

"Well, that does *sound* like a problem," I said. Harrison laughed. I felt like pumping my fist. I'd finally gotten him to acknowledge one of my puns. Oh, why weren't the others here to witness this?

"I hear it's an epidemic," Harrison said and winked at me.

This time I laughed and Tuesday glanced between us as if we were crazy.

"Harrison!" She stomped her foot. Yes, she really did with all the flair and drama of an outraged three-year-old. "I need to talk to you in private *right now*."

Harrison heaved a sigh. It was clear there would be no getting rid of her. He looked at me as he stepped back from the counter.

"I'll call you later," he said.

"Okay," I said. "Remember I'm a really good listener."

He laughed again and I felt like everything was right in my world, even though he was leaving with her. I wondered what she wanted. I couldn't shake the feeling that she was not to be trusted and not just because they had a history together. She put off a devious vibe and I sincerely hoped Harrison picked up on it, too.

The thought of Harrison taking the fall for the real murderer was completely unacceptable. I turned and went back into the workroom to talk to Viv. We needed to figure out how we could help Harrison whether he wanted us to or not.

Chapter 10

"Call Harrison and see if he is still with her," I said.

Viv looked at me with an annoyed glance. "How am I supposed to do that?"

"Just chat him up," I said. I waved her phone in front of her face. "But sound casual."

"Like he's not going to figure out that it's you putting her up to it, yeah?" Fee asked.

"He might not," I said.

The three of us were standing in the front of the shop. Harrison and Tuesday had left twenty minutes before, and as soon as Fee had arrived downstairs to start her shift, I had begun to badger Viv about following Harrison and Tuesday.

Fee rolled her eyes and began hand-stitching tiny seed pearls to the edge of a length of amethyst tulle that she was using to decorate a mother of the bride hat. It was going to be spectacular.

"Hi, Harrison, sorry to bother you," Viv said into her phone.

Fee and I both watched her as if we could figure out what Harrison was saying by her facial expressions.

"No, no emergency," she said. "We were just thinking we should remind you that we planned to meet up at Nick and Andre's tonight and wondered if you could still make it."

I raised my hands in a gesture of what are you doing? We needed his location now not later. She frowned at me and turned her back on me.

"Sounds great," she said. "So, are you still with her?"

I made an outraged noise. Seriously, the woman had zero skills in the art of covert information gathering.

"And where are you?" she asked.

Now I did a face palm. Why didn't she just say we were planning to stalk them?

She looked over her shoulder at me. "At your apartment?"

Now I gasped and so did Fee. Tuesday having Harrison alone in his apartment was not good, not good at all.

"All right, tonight then," Viv said and she hung up.

She tossed her phone onto the counter.

"Well, that was bloody uncomfortable," she said. "They're at his place."

I headed for the door. "Fee, watch the shop, come on, Viv."

"What?" Viv asked. "I have work to do and you're being an awful bossy boots."

I paused to stare at Viv and Fee. They were not getting it. "Tuesday could be the killer and Harrison is alone with her. Let's go!"

At this both Fee and Viv jumped. I realized my bark had been a bit ferocious, so I tried to tone it down.

"Now!" I yelled. Okay, tried and failed. Still, it got Viv moving. She grabbed her coat and her handbag, shouted instructions at Fee and followed me out the door.

As we jogged through the neighborhood to Harrison's place on Pembridge Mews, the sky grew increasingly dark and the wind picked up. Neither Viv nor I had thought to bring an umbrella, as if we didn't know better living in a city known for its rain.

Harrison had a second-story flat, so with any luck his curtains would be drawn back and we'd be able to see inside. I tried not to think about what we might see if Tuesday had her way—with him, that is.

We loitered under a tree across the street. The curtains were drawn back but the angle was no good. We couldn't see anything.

It began to drizzle and Viv's long blond curls started to poof into their natural frizzy state. She gave me a look that said she was very unhappy and then she dug into her purse until she found a scarf, which she wrapped around her head. My hair was getting sodden as well, but I knew I didn't have a scarf in my bag.

"You don't happen to have another one of those, do you?" I asked.

"No," she said. The look she gave me was dour.

Okay, then. I glanced around to see if there was a better

vantage point in the area. The steps to the house behind us would give us a bit of a boost. I gestured for Viv to follow me and we trudged up the steps.

Ah, now I could see into Harrison's place. I saw him pass across the window. His shoulders were hunched and he ran his hand through his hair. It was his usual look when he was agitated. I tried not to be thrilled that they were clearly not having a good time. I failed.

"Stop smiling," Viv chided me. "It's bucketing out here and we're spying on our friend who is obviously fine. There is nothing to smile about."

I glanced around me. Viv was right. The drizzle had turned into a full-on soaking. My hair was streaming water and my coat was drenched, but I didn't care.

The door opened behind us and an elderly man glared at us through the crack in the door.

"Who are you?" he asked.

Viv and I exchanged a glance. We couldn't say we were using his stoop to spy.

"I'm Scarlett," I said. I gave him my most winning smile, which was lacking its usual charm given my drowned rat appearance. "And this is Vivian."

"What do you want?" he asked.

His hair was sticking up in tufts on his head and he was wearing a baggy gray cardigan over a dress shirt and slacks with slippers. He looked toasty warm and dry and I felt a spurt of envy.

"We're lost," Viv said. "We're just trying to get our bearings."

"Well, do it somewhere else, or I'll call the police," he snapped. "Go on, get off with you."

He gestured us away with his hand and when we stepped down the stairs he slammed the door behind us.

"Rude!" Viv cried out.

"Shh!" I hissed. I grabbed her arm and pulled her behind a parked car.

"What is it?" she demanded.

"Look!" I cried. I pointed across the street where Tuesday Blount was coming out of Harrison's building. She paused to put up her purple umbrella, of course she had one, and then strode down the sidewalk toward Notting Hill Gate.

"Thank goodness, now let's go home," Viv said.

"No, we have to follow her," I cried.

"What?" Viv asked, incredulous.

I didn't answer but dashed across the road, giving Viv no choice but to follow me. She caught up to me at the crosswalk near the stairs to the underground.

"Have you lost your mind?" she asked.

"I just want to know what she's up to," I said. "She had to talk to Harrison in private and now she's hurrying off to go who knows where. I say it's suspicious behavior."

"You just don't like her because she's Harrison's ex," Viv said.

"Be that as it may," I said. "We need to know what she is doing in case she is trying to set up Harrison for Win's murder."

Viv sighed. We followed Tuesday's purple umbrella all the way into the underground. I grabbed one of the newsmen's free papers on the way in and used it as a shield to hide my face should Tuesday look back at me. She did not.

I was careful to keep several people between us at all

times. Still Viv and I managed to jump onto the same train car as Tuesday. I opened the paper and found myself face-to-face with an ad for men's underwear. Awesome.

Viv wrapped her scarf more loosely about her head, trying to hide her face. We were on the Central Line and I noticed when I peered around the paper that Tuesday wasn't taking an available seat but was staying by the doors. I figured that meant she was getting off soon. Sure enough, when we pulled up to the Bond Street platform, she darted out.

"Go, go, go!" I ordered Viv.

The crush of people getting on the train made it tricky to get off. We muscled our way through the crowd and found Tuesday switching to the Northern Line platform. We joined her while carefully keeping our distance.

The electronic board above told us the train would be arriving in three minutes. We followed Tuesday onto it and it went much as before with her switching to the Victoria Line and us following like eager little puppies.

"You are aware that this could go on all day," Viv hissed as we pulled into Victoria Station.

"It won't," I assured her.

Tuesday left the platform and headed up into the station. We followed as closely as we could. She circled a kiosk and I motioned for Viv to go one way while I went the other. When we met on the other side, there was no sign of Tuesday.

I scanned the area but there were so many people bustling about the enormous station, I couldn't get my bearings and I couldn't locate the annoying brunette.

"That's it then," Viv said.

She began to walk away and I was forced to follow her. She didn't look the least bit sorry to be ending our mission, and I was annoyed with her lack of commitment until I realized she wasn't headed back to our platform.

"Where are you going?" I asked. "Do you see her?"

"No," Viv said. "But I do see a lovely cheese and onion pasty with my name on it. I think I deserve it after that soaking we took."

I followed the direction of her gaze. Sure enough, tucked into the side of the station was The Pasty House. The display case in front showed stacks and stacks of the half-moon-shaped pies. I saw a chicken and mushroom and figured Viv was right. We deserved some comfort food to bolster our spirits.

We paid for our pasties and coffee and found a small café table and chairs. I shrugged off my jacket, hoping it would dry a bit while we ate. The crust was flaky and the inside was flavorful without being overdone. It was perfect rainy day, big disappointment food, and yet, I didn't feel any better.

I don't know what I had been expecting to figure out by following Tuesday. A secret lover? A rendezvous with a tabloid reporter? Something.

"You know Harrison is over her, don't you?" Viv asked.

"That's none of my business," I said.

"So we're following her because . . ." Viv's voice trailed off but before I could answer the devil herself plopped down in the empty seat at our table.

"Because you're busybodies and you're sticking your noses in where they don't belong," Tuesday Blount said as she eyed us with supreme disdain and loathing.

Chapter 11

I choked on a bit of crust and Viv thumped me hard on the back. I waved her off and took a sip of my coffee to dislodge the crumb.

"How did you know we were following you?" I asked. It seemed pointless to deny it.

"Oh, please," she said. "You two are as subtle as a kick to the shins. I saw you as soon as I left Harrison's."

"How is he?" Viv asked.

I figured that like me she thought Harrison might be more forthcoming with Tuesday since they were colleagues and Tuesday had known Win as well.

"Fine," Tuesday said with a shrug. "He expects the police will have it sorted in no time."

"You don't agree with him?" I asked.

Tuesday turned to look at me. It was clear that it pained

her to give me her full attention. That she didn't like me was obvious in the tiny curl of her upper lip which was almost a sneer but sheer politeness kept it from bursting into full bloom.

"You care about him," she said. She tossed her head and her black bob fell perfectly about her face.

The embarrassed heat that warmed my face outed me, making any sort of denial useless.

"He's our business manager," I said with a shrug. So lame.

She narrowed her eyes. "He says you two aren't dating."

"We're not," I said. Why it bothered me that Harrison had told her we weren't a couple, I can't say, but it did. A lot.

"I'm not dating him either," Viv said. She took another bite of her pasty and gave us a bland look.

"Look, I'm sorry I came on so strong at the party," Tuesday said. The crinkle in her nose made it clear that these words did not pass her lips without some internal strain. Good.

"Apology accepted," I said because I can be very gracious like that.

"Whatever it is that you and Harrison are or are not . . ." Tuesday paused and I noticed that she emphasized the *not*. "The fact is Harrison is in deep trouble and I'm in a much better position to help him than you."

"How do you figure?" I asked. I bit a mushroom in half like it was her head and ground it between my molars.

"I work with him," she said as if I were too stupid to live. "I can keep an eye on him and anyone around him all day long."

I took a slow sip of my coffee, hoping it would keep me

from slapping her smug face when she dragged out the words "all day long."

"That seems reasonable," I said. Viv cast me a curious look, but I ignored her while I brushed some pasty crumbs off my lap. "Since we'll be watching him all night long."

Tuesday drew in a sharp breath. One point to me or maybe two since that was a particularly good hit.

"But I thought you weren't a couple," she said.

"We aren't, but we are business associates and neighbors and our social circle is pretty tight," I said. "We frequently spend our evenings together."

"It's true," Viv said. "In fact, aren't we all going to Andre and Nick's for a nosh tonight?"

"Yes," I said. "Oh, I hope he makes his stuffed mushrooms again."

"And his canapés," Viv said. She looked at Tuesday. "Nick's a fabulous cook." And then she glanced back at me and said, "We should bring wine."

"Definitely," I agreed. "Unless it's Harrison's turn for wine, we should text him to be sure."

"On it," Viv said. She pulled her phone out of her purse and began to type.

"Don't mention that I'm with you . . . please," Tuesday said.

I was encouraged to see that she looked a bit panicked. Maybe she and Harrison were not as close as she wanted us to believe and Harrison wouldn't be too keen to have her talking to us. I held up my hand at Viv and she lowered her phone.

"Tuesday, can we let go of the posturing?" I asked.

"Obviously, we're all worried about him. Tell us what you know so we can help."

"How are two little hatmakers going to help?" she scoffed.

"Was that nice?" I asked.

"Like following me was nice?" she countered.

I pursed my lips. I really wanted to tell her to shove off but that wouldn't help the situation at all.

"Who hated Winthrop enough to want him dead?" I asked. I was done being coy. She needed to either put up or shut up.

"You mean other than Harrison?" she asked.

"He didn't want Win dead," Viv argued. "Sure, they were office rivals but he certainly wasn't angry enough to kill Dashavoy over business."

"Maybe it wasn't business," Tuesday said. She turned a vicious glance my way. "What exactly happened between you and Win anyway?"

"Me? Nothing," I said. "How am I involved in this?"

"They fought over you," Tuesday said. She made it sound as preposterous as polar bears sunbathing in Hawaii.

"No, they didn't," I said. "Win got grabby and Harrison checked his behavior; that was all."

"Why did Win grab you?" she persisted.

"Probably to get a rise out of Harrison," I said.

"But why?" Tuesday persisted.

"Why don't you ask Harrison?" Viv asked.

"I did but he seems to think it was just Win being his usual annoying self."

"But you don't?" I asked.

"Win is . . . was always sneaky," Tuesday said. There was a bitterness in her tone that made me suspect that she'd had more than her share of run-ins with Winthrop Dashavoy. "It was not in his nature to be so flagrant with his bad behavior unless it suited his purpose."

"He was drunk," I said. I remembered the reek of alcohol on his breath and I shivered. Bleh.

"He was always drunk," Tuesday said. "Even at work he was known for cornering the new girls in the mailroom for a quick grope but he was always very careful about it. He wasn't careful at the party. Why?"

We were all silent and Viv and I exchanged a look. I knew Viv and I were thinking the same thing. Tuesday had been a new girl once and she'd probably had to put up with Win's grabby hands at the time.

"So you think there is a reason that he was particularly awful that night," Viv said.

"Yes," Tuesday said. "Win was a mean, manipulative, deceitful prat, and no one liked him, and believe me no one is really mourning his absence from the office now."

"Except for Reese," I said. "She seemed distraught at his death. Harrison said Win was her husband's protégé and that she felt quite maternal toward him."

"'Maternal' isn't the word that leaps to my mind," Tuesday said.

"What do you mean?" I asked.

"I walked into Reese's office once and Win was already there," Tuesday said. Then she paused as if recalling the moment in great detail. She shook her head and her silky bob brushed her cheeks, drawing my gaze to her striking cheekbones. Annoying.

"And?" I prompted.

"It was not a mother-son vibe in that room," Tuesday said. "More like a cougar stalking a deer."

"I'm going out on a limb here and guessing that Reese is the cougar," I said.

She gave me a *duh* look. Gah, I didn't like Tuesday Blount, not even a little.

"That doesn't mean that they had anything going," Viv pointed out. "It could have all been wishful thinking on Reese's part."

"No, Win would use any advantage he had," Tuesday said. "And sleeping with the woman who owned almost half of the company would be quite the advantage."

"It would certainly be job security," I said.

Tuesday grunted an acknowledgment.

"The problem is that Harrison had a very public row with him right before he was killed," Viv said.

"And they've been rivals since boarding school," I added.

Tuesday's eyes narrowed. "Harrison told you about that?"

"How else would I know?" I asked. I tried not to sound smug, really I did. Okay, not my best effort.

"Harrison doesn't usually share that information," Tuesday said. She gave me a considering look as if I warranted more serious attention now.

"If he was this difficult with his co-workers, how was he in his personal life?" Viv asked. "For that matter, what about his clients? He can't have stayed on everyone's good side."

"Oh, he didn't," Tuesday said. "The list of people who

had a beef with Winthrop Dashavoy is as long as the phone book."

I blew out a breath. I didn't like this. It would be too easy for Harrison to become the readymade target. Not that I thought the Metropolitan Police were like that but still there was no denying that Harrison had inadvertently made himself a fabulous person of interest for the investigation and I couldn't help feeling as if it was all my fault.

As if reading my mind, Viv said, "I am quite sure that the detective inspectors will find the culprit. There has to be some sort of evidence, a witness, something, that will tell them who really killed Winthrop."

"What about Tyler Carson?" I asked Tuesday.

Her eyes went wide and then shuttered as if she was hiding something. "What about him?" she asked.

"What was his relationship with Win?"

"I don't know," Tuesday said. She spoke quickly and didn't meet my eyes.

"That's it," Viv said. She stood and gathered her purse, cinching her scarf about her neck. "This is pointless."

"What? Why?" Tuesday asked.

"You, my dear, are a terrible liar," Viv said.

Chapter 12

Viv's blue eyes, the same shape and shade as mine, snapped and sparked with frustration as she leaned over the table and got in Tuesday's face.

"Do you really think I don't know that you broke it off with Harrison because you were having an affair with Tyler?" she hissed.

I gasped.

Tuesday went a pasty shade of gray that reminded me of cold oatmeal.

"That is neither here nor there," she said. Her voice was faint and I would have felt sorry for her if I'd liked her. Luckily, I didn't.

"I'd say it's very much there," I said. "How many people knew you were sleeping with Carson?"

Tuesday looked at me and the loathing she had felt for

me before flamed into genuine hatred. "This is none of your business."

I stood beside Vivian and glared down at her. "Harrison is our partner and friend. It is very much our business, because I am betting that if Win knew about your relationship with Tyler, he wouldn't hesitate to use it against both of you."

I didn't think it was possible, but Tuesday went even paler and I wondered if she would soon be transparent. Either way, it confirmed what I suspected, which was that Win knew about the affair and he had used it as leverage.

"What happened?" Viv asked. "Did he go to Tyler's wife and tell on you or did he just threaten to do it?"

"Oh, please," Tuesday snapped. "As if Ava the pill-popping paralytic would even care if her husband stepped out on her."

We said nothing, just stared at her. She stood and faced us across the table. Her hands were shaking as she pulled on her gloves so I knew she was not nearly as blasé as she pretended to be.

"He did, didn't he?" I asked.

"Empty threats," Tuesday said. "Any relationship that may or may not have existed between Tyler and me was over before it started. Good day."

With a twirl of her coat, she stormed away, leaving Viv and me gaping after her. She disappeared into the crowd and a harried-looking couple with two small children crowded us for our table. Viv and I moved away so they could take it.

Viv glanced at the electronic board that posted arrivals and departures from the station as well as the current time.

"We'd best get back," she said. "Fee's been on her own long enough."

"Should we bring her something?" I asked.

"Let's get something closer to home," Viv said.

We worked our way through the crowd to our platform. I kept glancing around for Tuesday, which was ridiculous because the financial district was in a different direction and there was no reason she'd be on our train, unless she was going back to visit Harrison again.

I shook the thought off. She wasn't going to go back to Harrison's. I was sure of it, mostly, but a little pinprick of jealousy kept jabbing my insides, making me surly and a little mean.

Viv and I found seats on the train and I turned to her and asked, "So you're the expert married one; how would you feel if your husband cheated on you?"

She turned and looked at me as if I had three heads, but I wasn't in the mood to play.

"Oh, come on," I said. "Pretend you're Ava. How would you feel if your husband picked up with a woman at work?"

Viv's temper was beginning to heat. I could tell because she always fidgets when she is processing her ire and right now she was twisting the end of her scarf between her hands. I wondered if she was pretending it was my neck.

"I don't know," she said. "Obviously, my marriage is different than the Carsons'."

"Does Aunt Grace know you're married?" I asked. Viv's mother, my aunt Grace, lived up north in Yorkshire. She didn't like London and seldom came to visit, leaving the traveling to Viv. Although they were reasonably close,

I couldn't imagine Viv would have told her parents if she hadn't told me.

"No, I never told anyone," she said.

"Except Harrison," I said.

"I didn't tell him so much as he found out," she said. "He's never known anything more than the fact that it happened. Why are you asking me about this now?"

"Because I'm cranky," I said.

"Clearly," she agreed.

"And because I kept thinking you were going to open up and tell me about it yourself when you were ready, but now I am thinking that you're never going to tell me anything and life is uncertain, look at Winthrop Dashavoy. I'll bet he didn't expect his own death to be the premier event at the Carson and Evers bonfire party, and if you don't tell me about your marriage and something bad happens, I may never know what possessed you to marry, I'm sorry, what's his name?"

"So all of this"—she paused and gestured at me with her hands—"is because you're afraid you're going to die before finding out who I'm married to?"

"Yes," I said.

"But you'll be dead," she said. "What will you care then?"

"You are a cold woman, Vivian Tremont, colder than cold in fact," I said. "You're frozen solid."

A look of hurt flashed across Viv's face and she turned away from me. Instantly, I was filled with regret for my words, and I wanted to apologize but the part of me that was righteously injured because she hadn't confided in me about her marriage refused to knuckle under and apologize. I was beginning to think we'd never get past this.

The train rumbled through the dark underground. I glared at the passengers around us, the man on his smartphone, the businesswoman in the power suit, the hipster reading a book, the grandmother with two girls, who reminded me of Viv and Mim and me twenty years ago. I bet they didn't keep secrets from their best friends. Yes, I was in a full sulk.

I wondered what Mim would make of all this right now. Would she approve of Viv's secret marriage? Or would she say I was bang out of order, one of her favorite expressions, for pushing Viv so hard for answers?

Given that Mim had been the same creative free spirit as Viv, I had a feeling I wouldn't like the answer to my question. Knowing Mim, she'd say to give Viv time and that she'd come around when she was ready, even if it took years.

That line of thinking was fine if you were a patient person. Sadly, I am not. I want what I want when I want it. It's a flaw that I am working on, but when it came to finding out what was going on with Viv, the sister of my heart, I had even less patience than usual.

Perhaps it would be different if she were deliriously happy and flitting around like a magpie with a diamond, but she wasn't. She was quiet, withdrawn, aloof, and there was a pervasive sadness about her that wasn't natural at all for the Viv I had always known and loved.

Maybe it was selfish, but I just wanted my cousin back. I wanted her to be present in our shared business and our life. I didn't want any secrets between us, but until she told me exactly what was going on in her life, there was a chasm between us as wide as the Thames River and I had no idea how to bridge it.

"Viv—" I began but she interrupted me as the train pulled into High Street Kensington Station.

"Forget it," she said as she stood and moved to the door.

"Where are you—" I didn't get a chance to finish.

Viv stepped off the train and I scrambled after her, jumping onto the platform just before the doors shut. We had been on the Circle Line headed back to Notting Hill Gate. This was a stop short of our destination and put us smack in the midst of Kensington.

As Viv pressed through the crowd toward the exit, I followed feeling like a sad little puppy. As we exited onto the street, I caught her elbow and brought her to a stop.

"What are we doing here?" I asked.

I expected her to rip me a new one for pressing her about her marriage. Instead she said, "We need to know more about the Carsons."

I shook my head as if my ears were ringing and I couldn't have heard her right.

"You've lost me," I said.

"From what Tuesday told us and didn't tell us, the Carsons seem awfully suspicious to me, especially Ava," she said. "I just can't shake the feeling that she's got some sort of ulterior agenda happening. The way she swept off with Andre and Nick at the party almost as if she was planning to use them as an alibi."

I stared at Viv. Truly, I couldn't have been more surprised if she'd announced she was giving up millinery to join the circus. Then again, this was Viv of the secret wedding, so actually the circus wouldn't surprise me at all.

"This is very sleuthy of you," I said. "Have you been watching too much *Grantchester*?"

"Maybe," she conceded. "Fee and I did do some binge watching the other night when you were out with Nick and Andre. I think Fee has a crush on the vicar."

I nodded. I could see that. "So what's your plan?"

"Don't have one," she said. "But it is a shame I lost my yellow cap at their party, isn't it? And just when Elise Stanford said she wanted to run a segment on winter hats."

"You did?" I asked. "But I could have sworn . . ."

My voice trailed off as she stared at me.

"Oh," I said. "Now I get it."

"That's a relief," she said. She turned and began to walk and I fell in beside her. "You were beginning to worry me."

"In my defense, I thought you were angry with me for pressing you about your personal life," I said.

"I'm not angry, I'm annoyed, there's a difference," she said. "But Harrison is a bigger concern right now. Tuesday was right about one thing, with the hostile history between Winthrop Dashavoy and Harrison dating all the way back to their school days, Harrison makes a very tasty suspect and even the best copper would have a hard time looking away from that."

I felt my hopes for Harrison's future fracture and fall into the toes of my shoes. Viv was right. Unless we could find another suspect, Harrison was doomed.

Chapter 13

The Carson estate looked different in the cold, watery light of midday. There were no twinkling lights or lamps warming the front entrance and even the pumpkins and cornstalk decorations seemed withered and withdrawn.

Viv walked up to the front door with no hesitation and pressed the doorbell. It seemed to me that a place like this would have better security, you know, to keep the riffraff like us out. I glanced at the panel where the buzzer was and noted a tiny red flashing light, sort of like an electronic eye watching us. I resisted the urge to straighten my clothes at what I was sure was a security camera.

A voice spoke out of the box, and I recognized the butler Price's voice.

"Carson residence, how may I assist you?" Mr. Price asked.

"Good afternoon, sorry to trouble you, but I'm hoping to retrieve my hat, which I left here the other evening," Viv said. "I wouldn't bother you, but I am a milliner and it is a very important design."

There was no response and I braced myself for rejection, it hurts no matter who does it to you for whatever reason, but I needn't have bothered.

"You were the ladies in Mr. Wentworth's party?" he asked.

"Yes, Vivian Tremont and my cousin Scarlett Parker," she said. "We own Mim's Whims."

"One moment, please," he said.

And then as if we had spoken the magic words, the large door swung open and Price bade us to enter and speak with Oz the great and powerful, or in our case Ava, the wife, aloof and wasted.

Price led us through the immense foyer with the sparkling chandelier overhead, through the large room with the Rothko painting on display that I remembered from our first visit to the house. He strode down a short hall to the left and opened one of two gorgeously carved wooden doors, gesturing for us to precede him into the room.

"If you'll wait here, I'll send someone in to assist you directly," he said.

It was a lavish drawing room with floor-to-ceiling windows, draped in crimson velvet, that overlooked the side lawn. The furniture was a mix of ornately upholstered gold suede armchairs mixed with dark brown leather couches with plush crimson pillows. The walls were painted a matte ecru, which made the expensive paintings lit from above and below pop on the walls.

Several potted palms filled the corners with greenery, but the thing that caught my attention and held it was a large eight-foot-high marble statue placed in front of the center window. I crossed the room toward it as if it beckoned.

I tried not to gape, really I did, but it was hard when I could tell at a glance that the statue was Ava in the raw, as in naked, butt naked. I heard Viv grunt beside me and knew that she recognized the statue as well.

"That's taking stony silence to all new levels," Viv said. I chuckled.

"She can't help it," I said. "She's clearly caught between a rock and a hard place."

Viv snorted and I pointed at her. "You laughed."

"No, I didn't," she denied. "That was a sneeze."

"It was a snort!" I said. "Come on, you have to give it to me; it was a good pun."

"Oh, all right," she said. "But only because I think the rest of us must be rubbing off on you."

"Ahem."

A discreetly cleared throat brought our attention around to the door. A woman in a severe black dress with sensible shoes stood watching us.

"Good day, I'm Mrs. Bailey, the housekeeper," she said. "Mr. Price said you required assistance?"

Viv looked as if she'd forgotten why we'd come and I saw her studying Mrs. Bailey as if she were fitting her for a hat.

"Um, er, yes, we lost a hat the other evening during the unfortunate incident," I said. Mrs. Bailey gave me a small nod, letting me know she understood what I was talking about, and I felt a flash of pride at my mastery of the British art of understatement.

"Can you describe it?" she asked.

"Yes, it was a yellow cap, wool, with a short brim," Viv said. "And a bit slouchy in the back."

"I'll go and check the coatroom," Mrs. Bailey said. "Would you care for some tea while you wait?"

"No, thank you," I declined for both of us. I glanced at Viv and she nodded, indicating she was passing as well.

"Please make yourselves comfortable," Mrs. Bailey said. "I'll return directly."

She closed the door softly behind her, and I wondered if that was her way of telling us to behave. I sat on the edge of one of the plush-looking chairs. Viv took the one beside me. I bounced up and down a bit. It was like landing on concrete.

"Seems like these should be more squashy, don't you think?" I asked.

Viv tried her chair out. "Yes. Maybe the sofa is softer."

She rose and crossed to the couch. I could tell by the way she winced when she sat that it wasn't any better.

"Maybe they bring people in here because they don't want them to get too comfortable and overstay their welcome," I said.

"Well, it's working," Viv said. "As if the naked statue isn't off-putting enough, I don't want to be that up close and personal with my hostess's bare breasts, do you?"

"Hmm, that doesn't bother me as much as the feeling that she's watching me," I said. Whoever had carved the statue had managed to make it appear that the marble eyes had a bead on you wherever you were in the room.

It reminded me of the raven carved into the wardrobe in the corner of our shop. His beady little wooden eyes had the same effect on me.

I rose from my hard seat and walked across the room. Glancing over my shoulder, I felt the statue's watchful gaze on me. I switched directions and went the other way, and I swear it tracked me. I shivered.

"You're right," Viv said. She rose from her seat and stood beside me as if there were safety in numbers. "It's just creepy."

"Well, thanks for that!"

The voice was shrill and very dramatic, and I knew without turning around to whom it belonged. Ava Carson.

"So sorry," I said as I spun about, putting on my brightest people pleaser smile. Years in hospitality had trained me to be an excellent smoother-overer. "We shouldn't have been talking about the unfortunate incident the other night, very rude of us to call it creepy, please forgive us?"

I felt Viv turn her head to study me. I ignored her for fear that I might give us away.

"Oh, I thought you were talking about . . . something else," Ava said. She was standing in the shadow of the open door as if uncertain as to whether she wanted to come in or not.

"How are you, Mrs. Carson?" Viv said. "We do apologize for intruding upon you without notice."

"It's fine," Ava said. With that, she seemed to make up her mind and she stepped fully into the room.

I gasped as she sashayed toward us. This was not the blond bombshell wearing lavender cashmere from the other evening. Oh, no, this was a woman who appeared to have been on an all-night bender. Her red lipstick was smeared to one side of her lips, her mascara was flaked across her cheeks, and her blond hair stood up straight in the back but was flat across her forehead as if she'd just gotten out of bed. She was wearing a thick velour robe of deep purple with a lighter satin piping along the edges and sash, and she was barefoot.

We must have been staring, okay, yes, we were staring, because she sneered at us, and asked, "What?"

"Purple is a very good color for you," Viv said. "Not many blondes can carry it off."

"That's because I'm not really blond," Ava said.

She reached into the pocket of her dressing gown and pulled out a cigarette case from which she withdrew a black cigarette with a gold foil filter tip. She did not offer either of us one for which I was profoundly grateful; even with a swank gold tip I was not enticed to take up smoking.

Ava put the case back and used a sparkly lighter, also from her pocket, to light the cigarette. She inhaled and blew out a thick plume of smoke. She kept the cigarette between two fingers in front of her mouth and rested her chin on her thumb while she considered us.

Her gaze went from fuzzy to sharp as if she was fading in and out of the moment. I had a feeling if we wanted to ask her any questions about the other night, we'd better be quick about it.

"We lost one of our hats," I said. "The yellow one? We were hoping it might be here."

Ava turned her back to me and walked over to the statue by the window. Even beneath her robe, I could see that she managed to move her hips in a swivelly, swervy come-hither way that my behind would never master not even with lessons. Impressive.

She gazed up at her profile rendered in marble. The sculptor had done an amazing job capturing her likeness right down to the tiny divot at the end of her upturned nose.

"Carson had this carved for my birthday when we were first married," she said. "November fifth, bonfire night, is my birthday. It was not exactly a happy birthday this year or maybe it was."

Okay, that was creepy. I glanced at Viv, who gave me an alarmed look before blanking her features and turning back to Ava, who was still staring at her likeness.

"He loved me then," she said. Her voice sounded wistful.

I felt the discomfort of being an unwilling confidant, sort of like wearing a jacket that was too small as it pinched and squeezed, making me want to wriggle out of it.

"I'm sure he still does," Viv said. She was not as skilled in fibbing as I was and it showed.

"No, he doesn't," Ava said. She stroked her hand over the abdomen of the statue. "Being unable to bear children will do that to a marriage; suddenly the man starts looking at younger, more fertile women. It can't be helped. It's the nature of men."

I wanted to protest on principle that no man stopped loving a woman just because she couldn't have children, but I knew it was a lie just as I knew there were women who had left their men for similar reasons.

"I don't think—" Viv began, obviously unable to resist protesting Ava's assessment.

"It doesn't matter," Ava said. She spread her arms wide

to encompass the entire room and all that was in it. "Look around you. I have everything a girl could ever want. Everything." She paused and looked at us over her shoulder, and in a voice that was worthy of a D-list actress, she cried, "I will not let them steal my joy!"

Oh, boy. I had a feeling we were headed down a slippery slope of crazy, and it was best to get our conversation on track. Viv had said she didn't trust Ava Carson, that she had swept up Andre and Nick as if she was aligning an alibi. I thought that was an astute observation, but when I looked into Ava's blank gaze I wasn't sure how much brainpower she had available for subterfuge.

Of course, Tuesday Blount obviously loathed Ava and had no problem casting her in the role of villainess, but since I had no affection for Tuesday, I didn't give her opinion much credence.

I glanced at the grandfather clock ticking in the far corner. The housekeeper had been gone for fifteen minutes and would be back shortly no doubt. I decided to cut right into the heart of it.

"Has there been any news about Winthrop Dashavoy's death?" I asked.

Out of the corner of my eye, I saw Viv stiffen in surprise. My blunt American ways were showing again, but I figured that was exactly what would let me get away with the question.

Ava lowered her arms and turned toward me. She took a long drag off her cigarette and blew out a plume of smoke. The sunlight from the window illuminated the blue-gray swirls until they dissipated. She tapped the ash into a crystal ashtray that probably cost more than Viv and

I made in a month and then she lowered her head and glanced at me from under her long lashes.

I suspected the look was supposed to be coquettish, but with her makeup in smears and one of her false eyelashes dangling, it took on a sad caricature of charm. I knew I was supposed to feel beguiled but what I felt was repulsed with a dash of pity.

"You know who strangled Win," she said.

"Me?" I asked. I pointed to myself in confusion.

"Yes, you," she said. She stubbed her cigarette out in the ashtray. She walked around her statue, passing her hand lovingly over its alabaster curves as she went.

"How do you figure that?" I snapped. My usual people skills had abandoned me and I felt Viv step closer to me as my temper got the better of me. I wondered if she thought she was going to have to tackle me to keep me from doing Ava Carson an injury. Not the craziest thought.

"Why, because you're in love with the killer," Ava said. She leaned against her marble image and stared at me with an intensity that made my skin itch. "Harrison."

Chapter 14

"All right, let's get some things straight. Number one, I am not in love with Harrison, and number two, he is not the killer," I huffed.

Ava looked past me at Viv. "You know I'm telling the truth."

Viv threw her shoulders back and glared. "I know no such thing. Harrison is not a murderer."

I noticed that she didn't deny my love for Harrison, which I thought was a tactical mistake. I was right.

Ava came at us, sort of like a big cat stalking its prey but wearing a purple robe, which made her look a bit ridiculous frankly. From the smirk on her face, she seemed to be taking a perverse delight in needling us.

"Oh, is that how it is?" she asked.

She stopped right in front of us and planted one hand

on her hip as she looked at Viv. I noticed Ava had the crazy eye thing going, you know, like she wasn't really dialed in to this reality. "You're in love with Harrison and you don't want your precious little cousin to have him."

"You are way off the mark," Viv said. "Harrison is my friend and I know he could never ever do anything like strangle the life out of a colleague. You, however . . ."

"What?" Ava leaned closer and I caught a whiff of morning breath tainted with cigarettes that made me gag.

"She's thinking you could have killed him," I said, because I'm helpful like that. "I'd have thought poison would be your chosen method, though. It is for most women as it's less messy and doesn't require quite so much upper arm strength."

"You're daft," Ava snapped at me.

She stepped back, looking angry. The bright red flush on her cheeks looked so much better than the washed-out pasty thing she'd had going on, but I wasn't sure how to work that into the conversation without sounding insincere.

"There's only one person with anything to gain from Winthrop Dashavoy's death and that is Harrison Wentworth," Ava said. "They were rivals in the office"—she paused to look me over with scathing contempt—"as well as outside the office. It had to be Harrison and, honestly, the man should be awarded a medal!"

With that, she swept past us out the door without saying good-bye or get the hell out, both of which I had expected, although maybe the get the hell out more than the other.

"Is it just me, or did we just survive a typhoon?" Viv asked.

"Not just you," I said. "We did."

We were both silent, trying to get our bearings after such a rocky encounter. I waited until I was steady and then said, "She really thinks it was Harrison."

"I know." Viv nodded.

"If she thinks it, then—" I started the thought but couldn't finish it.

The truth was if Ava was this decided that it was Harrison then I had a feeling most everyone at Carson and Evers felt the same and if they did then the police were bound to center their investigation on the likeliest suspect. Harrison.

Mrs. Bailey returned with the news that Viv's hat was nowhere to be found. She was so genuinely aggrieved about it that I felt badly that we had tricked her. Viv must have felt the same because she thanked Mrs. Bailey profusely and then gave her a business card, telling her that anytime she needed a hat she could come into the shop and pick one out on the house. Yeah, guilt makes a liar generous when repenting.

By the time we got back to the shop, Fee looked like she wanted to strangle us. I was pretty glad I wasn't wearing a necktie and I removed my scarf posthaste. All was forgiven when Viv handed her a takeaway bag from Nando's with a butterfly burger in it.

Fee made a grumbling noise that sounded like thank you and disappeared into the workroom with her lunch. The shop was quiet. Two ladies were standing in front of a mirror in the corner trying on a few of Viv's more outrageous fascinators. The giggles they were emitting made me smile and I realized it was probably one of very few that day, which was depressing but I refused to dwell on it.

Viv sank down on the chair beside me and leaned her head back. She was the less sociable of the two of us so I figured if I was feeling drained she must be utterly wrung out.

"I wish I felt as if we'd learned something useful today," I said. "I feel like all we did was spin our wheels a bit and we landed in the same spot where we started."

"We made enemies of Tuesday Blount and Ava Carson, don't forget that," Viv said. She didn't lift her head or open her eyes while she spoke and I wondered if she was drifting off to sleep.

"Not frenemies?" I asked. "I was hoping for some sort of mutually respectful loathing."

"Maybe with Tuesday but not Ava," Viv said. "I get the feeling she's the sort of woman who doesn't have girlfriends."

"I never trust those types," I said.

"Me either, but at least they're honest," Viv said. "An even worse sort of woman is the one who specifically picks her friends because they make her prettier, richer, smarter, etc."

"Oh, I've had a few of those," I agreed. "Remember my college roommate?"

"She was a horror," Viv said. "She took your clothes, your food and your boyfriend."

"In that order," I said. "And all the while she pretended we were friends. Ugh, I was so happy when I moved out. I don't think my self-esteem was ever so hard hit, well, except when I found out my rat bastard boyfriend was still married, but I've moved on, really."

"Have you?" Viv asked.

She didn't move but her eyes opened and I could feel her watching me with concern.

"Yes, definitely," I said.

"No lingering pangs or longings?"

"God, no," I said. "Well, I'd still like to back over him with my car if the opportunity presented itself, but I've stopped fantasizing about it daily, so I think that's an improvement."

Viv laughed. It was as sparkly and ticklish and colorful as the feathers on the fascinator one of the ladies had perched on her head. I realized I hadn't heard her laugh much over the past few months and it warmed me from the inside out.

"Have I told you how glad I am that you're here, Scarlett?" she asked.

"Yes, but it never hurts to hear it again," I said. I reached over across the small table between us and squeezed her hand. "I'm glad I'm here, too."

We shared a smile and I felt as if we were finding our way back together again.

"Miss, oh, Miss!" One of the ladies waved at me.

"Duty calls," I said to Viv.

"Yes, it does," Viv said.

I rose from my seat and Viv did the same, but while I crossed the shop toward our customers, she turned and headed back into the workroom. Customer service really wasn't her thing.

As I glanced at the two ladies, I noticed they had a marked similarity in appearance, the same pretty blue eyes and matching dimples in their left cheeks. I wondered if they were sisters.

"I need your opinion, Miss," the first one said. I noted right away that she had an American accent. "My cousin thinks I should be bold and buy the hat with the bright fuchsia feathers, but I am more partial to the quieter shade of green. What do you think?"

"That you're going to blend right in with the curtains," the other woman said. She was clearly a local judging by her London accent.

"I didn't ask you," the first one said. She pushed her glasses up on her nose and turned back to me. "I'm Carol Landers and this is my cousin Mary Tavistock."

"A pleasure," I said. "I'm Scarlett Parker and my cousin Vivian Tremont is our hat designer. We're cousins, too, one American and one British."

They did not look nearly as interested in the fact that we were two sets of female cousins from two different countries as I was.

"That's nice, dear," said Mary. "Now convince her not to be as drab as dishwater and go with the pink one."

The bossy one was definitely most like Viv. I mean just because you have a sense of style doesn't mean you should force it upon others. Viv and I had this conversation repeatedly, and yet, she still had episodes where she bullied one of our clients into some elaborate creation of hers that they were uncomfortable with and I had to mediate an acceptable outcome.

"Maybe if you told me a bit about the event, I would be better able to determine which hat would be most appropriate," I said.

"We've been invited to high tea with the Countess of Wessex," Mary said. "And I don't want Carol to go unnoticed. She needs something bolder than her usual quiet colors."

"I'm just not sure," Carol said. She was pretty with short-cropped dark brown hair and sparkling eyes that made it seem as if she didn't take life too seriously.

"If that shade of hat is too bright"—I paused and gestured to the bold pink confection Mary had put on the counter beside her cousin—"then how about a lighter shade of pink or a different color altogether? Viv has made a wide variety of hats, and I'm sure we could find something that will work."

"Well . . ." Carol bit her lip. "Maybe."

I led the two ladies to a cupboard in the back. At the height of wedding season, Viv and Fee had hired on extra help to meet the demand. The extra hats, which covered every hue of the rainbow, had been stored back here to be refurbished for the next season.

I sincerely hoped I had something that would suit Carol, because I wanted her to have a successful high tea that she would remember fondly.

I moved aside several hats until I found the clutch of moderately bold ones. Viv and Fee had created everything from the palest pink with a blusher to a studded dazzler in vivid purple that was so bright I was surprised it didn't light up.

Naturally, Mary liked that one. Carol shook her head in horror so I pushed it to the back. We were left with a variety of others that I thought would do nicely.

"That one," Carol said.

To my surprise, she chose a unique pumpkin-colored pillbox hat fashioned out of sturdy felt with a burst of brown and white feathers on the front with two longer pumpkin-colored feathers curling away from the front in a charming accent.

"Oh, I like that one," Mary said. "Try it on."

We moved to one of the many mirrors in the shop and Carol put the hat on. It didn't sit quite right.

"May I?" I asked.

"Please," she said.

I stood behind Carol and moved the hat to a jaunty angle on the side of her head. "A nice hat pin will hold it in place and give it some sparkle."

"It's perfect," Mary said. "You will be the talk of the tea."

"Oh, I'm not comfortable with that," Carol said.

"Just smile and you'll be fine," I said. She really had an infectious smile; everyone was going to love her.

"Shall I box it up for you?" I asked.

"Yes, please," she said.

"Mine, too, please," Mary said.

I took both of the hats and set to work behind the counter, boxing them up in a nest of tissue paper inside our sturdy round boxes with the blue silk cord for a handle. It was an updated box from the ones Mim had used forty years ago, but it still had the blue stripes and the name "Mim's Whims" scrawled across the top of the lid.

There was a decided nostalgia to using the hatboxes that I enjoyed. I supposed I had a romanticized view of the past, but I liked sturdy hatboxes, milk in glass bottles, daily newspapers, men in fedoras who opened doors for a lady, jazz on the radio and a nice fruit-laden cocktail at the end of the day. Not for the first time I wondered if I was living in the right century.

"Do you teach any hat-making classes?" Mary asked.

"Occasionally, my cousin will do a small fascinator-making session at a hen party," I said. "Why?"

"We have a friend in Paris, Lucas Martin, who runs an art school," Carol said. "We were just there, taking a class in watercolors."

"That sounds lovely," I said. And it did. Paris. I'd been in London for eight months and had not made it across the English Channel to France. Now that I thought about it, my priorities were completely out of whack.

"Lucas is a very dear man," Mary said. "I am going to tell him about your shop and see if he is interested in having you come and teach."

"Oh, I don't—" I began but the cousins weren't listening.

"You just want an excuse to call Lucas," Carol teased her cousin. Mary shrugged and then grinned. She winked at me. "I'll be in touch."

As the ladies departed with their hatboxes dangling on their arms, a man approached the door. He was wearing an overcoat and a trilby, which is basically a short-brimmed fedora. I watched as he opened the door for Carol and Mary and doffed his hat as they passed him. Both ladies twittered like two little birds over a crumb and I realized I wasn't the only one who liked a door held open or a man in a hat.

Once the ladies were clear, the man entered, removing his hat as he did so. Recognition with a feeling of foreboding hit me low and deep.

"Good afternoon, Inspector Simms," I said.

"Hello, Ms. Parker," he said. "Mind if I have a word?"

Heck, yes, I minded. It was always bad news when he

used a formal greeting with my surname. There was only one reason I could figure that he was here and that was to blame Winthrop Dashavoy's death on Harrison, and I refused to go along with it. In fact, I planned to do everything in my power to stop it.

Chapter 15

Of course, I didn't say any of that. Instead, I offered up my sincerest "help the customer get to yes" smile and said, "Absolutely, how can I help you?"

Inspector Simms was built solid, with shoulders wide enough to carry around the grief that came with his position. I liked that about him. His thick head of dark hair was matted from his hat and he ran his fingers through it as if to fluff it up.

His light brown eyes were serious and not a little intimidating under the thick eyebrows that met in the middle in a menacing line on his prominent brow, although in the time I'd known him he'd never once menaced, if that counts for anything.

It was a good thing that I knew him; otherwise I might have been nervous. Instead, I remembered the time he and

Inspector Franks had popped into the shop, eaten their fill of tea and crackers and left without ever arresting anyone, namely Viv, even though there were a couple of times where it wouldn't have been completely out of order to do so.

"Excellent," he said. "About the night of the Carson bonfire party . . ."

He paused and I wondered if he was hoping that I would just start talking and tell him who killed Winthrop Dashavoy, as if I wouldn't have done that already if I'd seen it.

"Yes?" I asked.

"You said that you were with Mr. Wentworth," he said.

"That's right," I said.

I forced myself to meet his gaze and not look away. I have heard that everyone has a tell when they are fibbing, and I'm not sure what mine is, but I knew that looking away from someone was considered suspect so I made sure not to do that. Also, I didn't blink. This seemed to convince him.

"So other than the time Mr. Harrison was away getting drinks, which you both mentioned was when you were approached by Mr. Dashavoy, then the two of you were together," he clarified.

"That's right," I said. Still I didn't blink or look away.

Now his unibrow lowered over his eyes. "That's interesting because I have it from Mr. Wentworth that after the scuffle with Dashavoy, he left you again for a few minutes."

Damn Harrison, why did he have to go and tell him that? I was supposed to be his alibi. What an idiot!

"I'm sorry but you said 'other than the time Mr. Harrison was away getting drinks' so I assumed you meant both times we were apart since he left me to get drinks both times. In fact, the second time he was gone no longer than a few minutes since he was just retrieving the drinks he had bought earlier from a nearby bar."

"No longer than a few minutes?" Simms asked. "Are you quite sure?"

"Yes," I said.

"How?" he asked.

"I'm sorry?" I asked.

"How do you know how long he was gone?" he persisted.

I glanced around the shop. It was empty, not a customer in sight. This was not helpful. I thought back to the party and the time Harrison had left me to get our beverages.

I knew it had been less than a few minutes. How? Well, because I had watched him. Could I say that? Would that even sound plausible? Did it matter if it helped Harrison?

"I know because I watched him," I said. "I never let him out of my sight."

Simms's brow rose and he straightened up a bit.

"Any particular reason why?" he asked.

This time I glanced away. Vulnerability is not an emotion that I wear well. I don't like to let my soft underbelly show; rather I like to hide behind the polished veneer of an independent professional young woman even if it does feel like a façade most of the time.

When I'm honest with myself, I know that I was drawn to the hospitality industry because I like to feel needed. It makes me feel important and fluffs up my self-esteem to help someone else. Otherwise, people might think I'm emotionally needy, and I just couldn't stand that.

Now, admitting that I had been watching Harrison to make sure that Tuesday didn't get near him made me feel like a stupid schoolgirl with her first crush. It was mortifying to admit that I liked him that way and was feeling turfy about him.

"Were you worried that he and Dashavoy were going to mix it up again?" Simms asked. "Is that why you watched him? Did you have a feeling something bad was going to happen, Scarlett? I need you to be honest with me."

"Ugh," I groaned and leaned my head back as I studied the ceiling. Yes, one part of me was looking for an escape hatch that I knew wasn't there.

"Scarlett, you aren't helping him if you lie for him," Simms said. His voice was filled with paternal concern, a trick I assumed he had learned from his partner, Inspector Franks, since I knew Simms was single, without kids, and not much older than me.

"I'm not lying," I said. I could feel how hot my face was and I resented that the truth was being embarrassed out of me so I sounded a bit snippier than I would have liked. Again, vulnerable is not my comfort place. "The truth is I was watching Harrison because, oh, man." I paused before continuing, trying not to choke on the mortification that was forthcoming. "Because I have a crush on him and there was another woman there who was interested in him, and I wanted to make sure she steered clear, all right?"

Simms blinked. He looked nonplussed and then a small smile tipped the corner of his mouth.

"I thought there was something going on with you two," he said.

"You did not," I said.

"Yeah, I did, weeks ago, in fact," he said. "But I thought it was more him shining on you than you on him."

"Well, now you know," I said. "And I would appreciate it if you wouldn't say anything."

"Don't see why I would." He shrugged. "But you are absolutely sure he was never out of your sight after the fight with Dashavoy. I'll have your word, and I know I don't need to remind you that if you lie, you'll be charged with impeding an investigation."

"I would never!" I protested. "I kept my eye on him for all but a matter of seconds, and I saw him talking to a stout man in a bright green jacket. I'm sure Harrison could give you his name if he hasn't already." Okay, I was mostly sure but that had to be close enough, right?

Simms nodded. "I didn't think so but we have to make certain. There is one more thing."

I noticed he looked ill at ease, and I braced myself.

"What's that?" I asked.

"Is there anyone who can verify your whereabouts after the tussle with Dashavoy? Anyone other than Wentworth?"

I hadn't seen that coming. I thought back to my time waiting for Harrison. He was the only person who might have noticed me and he was off getting wine and sharing laughs with old men.

My throat felt very dry when I answered, "Um, no."

Simms left shortly after that. He didn't ask to talk to Viv or Fee, and I wasn't sure how I felt about being the one singled out for a chat. Then again, I was the one who had tussled with Dashavoy before Harrison came to the rescue so I supposed it made sense.

As Simms disappeared from sight, I had a horrible thought. What if Simms hadn't been here to discuss Harrison's alibi? What if he had really stopped by to go over mine? I was the one Dashavoy had gotten grabby with, so it stood to reason that I was the one who might have been holding a grudge.

Maybe the police thought that in a fit of ire, I strangled Dashavoy for excessive groping. I am a redhead and I had an embarrassing history of losing my temper in public, maybe they thought this was just another example of my instability. I'm not gonna lie the thought hurt.

Disquiet filled me as I realized Simms had been questioning me, not to discover Harrison's whereabouts, but rather to pinpoint mine. Perhaps Simms thought I was Dashavoy's killer.

The horrible idea took root like an invasive weed in my brain and no amount of tugging could dislodge it.

Chapter 16

There is nothing a dirty martini can't put into perspective, or so I told myself as Nick handed me my second martini of the evening, heavy on the olives.

Viv and I were ensconced at the bar in the corner of Nick and Andre's studio. Miles Davis was playing in the background, making his trumpet weep while night settled onto Portobello Road, tucking us in under its wing like a mama bird putting her hatchlings to bed. We were not listening.

"Has there been any news about Dashavoy's death?" Andre asked.

Viv and I exchanged a glance. I had told her about Inspector Simms's visit and my alarming realization that I might be a suspect.

"No news as yet," I said. "But they do seem to be checking every possibility."

Andre met my gaze across the bar. One of his eyebrows went up just a little bit higher than the other.

"Harrison?" he asked.

"Me," I said.

Nick gasped.

"I know," I said. "Can you believe it? As if I could ever murder anyone."

They were all silent, even Viv. I glanced at each of their faces but no one was meeting my gaze.

"Do not tell me that you believe me to be capable of murder," I said. "I swear I will go out and find all new friends if you do."

"You do have a temper, Scarlett," Nick said.

"And if someone you cared for was in jeopardy . . ." Viv began.

"I could see you doing some damage," Andre interrupted. "You're tougher than you look."

"So you all think I did it? Is that it?" My voice hit a high note that I think rated on the low register of the hysterics range.

"No!" Viv said. "We're just saying that anyone under the right circumstances might be driven to murder."

"Well, this was not the right circumstances," I said. "I'd knee a man in the privates for being too grabby, not strangle him."

"Of course you would, pet," Nick said. He patted the back of my hand and I felt a teeny bit better.

"I wish the police were as certain as you," I said.

"There has to have been someone at the party who had a stronger motive to murder Winthrop Dashavoy than you," Viv said.

"Well, I just happened to be chatting up one of my patients today, Ophelia Thift, of the Kensington Thifts," Nick said. "And she had some dish about Dashavoy that really came out when the nitrous oxide went in."

"And this is the first you're mentioning it?" I asked. "Nick, we've been here for an hour already!"

"Ophelia? Isn't she that horrid woman who likes to toss her badly processed brown hair over her shoulder and wear cute little flowery dresses like she's twenty-five instead of forty-five?" Viv asked.

"The same," Nick said.

"Not a bestie?" I asked Viv.

"Not in this life or any other," she assured me. "She's all fur coat and no knickers. You know her type—when you meet them at a party they give you the cold, limp hand and then look past you to see if someone more important is hiding behind you."

I nodded. I'd met Ophelia's kind before; in fact, I was quite certain that Tuesday Blount fell into that category.

"She's just a source, darling," Andre said. "Don't dwell on it."

"You're right," I agreed. I turned to Nick, who looked ready to bust. "What did you learn?"

"Winthrop Dashavoy had a little side business," Nick said. "According to Ophelia, he was into pharmaceuticals."

"Like investing in them?" I asked. Yes, because I am obtuse like that.

"More like pushing them, I imagine," Andre said.

"You mean he was a drug dealer?" Viv asked.

"Sort of," Nick said. "Apparently, Ophelia's friend Deena Parsons, also a client of mine, has a small OxyContin problem, and when she's in need, one of her sources is, or rather was, Winthrop Dashavoy."

"This is fantastic!" I cried.

"That Deena is a pill popper?" Nick asked. "How do you figure?"

"No, no, not that," I said. "If Win was supplying prescription pills to desperate people, then that gives us a whole list of people who might have wanted him dead."

"We can start with Ophelia and Deena," Viv said.

"And if we can figure out where he was getting his pills from, that's a whole new lead," I added.

"Wait, wait, wait." Andre raised his hands in a stop gesture, which was somewhat diminished by the Jameson on the rocks he held in his right hand. "You are not meeting with anyone except Inspector Simms to tell him what you know."

"And you can't tell him that I told you," Nick said. "Patient confidentiality and all."

"I thought that was for doctors. Is it true for dentists, too?" Viv asked.

"If you want this dentist to still be able to get the dish for you, then yes," he said. "I can't have a reputation as a goss; people will stop telling me their secrets."

"Of course we won't tell where we heard," Viv said. "We'll make it sound as if it's just some tearoom chin wagging we overheard."

"But we want them to take it seriously," I said.

Bang. Bang. Bang.

I jumped and spilled my beverage over my fingers. I glanced at the front door and saw Harrison, standing there looking particularly grumpy.

"Blast! He scared me," Andre said. He grabbed a

cocktail napkin and dried off his fingers while Nick went to unlock the door and let Harrison in.

"I have a feeling this is going to be unpleasant," Viv said. She glanced at me and I knew she was thinking what I was, that Harrison knew about our field trip to the Carson house.

"What were you two thinking?" Harrison roared as soon as Nick pushed the door open. Harrison shouldered his way into the studio and strode toward us.

"That I really prefer to lap my drink off of the bar, thank you so much," I said. I gave him a dark look as I swabbed up the mess my martini had made when I was startled by him.

He pursed his lips and inhaled through his nose as if struggling to keep his temper in check.

"You know what I'm talking about," he said. He cast a dark look in my direction and then in Viv's.

"Ava blabbed, didn't she?" I asked.

"If by that you mean that she mentioned to Tyler that you two dropped by to see if Viv's hat was there, then yes, she blabbed," he said. "Do you have any inkling of the problems you have caused?"

"Problems?" I asked. "We went looking for a hat, how is that a problem?"

"We didn't find the hat," Viv said. "That's a problem."

I had to give her points for trying to keep the façade going.

"No doubt because the hat is safely back on its shelf in the shop," Harrison said.

"There might have been a small oversight in that regard," I agreed.

"Small oversight?" he asked.

His voice was rising in volume again and I noticed that Andre and Nick were watching the exchange as if they had box seats at the theater.

"You don't need to yell," I said. "My hearing is perfectly fine."

"Really, Ginger?" he asked. "Because I am quite sure that I told you to stay away from this situation, and yet, here you are insinuating yourself right into the middle of a murder investigation."

"I am not," I said. "Viv and I are just trying to help."

"I don't need your help," he argued.

"Yes, you do," I said. "Your history with Dashavoy makes you a prime suspect. You need all the help you can get."

"You don't understand me. We don't know who killed Win, which means the killer is still out there and the situation is dangerous. I don't want any of you near this mess," he said. "I don't want you to get hurt."

He was being thoughtful and protective. I should have been touched. I was not. I was furious.

"Well, that's rich, Harry, since you certainly don't seem to mind when Tuesday inserts herself into the investigation," I snapped. Yeah, I know, temper, temper.

"Scarlett." Viv's voice was full of warning but I was too far gone to register it.

"Tuesday's role in this is none of your business," Harrison said. "She worked with Win, too. She has a vested interest in finding out what happened to him."

"That's just what she said," I argued. "As if she has more right to help you than we do, when we're your friends while she is just an annoying ex-girlfriend, which is exactly what I told her."

"What?" Harrison snapped. "When exactly did you speak with her?"

Uh-oh. I glanced down at my beverage just as Viv let out a long-suffering sigh.

"How about a drink, old man?" Nick clapped Harrison on the shoulder. "I think you're going to need it."

Harrison's green eyes were like lasers and I could feel them boring into the side of my skull even as I resolutely refused to look at him.

"Best make it a double," Andre said. "We have some news, too."

Once Harrison had shrugged off his overcoat and had two fingers of Jameson on the rocks in a glass in his hand, we all moved away from the bar and sat on the stylish couch and chairs Nick had insisted on adding to the studio.

Viv and I recounted our conversations with Tuesday and Ava while Nick told Harrison about his information from Ophelia.

Harrison listened without interrupting. I wasn't sure if it meant he was madder than ever or if he had calmed down enough to hear what we had to tell him without feeling the need to yell at us again.

When Nick finished his tale, Harrison downed his drink in one long swallow. Then he shook his head as if he could make it all go away like a dog shaking rain off his fur.

"Someone strangled Winthrop Dashavoy," he said. "I loathed the man but I never would have wished that on him."

"I'd wager someone knew that there was bad blood between you and decided you would make the perfect scapegoat," Andre said. "But who?"

"My first guess would be a man," Nick said. "It takes a lot of muscle to snuff someone out via strangulation."

"But Dashavoy was very drunk and he'd already sustained an injury," I said. "Honestly, I think I could have taken him out at that point if I were the sort of girl who would do that type of thing."

They all looked at me, and for the first time that evening, Harrison's mouth moved up in the corner just the tiniest bit but I took it as a good sign.

"I imagine you could do anything you put your mind to, Scarlett," he said.

Why this praise made my heart take flight in my chest, I have no idea, but I really felt as if Harrison meant it and it flattered me, even though, yeah, he was agreeing that I could murder someone. Hmm. I frowned at him and he winked at me, which made it all better. I'm easy, I know.

"Any chance that Deena and Ophelia were at the bonfire?" Viv asked. "That would certainly give us a starting place."

"No idea," Harrison said. "Are they clients?"

Nick shrugged.

"We need a guest list," I said. "Then we can cross-check it to see who might have been buying pills from Winthrop and who might have had a reason to kill him."

"But why would they kill him if he was supplying them with pills?" Viv asked.

"Maybe he ran out or refused or was trying to get out of the business," Nick said.

"Who would know that?" I asked.

"Reese?" Viv offered. "If what Tuesday said was true and the feelings Reese had for Winthrop were not motherly but rather were lover-like, then she might have known what he was doing."

"Oh, no, I can't see that. He's like a son to her. Besides I can't believe she would put the business at risk like that," Harrison said. I could see his jaw clench repeatedly, a sign I had come to recognize as meaning he was highly agitated.

Nick must have sensed it, too, because he retrieved the bottle of Jameson and poured a healthy splash into Harrison's glass.

"Well, that's the rub, isn't it?" Nick asked. "Do we, any of us, really know what someone else is capable of, whether they be a business partner, a friend or a lover?"

We were all silent and I noticed that none of us were making eye contact, choosing to study our drinks while we contemplated the truth of Nick's words.

"No, clearly we don't," Harrison said and he frowned down into his drink, looking forlorn.

The talk moved away from Winthrop Dashavoy's murder. Nick went to the little kitchenette at the back of the studio to retrieve some canapés he had made while Viv and Andre talked about a mutual acquaintance who was a fashion designer.

Harrison took his drink and walked over to the front window. He leaned against the wide wooden sill and stared out into the night. His dark brown hair fell over his forehead and he gazed down into his drink as if trying to find answers in the ice cubes.

It wasn't a conscious decision on my part to move to his side. It was just where I knew I was supposed to be.

"I'm sorry, Harry," I said.

He tipped his head to the side and studied me. "What do you have to be sorry about, Ginger?"

"I'm sorry that you're going through this," I said. "I know it's uncomfortable to be so scrutinized by, well, everyone."

Despite myself, I shivered. The sticky icky feeling of shame welled up inside me before I could beat it back. My own public humiliation was still pretty fresh and its claws were sharp.

Harrison lifted his left arm and I slid into his side while he wrapped his arm around my shoulders and held me close. I felt him press a kiss into my hair, which made my heart thunder in my chest.

"Shame," he said. "That's what you felt."

"Yep," I said. "Still do when I think about it."

"I had no idea," he said. "It's weird to feel shame about something you had no part in other than having an unfortunate association, well, and for being in the wrong place at the wrong time. I'm sorry."

"What do you have to be sorry about, Harry?" I turned his question back on him.

My voice sounded scratchy and I kept my gaze fixed out the window and not at him because I felt as if looking into his eyes would make me more exposed than I could handle right now.

"At the moment, I'm sorry I didn't ask you out before you took that vow of celibacy," he said.

I did not expect that. I glanced up at him and saw the teasing glint in his eyes. It made me laugh.

"Our timing is pretty lousy," I agreed.

"It's all right," he said. He tucked me in closer and rested his head on mine. "Everything is going to be all right."

Comforted and cared for, that was how Harrison made me feel, and this was the most content I had felt in months. I was pretty sure I could have stayed in the circle of his arm forever.

"Scarlett, Harrison, quit dawdling by the window," Nick bellowed from across the room. "You have to eat some canapés before I eat them all and they land right on my arse."

I stepped away from Harry with great reluctance.

"You okay?" I asked him. I hated that our moment had been interrupted and a part of me knew exactly where I wanted to stuff Nick's canapés. No, that wasn't nice, but I wasn't really feeling nice.

"I will be," he said. "It chafes that I'm a suspect, but I know I'm innocent." He glanced at our friends and then at me. "The people who matter know I'm innocent."

"We do," I said. "We really do."

"Walk me out?" he asked. His hand was still on my back and I got the feeling he was hesitant to let me go, too.

"Sure," I said. He retrieved his overcoat and we made our way to the door. I called over my shoulder, "Harrison is calling it a night."

"Oy, so soon?" Nick asked. "But you didn't eat any-thing."

"I don't want it to dilute my alcohol," Harrison joked.

Viv gave him an understanding smile and a wave and Andre nodded and said, "Be good, mate."

I racked my brain, looking for something positive to say that would make it all better, but I was stuck for words. The fact was Harrison looked awfully guilty and I knew it was partly my fault because of the scuffle between him and Win.

Even though we had a solid relationship with Inspector Simms, I knew that my vouching for Harrison was suspect just because he was our business partner and friend. Damn.

I unlocked the door and Harrison pushed through it. I was about to say good night, when he grabbed my hand and pulled me out onto the sidewalk, letting the door swing shut behind us.

Harrison draped his overcoat around my shoulders and pulled me around the side of the building and into the shadows.

"For the next ten minutes, can you do me one favor?" he asked.

"Sure," I said, thinking he wanted me to listen to him talk. Me not talking was definitely a challenge, but I was game.

"Can you lift the ban on no dating?" he asked.

My jaw slid open in surprise and the word "yes" floated out on a soft sigh and then he was on me. He cupped my face in his hands and pressed his lips to mine in the softest greeting possible. It wasn't enough.

I grabbed his shirtfront and pulled him close. The kiss took on a desperation that sent heat rocketing through my system, short wiring any common sense I may ever have had.

By the time we came up for air, I had his necktie in a stranglehold and I was using it to keep myself from melting into a puddle on the pavement at my feet. His hands gripped my hips, keeping us just far enough apart to keep the kiss from being obscene. Pity.

He rested his forehead against mine and our breath

mingled while we tried to ride out the firestorm of hormones flaming between us. Meanwhile all I could think was, What the hell was that?

But then, I knew. His kiss had seduced and beguiled but there had been an underlying panic in it and I realized that he had kissed me because the future was uncertain, because he feared he might go to jail and this might be his last chance.

I let go of his tie and threw my arms around his neck. I buried my face in his shoulder and let him wrap me tight against him in a hug that didn't leave room for even a molecule between us.

"You will not leave me," I said. "No matter what happens, you will not leave me."

"Ah, Ginger, you are a wonder," he whispered. I heard the smile in his voice and I leaned back to see it on his face. His gaze moved over my face, taking in every eyelash and freckle. He traced my lower lip with his thumb. "I have two more minutes until you're unavailable again."

This time I kissed him with all of the pent-up longing and panicky desperation I felt. I wondered if this uncertainty was what partners felt like when they sent their mate off to war. It was unacceptable. Harrison didn't know it yet, but I had never been more serious in my life. Even if I wasn't ready to date, I would not let him leave me. Period.

Chapter 17

"He's a mobster, isn't he?" I asked Viv. We were sharing a breakfast of cranberry scones that Nick had packed up for us the night before, and I thought if I could catch Viv before her morning tea, she might be fuzzy enough to let something slip.

"What? What are you . . . Oh, the husband. Scarlett, you know I refuse to talk about this," she said.

"I know and it occurred to me last night that it has to be because he's into something bad," I said. "So just tell me, is he a mobster?"

Viv looked at me like she was debating running into her room and locking the door just to get away from me. I grabbed her hand. She was not going to get away that easily.

"I can't believe that after snogging Harrison last night

you could even engage your brain to contemplate my life," Viv said.

I gasped. She knew we'd kissed! Then I caught on. This was a distraction tactic. So obvious.

"Snogging Harrison?" I asked. I made sure I was all wide-eyed innocence. Viv didn't buy it. Yeah, probably because my face went flaming hot and even I knew I was blushing.

"So can I assume you two are dating?" she asked.

"We were for ten minutes," I said.

She looked bewildered.

I sighed. "He asked me to lift my no dating ban, but only for ten minutes so he could kiss me."

"That is so disgustingly romantic, I might toss up my breakfast," she said. Then she grinned. "So how was it?"

And just when I thought my face could not get any redder. Seriously, I patted my cheek to make sure flames weren't coming out of my pores. They were not.

"No more trying to change the subject," I said. "Tell me if your husband is a Mafioso."

She looked down at my hand on hers. "No, he's not in organized crime."

I let go of her, thinking that finally she was going to crack and tell me everything. Instead, she fussed with her tea and then turned and left our kitchenette with her mug cradled in her hands.

"It's far worse than that," she said. Then she went into her room and shut the door behind her.

Worse? Than a mobster? Was that even possible? I wanted to howl with frustration. Instead I stuffed a cranberry scone in my mouth with clotted cream on top and chewed until the desire to bang my head against the wall passed.

I was standing at the counter in the front of the shop, working on my laptop, when Fee came bustling in with a huge parcel under her arm. This was not entirely unusual as she frequently picked up supplies for Viv.

"All right, Scarlett?" she asked me as she hurried by.

"Good and you?" I asked. Of course, my first thought was that Viv had told her about Harrison and me, but that was silly since as far as I knew Viv hadn't spoken to Fee yet that morning. Still, there was something off about Fee's expression.

"What do you have there?" I asked, thinking I could draw her out and get her to open up to me.

"This?" Fee asked. She clutched the brown paper bag to her chest as if I'd made a grab for it. "Nothing!"

I frowned at her. "Okay, no need to freak out."

"Oh, sorry," she said. She blew an orange curl out of her eyes. "I'm just a bit tetchy, yeah?"

"Sure," I said. "I guess we all are."

She hurried into the back room, and I returned my attention to updating our website. A couple of years ago, Viv had hired a web designer but when I arrived I noticed that our updates lagged by weeks, so I had fired him thinking I could do it better. The learning curve had been steeper than I anticipated, but at least now when things weren't put up in a timely fashion, I only had me to blame.

Andre and I had recently done a photo shoot of Viv and Fee's upcoming spring collection and now it was up to me to load the pictures and give them clever captions. This was where I had to be careful because Viv could be a little prickly about the names I picked for her hats, such as the smashed avocado.

Yes, she had created a brown and green beret that bore a marked resemblance to a flattened avocado. It was just a nickname; it wasn't like I was going to use it on the site. Still, she was offended. Artists.

I loaded the pictures and then I went to update the page that was our diary. This was where I listed all of the social events for which we had been commissioned to make hats. Viv had finished all of her bespoke holiday hats but there were still a few outstanding New Year's hats that had to be finished, and we had plenty of off-the-rack hats for those like me, who lived a bit more by the seat of the pants.

My thoughts strayed to Winthrop Dashavoy and the fact that he wouldn't be attending any parties this holiday season. I wondered how his family was dealing with his death. Did they know a different Win than the rest of us? Was he courteous, thoughtful and kind with them or was he just as awful to them as he was to the rest of the world? Did they know that he was a prescription drug dealer? Did they get their drugs from him, too?

So many questions flitted through my head it made it difficult to concentrate on the task at hand, probably because the task at hand was dismally dull. I wondered how Win had found himself in the position to be trafficking in prescription pills. That wasn't something a person just fell into like telemarketing.

Could he have had a prescription pill problem and it had evolved into selling his extras to others? But then, it seemed as if he had a substantial client base for the pills so where was he getting his supply? There had to be someone else involved but who could it be? A doctor taking a cut? A drug dealer using him as a front? The possibilities were endless.

Viv and I had talked about what Nick told us and we agreed that we needed to mention it to Inspector Simms. Harrison had insisted that we leave it alone and that he would be the one to mention it to the detectives as soon as he found some additional proof from work. I didn't think he could wait that long.

In fact, the more I thought about it, the more I thought Viv and I should call DI Simms right now. I saved the work I had done on the webpage and put my laptop under the counter. The shop was empty but I didn't want to leave expensive equipment unattended while I ducked into the back for a moment.

"Viv," I called as I stepped into the workroom. Both she and Fee started at the sight of me and I got the feeling they weren't pleased to see me. Kind of hurtful.

"Yes?" Viv asked. She was leaning over the table as if trying to block my view. I am not that easily deterred.

"What are you working on?" I asked.

She sighed. She glanced at Fee and then back at me. "Don't make fun of us."

"Why would I do that?" I asked. "Am I usually mean?" Smashed avocado aside, I thought I was always very supportive of their creative efforts.

"No, although . . ." Her voice trailed off and I knew she was thinking about the same hat.

"Let it go," I said.

"All right, we've gotten a last-minute commission by the, uh . . ." She paused and looked at Fee.

"Johnson family," Fee said. "From America."

"Yes, that's right," Viv said. "The Johnson family has asked us to create some Thanksgiving hats for them."

"Seriously?" I asked.

I approached the table, and sure enough, plastered to a couple of hat forms were the black wool brim and crown that together would make the well-known Pilgrim's traveler's hat. On the table next to it was a half-fashioned Native American headdress with feathers. They looked like something from my fourth grade elementary school play about Thanksgiving.

It was ridiculous but suddenly I was overcome with a bout of homesickness that almost took me out at the knees. Thanksgiving was my favorite holiday; it always had been.

I loved everything about it from watching the Macy's Thanksgiving Day Parade—who doesn't love to watch a giant Snoopy blowup floating down Seventh Avenue—to American football on TV and cranberry sauce with dinner, always the jelly from a can that kept its can shape, to the post-feast delivery pizza that my dad and I always ordered much to my mother's dismay.

Being British, she never really understood the whole "the meal isn't over until you hate yourself" glutton thing, but my dad and I had it down to a science.

"Where are they from?" I asked.

"Who?" Viv asked. She was watching me closely and I knew she could probably tell I was feeling a little homesick; despite her flighty ways, she was a good reader of people to whom she was close.

"The Johnsons," I said.

"Texas," Fee said.

"California," Viv said.

They looked at each other and Fee said, "They stopped in Texas on their way from California."

"That's right," Viv said.

"And they're having Thanksgiving here?" I asked.

"A small party, yes," Viv said.

"I wonder where they will manage to find cranberry sauce," I said.

"What sauce?" Fee asked.

"Cranberry," I said. "You can't have Thanksgiving without it."

"Oh, I thought it was about the turkey, yeah?" she said.

"Turkey, stuffing, cranberry sauce and pumpkin pie," I said. "These things are not negotiable."

"Well, I'm sure they have it sorted," Viv said. She looked at Fee. "Mrs. Johnson seemed very capable, didn't she?"

"They came into the shop?" I asked.

"Yes, one day while you were out," Fee said. "I think you were at the library."

"Oh." I felt unaccountably disappointed. It was silly but it would have been nice to talk to someone from home. "Next time they come in make sure I'm here, all right?"

"Of course," Viv said.

"Absolutely," Fee agreed.

They watched me for a moment and then Viv said, "Was there something you came in here for?"

"Oh, right," I said. "I was thinking about Winthrop Dashavoy."

Her face cleared and she nodded. "Go on."

"I think we should tell Inspector Simms about Nick's patient Ophelia Thift," I said. "The sooner the better."

"But Harrison wants to ask around a bit at work," she said.

"I know, but I'm worried that time isn't really on his side on this," I said.

"The Dashavoy family is powerful," Fee said. "They're going to want an arrest made soon."

"You're right," Viv said. "So how do you propose we go about letting Inspector Simms know what we've learned, because we have to leave Nick out of it as well."

The bells chimed on the front door. I felt a flash of irritation. Yes, I was supposed to be manning the front. Yes, this was our business. And yes, I was the people-pleasing face of the hat shop, but there was stuff going on and if I could just have a minute.

"Hello?" a deep voice called from the shop. It was clearly a man's voice, and I didn't recognize it.

I glanced at Viv. We had a few hats for men, just as a gesture, really, so we didn't get a lot of men in the shop unless it was a special order.

Her eyes were wide and she looked alarmed, and I wondered why . . . unless, she recognized the voice. Maybe it was her husband!

I raced for the door to the shop and Viv dropped the fabric she was holding and did the same. We hit the doorway at the same time and managed to wedge ourselves good and tight until I wiggled an elbow loose, and shoved her behind me as I pushed through the door.

"Hello, how can I help you?" I cried as I jogged across the shop.

The man standing in the center of the room looked both startled and amused as Viv tried to overtake me. Yeah, good luck with that, cousin. If this was her man, she didn't stand a chance of keeping him from me. Not now.

Chapter 18

Recognition hit me like a disappointing slap across the face. I glanced at Viv and saw her shoulders slump, although I wasn't sure if it was in relief or disappointment.

"Hello, Inspector Franks," I said. "Shopping for a new hat?"

His bushy mustache curved up when he smiled. He was Inspector Simms's partner, the senior investigator of their duo, and I assumed that he had just gotten back from his trip to York.

"When Vivian starts making ten-gallon cowboy hats, I'll be the first in line," he said. He poked a finger at a stylish emerald green cap with a long pointed feather that coiled around it as if it was a snake and he was trying to determine if it would bite.

"I think the Stetson Company has it covered," Viv said. "But I'm flattered that you think me capable."

Inspector Franks nodded. He smoothed his mustache with his thumb and forefinger while he contemplated us. I had no doubt that Simms had caught him up to date about the murder at the Carsons' party. I wondered if the inspector was looking for Harrison, but then why was he here and not at the offices of Carson and Evers?

"Simms told me it was quite a bonfire night," he said. He examined the blue hat perched next to the green one. Then he glanced at me with a look that was razor sharp. "Especially for you, Scarlett."

"Would you care for some tea?" I asked. I wasn't intentionally trying to change the subject or stall, but I did want to take a moment to get my head together.

"I thought you'd never ask," he said.

"Please, come and sit," Viv said. She gestured to one of the sitting areas. "I'll just go and start the tea."

Inspector Franks and I sat in two of the plush blue chairs that Mim had scattered in little groupings all around the shop. There was a small glass table between us with copies of the latest fashion magazines.

Viv liked to keep up to date on what was trending, and yes, she also liked to shred some of the latest haute couture designs. She felt that form and function had to meet in an article of clothing for it to be a substantial design; otherwise she felt it was reduced to being silly or dowdy, both of which were completely unacceptable to her.

Once she left, I turned to Inspector Franks. He was a good detective. We had met over a few unfortunate situations before, and I had learned that he was a thorough investigator, a nice man, and he had a rich baritone that he liked to exercise by singing country music at a local pub. In short, I trusted him.

"Inspector Simms told us you were vacationing up in York," I said. "Was it a nice visit?"

"Quite pleasant," he said. Then he glanced down at the table. "It's really more for my wife. Our daughter, well, things aren't as we'd like between us so every year around bonfire night, we go away to make it a bit easier."

"I understand," I said. "My mother is always telling me that she thought the growing pains would be over when I was an adult, but I don't suppose it ever really ends."

"No, I expect not," he said. He glanced back up and I noted he appeared to be making an effort to look cheerful, which made me feel even more empathy.

"Tell me what happened that night," he said.

I knew he meant the party, and I was happy to talk about anything that might distract him. I described the evening in detail, highlighting the fact that Harrison had not been out of my sight when he went to retrieve our wine the second time. Franks's face remained impassive through the entire interview.

Viv returned with a tray of tea and cookies and Franks gave her a grateful smile. She took the seat next to mine and poured the tea while I wound down in my story. I did not tell Franks that we had tailed Tuesday or popped in on Ava. I didn't want to throw too much at him at once, and I really didn't want to get in trouble.

"How is your sense of time?" Franks asked me.

"What do you mean?" I asked.

"Do you wear a watch? Do you consult your cell phone frequently?"

I frowned. "No, but what does that have to do—"

"Are you usually late or on time?" he asked. He took a sip of his tea and watched me over the rim of the cup.

"I'd say I'm mostly on time, but I occasionally run a few minutes late," I said.

"Why?" he asked.

"Probably, because I get distracted . . ." The words fell out of my mouth before I had the brains to snap my jaw shut. Damn it. I had just admitted that I get distracted. Now he would think I really didn't know how long Harrison had been gone and that I hadn't really been watching him the whole time.

Yes, I know I looked at the fire for a few seconds while Harrison was gone, but I was absolutely certain it hadn't been long enough for him to strangle Win, hide his body, and get back to my side, but now I sounded unsure. The urge to smack my own forehead was strong, but I resisted.

"Exactly," he said. "Funny thing time."

I was about to protest that there was nothing funny about it when he turned his attention away from me.

"Vivian, can you tell me what you remember about the night?" he asked.

Vivian nodded. Everyone who had been at the party had been questioned, so her information had already been taken, but I supposed if they had no concrete leads, Franks was forced to go over every testimony until something stuck out.

I held my cup of tea in my hands but I wasn't thirsty. I was using it as more of a hand warmer against the draft than anything else.

"How much time did you spend with Elise Stanford?" Franks asked.

If Viv was surprised she didn't show it, at least not as much as I probably did. Elise Stanford was a noted television personality—what could Franks's interest in her be?

"She took us to meet with her producer, Sam Kerry," Viv said. "They are planning to do a segment for the morning show on winter hats. She was particularly interested in the yellow cap I was wearing."

"Do you know her personally?" Franks asked. He appeared relaxed, but I noticed that his eyes never left Viv's face as if he didn't want to miss a bit of her answer.

"We've met at various functions," she said. "But we don't have any shared history."

"Did you know she was dating Winthrop Dashavoy?" Franks asked.

Viv and I both gasped.

"I'll take that as a no," he said.

He took a cinnamon chocolate cookie off of the plate and bit it in half. I could see crumbs and sugar crystals clinging to his mustache and I wondered if he combed it out every night or if he found stray bits of food in it every now and then sort of like a backup snack.

"They seem an unlikely couple," Viv said.

"How so?" he asked.

Viv looked at me as if she wasn't sure how to phrase what she was thinking. I wondered why she was looking at me and then I remembered that I am the schmoozer of our duo so she was probably looking to me to find the right words.

"He was a grabby-handed arrogant jerk," I said. "While she seems quite nice."

"Really, Scarlett," Viv clucked. "I could have done better than that."

I shrugged. Winthrop Dashavoy was a horrible person and if Elise Stanford was involved with him then I had to rethink my opinion of her as well.

"What could she possibly see in him?" Viv asked.

"Her morning show is suffering in the ratings," Franks said. "Dashavoy comes from old money and would have been a wealthy bird with which to feather her nest."

"She didn't seem that calculating to me," Viv said. "She's planning to bring a film crew by here in a few days. I don't know how I'm going to look her in the face, knowing she was tied up with him."

"You're a pro," I said. "Think about the publicity for the shop and you'll be fine."

"What day and time?" Franks asked.

"The day after tomorrow in the early afternoon," Viv said. "It's to be a pretaped session for the morning show the next day."

Franks pulled out his phone and made a note. I had a feeling he was planning to be in attendance for the taping.

"Were they officially engaged?" I asked. Memories of my tussle with Winthrop made me wonder if he'd meant Elise Stanford when he said he "wouldn't let her get away with it." I felt bad about offering her up to the police using Win's hateful words, but if it saved Harrison I was more than okay with throwing her under the bus. Turns out I have a dark side, who knew?

"Not officially," Franks said. "But it was clear she thought it was going that way."

"I didn't see her when his body was found," I said.

Franks looked at me and I saw one of his eyebrows rise just the tiniest bit. "That's an excellent observation. She had, in fact, already left the party when his body was discovered."

"Alone?" Viv and I asked together.

"Why do you ask?" Franks's voice was deceptively mild.

I exchanged a glance with Viv and knew she was thinking the same thing I was. She gave me a small nod. I took a deep breath. I did not want to sound as bitter as I had before; rather I wanted to sound as if I were operating from a place of cool calm reasoning, instead of ecstatic that there might be a much more viable suspect than Harrison.

"I'm sure it has already occurred to you that if Elise left the party alone with no witnesses then it stands to reason that she left after having heard about Harrison's scuffle with Dashavoy."

"Possibly," Franks said.

"And if she discovered why they had fought, she might have been furious with Win for embarrassing her. It's possible she could have had a confrontation with him and killed him. In a panic, she might have hidden the body in the effigy's place, thinking it would be burned before anyone realized what she had done."

"Why do I get the feeling that you would really like to hear that Ms. Stanford has no alibi?" Franks asked.

I blinked. Did I sound too eager? Did that look bad? Was he thinking I was trying to hide something and clinging to the hope that Elise Stanford took the fall for Win's death?

"Inspector Franks, Harrison is our friend as well as our business manager," Viv said. "Of course, we don't want to think the worst of Ms. Stanford, but since we are quite positive that it isn't Harrison, well, it has to be someone."

I frowned. Viv, my flighty artist introvert cousin, sounded so reasonable that I wondered if we'd suffered a sudden personality swap. I had no words and she sounded as smooth as whipped butter. Franks even grinned at her.

"It does have to be someone," he said. "But it isn't necessarily Ms. Stanford. As it happens, her producer, Sam Kerry, was by her side at the party and left with her. They say it was before the ruckus between Dashavoy and Wentworth."

"Can they prove it?" I asked. Eagerness be damned; I wanted a new suspect.

"Not as yet," he said. "We are trying to pin down the actual time."

"Excellent," I said. Both Viv and Franks looked at me. I gave them a sour look. "I just mean that she makes a fine suspect—much better than Harrison at any rate."

Franks leaned forward and put his empty cup on the tray. "The investigation is ongoing. We'll find out who did this."

"I have no doubt you will," I said. See? My people-pleasing skills were kicking back into high gear. I bit my lip and then figured this was as good a time as any to mention what we had learned about Win. "We did hear a rumor."

I glanced at Viv to see what she thought of telling Franks what Nick had told us. She nodded.

"Someone said that Dashavoy was known in some circles for dealing in prescription drugs."

"And someone would be who?" he asked.

"I can't recall." Viv tossed her long, blond curls and tipped her head to the side.

This is Viv's tell. She always does the head toss thing when she's fibbing. I know because she's used it on me, and I've seen her use it on men to blind them from the fact that she is fibbing. There must be something about the light catching in her pale curls that distracts them from pursuing the truth. I swear, it works every time.

"What about you?" Franks turned to me.

I did not have Viv's amazingly distracting head toss thing, which was why I always tried to stick as close to the truth as possible.

"It must have been someone at the party who mentioned it," I said. Nick was at the party so it was not a total lie; thus I could maintain eye contact with Franks and not even flinch.

He pursed his lips and nodded. With a grunt he hefted himself out of his seat and lifted his overcoat from the chair beside him. As he shrugged into it, Viv and I rose to see him out.

"If either of you think of anything else . . ."

"We will be in touch immediately," I promised.

We walked to the door as if this had been a date for tea instead of an interrogation. Okay, slight exaggeration but still. When Franks pushed open the door, I found myself grabbing his arm, stopping him.

"Is Harrison . . ." I wasn't even sure I knew how to verbalize what I wanted to ask so the words just hung in the air between us like a belch of exhaust from a city bus.

"A suspect?" he asked. He looked weary and a little defeated. "Yes, and unless some other information comes to light, I'm afraid he's our prime suspect."

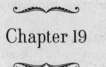

Chapter 19

"What are we going to do?" Viv asked me.

"Find out who else Dashavoy was selling pills to," I said.

"Because that should be easy," Viv said.

"I didn't say it was going to be easy, just that we were going to do it," I said.

"Please throw me an inkling of a plan, so that I can pretend you're not utterly cracked," she said.

"Tuesday is going to get us a list of people who were invited to the party," I said.

"Because she really struck me as being helpful like that," Viv said.

"Your negativity is kind of a downer," I said.

She waved her hand at me to indicate I should continue.

"Once we have the list, we can run the names by Nick and Andre and see what they know," I said.

"And if they don't have any ideas?"

"Then we broaden our circle and ask other people," I said.

"Like who?" she asked.

"Viv, you're being awfully persistent in your pessimism," I said. "First we need the list then we'll worry about sources of information."

"Fine, but if Harrison finds out . . ."

"He won't," I said. Admittedly, I sounded much more confident than I felt but at this point where was the harm?

"How are you going to get Tuesday to talk to you?" Viv asked. "We didn't exactly part on the best of terms."

"I'll make it worth her while," I said.

"With what?" Viv asked. "Are you going to promise to walk away from Harrison and leave him to her because that's about the only leverage you've got."

I sucked in a breath. I knew she was right. Was I willing to do that? Would I give up Harrison to save him? Did I really have a choice?

"If I have to," I said. It was tough talk. I really hoped Tuesday didn't use my friendship with Harrison as a bargaining chip, but if she did I'd have to play it wisely.

Viv sighed. "There is one thing you aren't considering."

I nodded for her to continue, still feeling a bit shell-shocked.

"Tuesday could be the murderer," she said.

"I know," I said. "And I know that if she is, this could put me in harm's way."

"Us in harm's way," Viv said. "I'm not letting you do this alone."

I thought about arguing but then realized that if the situation was reversed, I would demand the same.

"Fair enough," I said. "Just like I plan to be here when Elise does her bit for the morning show because she, too, could be our killer."

"Franks will be here," Viv said. She ran a finger over the same green hat that Franks had taken a poke at and a small vee appeared between her eyes.

"What is it?" I asked.

"Elise and her producer, Sam Kerry," Viv said.

"What about them?"

"I got the feeling when we were discussing the interview that they were more than co-workers," she said. "He was very protective of her, very solicitous, and not because she was the talent. It seemed more personal."

"Was Sam a big man?" I asked.

"Not especially," she said. "He was very average, average height, average weight, even average looking. He was not someone you would notice except that he wore a perfectly tailored suit and had that indefinable air of power about him."

"I know the type," I said. "He's a problem solver, someone who is usually behind the scenes pulling the strings. If things were dicey between Winthrop and Elise and it would impact her career, Sam Kerry might have felt compelled to step in and help her."

"You mean murder for her?" Viv asked.

I shrugged. We had seen some crazy stuff over the past

year. You expect when living in a city like London that you might have a few encounters with shady characters that were not always at one with the law, but we seemed to have a knack for being drawn into the misfortune of others that was becoming downright bizarre.

"If she was interested in Dashavoy for his money, then killing him wouldn't really help her, would it?" I asked. "Maybe there was something else going on there. He was raving about someone when he was being grabby with me. Do you think it was her? Maybe she wanted to end the relationship and he didn't."

"Or maybe she was one of his prescription drug clients," Viv said. "Maybe he was going to disclose her problem to the public."

"Oh, that's a motivator," I said. "For both her and her producer, a drug problem would kill her career and then where would either of them be?"

My phone was in a drawer under the front counter. I retrieved it and opened up a browser to the Internet. A quick search brought up the main number to Carson and Evers. I dialed it and waited.

"Good afternoon, Carson and Evers, how may I be of assistance?" a pleasant female voice answered.

"Could you connect me to Tuesday Blount?" I asked. "Please tell her Scarlett Parker is calling."

Viv's eyes went wide. I think she thought I was going to think it through or devise a crazy scheme. Yeah, no, those are for bad sitcom television whereas we clearly had a drama unfolding.

"One moment, please," the voice said.

It was more than a moment. In fact, the canned music

I was being forced to endure assured me that it was a lot closer to ten moments than one. I tried to be patient. Maybe she was in a meeting. Maybe she had run to the bathroom. Maybe Harrison was in the office with her. Right. Now.

I shook off the thought. Even if he was there, it was just work because he had made it very clear that she was the past with no chance of returning to the future.

"Hello, Scarlett," a familiar female voice, a very familiar smug-sounding female voice, answered.

Is it wrong that I wanted to reach through the phone and punch her in the throat? Okay, yeah, I already know the answer to that.

"Hi, Tuesday," I said. I felt very mature, too.

"What do you want?" she asked.

"The list of names of everyone invited to the bonfire party," I said.

"What for?" she asked.

"To determine who might have had both motive and access to Winthrop Dashavoy on the night of his murder," I said.

"Surely the police will be doing this already," she said. She sounded intrigued, however, so I took that as a good sign.

"I'm sure they are," I agreed. "But I don't think they know the players like I do."

"What do you know about the clients of Carson and Evers?" she snorted. Yes, she actually snorted.

"Given that I'm one of them, I know more than you think," I snapped. Yes, this was a total fabrication, but she was being super obnoxious so it felt as good a time as any to bust out a fib.

"Fine, if I get you the list, what's in it for me?" she asked.

"What do you mean?" I asked. "I should think helping Harrison out would be more than enough for you."

I went for indignant; meanwhile my stomach was curling in on itself as I suspected Viv's prediction was true and Tuesday was going to make me give up Harrison. Well, she could try but I wasn't going to make it easy for her.

"How about a new hat?" I asked.

Viv, who'd been blatantly eavesdropping the whole time, gave me a sour look. I imagined she wanted Tuesday to own one of her hats about as much as she wanted a person with lice trying them on, but sadly it was all I had to offer.

"Those overpriced rags?" she scoffed.

I took a moment to thank the Universe that I had not been stupid enough to put my cell phone on speakerphone. I could only imagine how Viv would have responded to having her hats, works of art really, called rags.

As her business partner and cousin, I should have leapt to her defense, but I am a horrible person and it didn't suit my needs to do so. So instead, I gave Viv an eye roll to indicate what a pain Tuesday was being. Viv narrowed her gaze at me and I wondered if she had been able to hear Tuesday. Uh-oh.

I circled around the counter and began to pace. I figured it would be much harder for Viv to snatch the phone out of my hands and curb stomp it like it was Tuesday's head if I stayed in motion.

"What would you like?" I asked.

"You know what I want," she said.

My stomach dropped into my shoes as I said, "Spell it out for me."

"Harrison," she said. "I want him back. I want you gone. You must convince him that there is no future for the two of you and then I will take over your account from him."

Now the room went fuzzy and I was seeing spots. It was one thing to demand that I back away from Harrison. I understood the desire to cut out the competition—that made sense to me and I couldn't say I blamed her for the maneuver. It was a whole other thing to mess with my business, however.

Harrison became our business manager when his uncle, who had been Mim's financial advisor, retired. Our families had been entwined through the shop for four decades. Could I really sever that just for a list of names that may or may not lead us to a suspect in a murder?

I glanced at Viv, who was watching me as I paced in front of the window. She looked concerned like she knew the price I was being asked to pay was steeper than I had bargained for. I didn't know what to do, and judging by the way my palms were sweating, my breath was short and my heart was racing, I was beginning to panic.

Chapter 20

It was then that the sweet smell of lily of the valley infused the air. It was stronger than usual as if it was trying to get my attention. I glanced over at Viv to find her sniffing the air. She looked at me and I could see the question in her gaze. She wanted to know if I could smell it, too. I nodded and she looked relieved.

We had nothing that carried the scent of lily of the valley in the shop. Viv used lavender sachets to scent the store as they were supposed to be calming and she figured it didn't hurt to try and mellow our customers upon arrival.

But lily of the valley was imprinted on both of our brains since it was the scent that our grandmother Mim had always worn. Even now just the smell of it made me feel as if I was being enfolded in one of her generous hugs.

It made me feel safe, and loved, and supported. It also cleared my head and now I knew exactly what I had to do.

"Forget it, Tuesday," I snapped. "You went too far. I was trying to help my friend but, you know what, I'll just share all of my information with the police and let them get the list of guests. I'll be sure to tell my friends Inspectors Simms and Franks how helpful you've been, not to mention Harrison. Won't he be thrilled to hear you're trying to take his clients away?"

"I am not after his clients and you know it," she snapped. "I am merely trying to sever the hold that a miserable, grubby little hat shop has on him. Of course, as soon as you became my client, I was planning to unload your pathetic little bonnet shop on another company."

"What is wrong with you?" I asked. "Are you really that dense? Don't you think Harrison would have noticed?"

"By then we would have moved on with our lives and you would be just a faded memory," she said.

"You really are delusional, you know that?" I asked. "You don't know Harrison at all if you think he is so fickle as to just forget about his friends, the people who care about him and who've had his back through this whole mess."

I heard Viv laugh and noticed that the smell of lily of the valley surged and then dissipated. I took it as a sign that Mim approved of the stand I had taken. It was absurd, given that I had no idea if the smell was actually Mim or not, but since I knew Viv could smell it, too, I chose to believe that it was Mim, visiting us from another realm, and I felt bolstered by the possibility.

"All right, don't throw a wobbler," Tuesday said. "I'll

see if I can get the names and then we'll see what you can do for me in exchange."

"Or you could just e-mail the names to me when you get them, because it's the right thing to do," I said.

Tuesday barked out a surprised laugh. "You are most definitely not cutthroat enough to exist in Harrison's world."

With that the phone went dead and I took it away from my ear. It occurred to me that I should have told her not to tell Harrison about my request, but I figured since I had called her directly that secrecy was implied. If not, well, how mad could he really get?

As it turned out, pretty mad. I was just locking the front door when he appeared. The stiff set of his shoulders should have braced me for his ire, but I held out hope that it might be the cold.

"What were you thinking?" he asked. Harrison stepped into the shop, looking positively irate. It took me a moment to notice the man who followed him. With his thick head of silver hair, square jaw, amused gaze and impeccable wardrobe, I should have recognized him right away. When I did I started. It was Harry's boss, Tyler Carson.

"Good evening to you, too," I said. I was rattled but determined to play it cool, at least for now, because the minute I saw Tuesday Blount I was going to give my yeller a solid workout. Okay, not really, but it felt good to pretend. "Good to see you, Mr. Carson."

"Ms. Parker," he returned. At least he wasn't yelling at me. And really given that Viv and I had entered his house under false pretenses, he had every right. I wondered if Harrison had told him the truth about that visit. Judging by his smile, I doubted it.

"Please call me Scarlett," I said.

"Tyler." He inclined his head.

"Can I get you anything, Tyler?" I cast Harry an alarmed look. "A glass of wine, a shot of Jameson, anything?"

"No, thank you," he said. "I did want the opportunity to apologize to you."

"Me?" I asked.

"You," he said. His smile faded and he looked grim. "Harrison told me about what Winthrop did to you, and I just wanted to let you know how very sorry I am that he touched you, frightened you or harmed you in any way. That behavior is reprehensible and that it should have happened under my roof, well, I am appalled."

"Oh, thank you," I said. He seemed so upset that I rushed to make light of how awful it had been. It's the people pleaser in me. I can't help it. "Please don't fret about it. I'm fine. The worst of it was having my face smashed up against his neck and suffering through the smell of his cologne. Someone really needs to teach men that less is more."

Tyler gave me a weak smile as if he suspected I was trying to make a joke of it.

"Really, thank you for your concern," I said. "But I'm fine. I promise."

"You're a remarkable woman," he said.

We exchanged a glance of understanding that while the moment with Win had been horrible, I was strong and fine and no damage had been done.

"This is all very nice, but we're not here for a social call, Ginger," Harrison snapped.

"I'm sorry, aren't we closed?" Viv's voice came from the back, getting louder as she walked into the room. "Whatever is the racket?"

"Harrison is throwing a wobbler," I yelled back.

Tyler looked like he was going to laugh but he stopped himself at Harrison's frown.

"Oh, dear, whatever for?" Viv asked. "Your British slang is coming along nicely, dear."

"Thank you," I said.

We both turned to look at Harrison, waiting for his explanation.

"Did you or did you not ask Tuesday for a list of guests to the bonfire party?" he asked.

"Oh, we did," Viv said.

I had not planned to jump into the truthful end of the pool so fast, but Viv is the more impulsive of the two of us. I just hoped we could swim our way out of this one.

"Whatever for?" Harrison asked. "You know the police are investigating any leads on the case and they already have the list. Surely you don't think you can track down every single person at the party and interrogate them better than the inspectors, do you?"

Okay, now I was mad. He was being arrogant, overbearing and insufferable. Yes, it was unfortunate that he was in the hot seat as far as the investigation went but that didn't give him leave to bring his boss into our place of business and dress us down like we were errant grade-schoolers.

"For your information," I said, "we have very valid reasons for requesting the list of names of all of the guests."

"Yeah?" he asked. "Give me one."

I noticed Tyler was looking distinctly uncomfortable during our exchange and I felt bad about that, I did, but it couldn't be helped. Neither could the absolute blank that my brain had become. I, the queen of the fibbers, had nothing.

I glanced at Viv, hoping she might have thought of something, but no, she looked at me with wide eyes. We were doomed.

"Really, Harrison, is it necessary to have such a go at them right now? We do have one of Dashavoy's clients to meet in fifteen minutes as you know," Tyler said. "Besides it's quite obvious why she asked Tuesday for the list of party guests."

"It is?" Viv and I asked together.

Tyler smiled at us. It was the sort of smile that opened doors, garnered free drinks, and in some cases, like Tuesday's I suspected, lifted skirts. Tyler had charm and panache by the bucketful and I doubted there was a person who met him who was immune.

"It's just good business," he said. "A guest list like that is exactly the kind of clientele you cater to so why not add their names to your own database? It's just the smart thing to do. I'd have done the same."

"You would?" Harrison, Viv and I all said together.

"Of course." He shrugged.

"Thank you so much for understanding, we weren't sure how to tell you and didn't want you to think badly of us," Viv said. She tossed her blond curls and stepped forward and put her arm through Tyler's. "You really are a savvy businessman. I feel so much better knowing that you approve."

Harrison stiffened and I knew Viv's words had found their mark. He looked as if he'd protest, but Viv turned Tyler away and they walked toward the other side of the shop. Tyler said something and Viv threw her head back and laughed. It appeared they had a mutual admiration thing going, so I turned my gaze back to Harrison.

"What are you thinking, barging in here and ordering us about? Just because you own the controlling interest in the shop doesn't mean you get to be a bully," I said.

It occurred to me that the last time I had seen him we'd been in a lip-lock of smoking hot proportions, but right now the only thing that was hot was my temper.

"I told you to stay away from this and then what do I discover—" he started but I interrupted.

"Discover? Don't you mean your ex-girlfriend went running to you to tattle on me the moment she hung up the phone?" I asked.

"Actually, I found her logging into Tyler's assistant's computer, where she was e-mailing the guest list to— surprise!—you," he said.

"So what?" I asked. I glanced over at Viv and Tyler where she was modeling a hat for him. He seemed charmed. I leaned closer to Harrison and hissed, "What do you care if we want the guest list for business?"

"Pah ha ha!" He barked a laugh completely devoid of humor.

Both Viv and Tyler turned to look at us, so Harrison and I bared our teeth. I did not think there was any way our grimaces could be construed as smiles but maybe they were far enough away that they couldn't see clearly, because they both smiled and turned back to the collection of hats Viv was showing him.

"Do not cling to that flimsy excuse Tyler gave you as the reason you asked for the list," Harrison said. "Neither of you is business savvy enough to have thought of it, and in the aftermath of what happened at the party, it would have been grotesquely bad form."

"I'm American," I said. "We have different social mores than you."

"Do not even try to hide behind that," he said. "You are working the case and we both know it."

"So what if I am?" I asked. "Listen, Inspector Franks was here today and he said straight up that you're the primary suspect because of the scuffle at the party. Even my vouching for you is being taken apart because I don't wear a watch and can't pin down our time apart exactly. Harry, I'm scared for you, really scared."

Maybe it was because my voice cracked or perhaps I looked as stressed as I felt, but the hard lines of Harry's face softened and he cupped my cheek.

"Oh, Ginger, don't be scared," he said. His voice was still low but it wasn't hissing anymore; rather it was a gentle whisper as if he couldn't bear to cause me any more anguish.

"Harrison, we really have to go," Tyler called from the door, where he and Viv stood waiting.

"One moment." Harrison stepped forward and kissed my forehead. "Don't worry. Tyler believes in me and that's saying something. He's even helping me consult with Win's clients as a show of faith. It's going to be okay."

I wished I had his confidence, but I couldn't help thinking that if we didn't find someone else to take his place as the primary suspect, and soon, Harrison was going to be put behind bars for a crime he didn't commit. Because no matter how you looked at it, even I could see he had both means and motive and how could you fight that?

Chapter 21

As expected, Inspectors Franks and Simms just happened to be in the neighborhood during Viv and Fee's segment with Elise Stanford.

While the cameraman and his crew person packed up their equipment after the shoot, Elise and her producer, Sam, chatted with Viv and Fee.

I paced in front of the doors since it was my job to keep out any customers who wanted to come in during the filming. Viv and Fee had spent the morning staging the shop so that when Elise and crew arrived, they managed to get the interview done in about twenty minutes. I had to give it to Elise, she asked insightful questions about the hat business, Viv and Fee's creative process, and what they projected the future of hats to be.

About halfway through the interview, I spotted Franks

and Simms, standing across the street. They looked as if they were debating whether to come over or not. I considered sticking my head out the door and inviting them in, anything if it would get Elise in the perp chair and Harrison out, but I resisted. The interview was to air tomorrow and interrupting it would be detrimental to the shop, no matter how much I wanted to see Elise hauled away in handcuffs.

It was nothing personal, I just wanted to save my future boyfriend, yes, I had decided Harry would be my boyfriend just as soon as my ban on men was lifted. And I did not want my first boyfriend in forever to be one I only got to visit in the prison yard for an hour every other Saturday.

The hats in the front window didn't need rearranging but I fussed with them anyway as it gave me something to do. Since I wasn't a designer and couldn't talk intelligently about hats, I had not been invited to participate in the interview. This was fine with me. If I never had a camera pointed at my face again in this life, well, I would consider it a blessing.

Franks and Simms both had cardboard cups of coffee. I watched as they stood next to each other, talking as the steam rose out of their cups. I wondered if they were reviewing suspects. I squinted and tried to read their lips but Simms was a mumbler and I couldn't see Franks's mouth through his mustache.

It would have really made my day if one of them had mouthed the words "She's our killer," but no, as far as I could tell, they were either debating the weather or comparing football scores.

I fluffed the enormous purple plume on a matching velvet mushroom hat. This was one of my favorites. Like the cloche, the brim went down but this one also went out like a mushroom cap, hence the name, and I had yet to meet a woman who did not look good in the style.

When I glanced back up to where the inspectors had been standing, they had moved and were crossing the street in our direction. I wondered if they had been waiting on some crucial bit of evidence before moving forward. I closed my eyes and fervently hoped that Elise was arrested, yes, because I am an awful person.

I hurried over to the door and unlocked it. The camera crew thought it was for them and they thanked me on their way out.

"See you at the station," the main guy called to Elise as they left.

"Editing room at three," she called back. She waved with a genuine smile.

As the last of the crew departed, Franks and Sims made their way inside.

Viv called out, "So sorry, we're closed. Scarlett, you're supposed to—"

"Good afternoon, Vivian, Scarlett and Fiona, isn't it? How are you?" Inspector Franks said.

There was a moment of surprise, well, not so much for me and Viv, but for everyone else, yeah, it was awkward.

"Oh, no, you're here to arrest me, aren't you?" Elise cried out. She put her fist to her lips as if to keep herself from saying any more. Then she fainted.

"Elise!" Sam Kerry, her producer, caught her right before she would have cracked her head on one of our tables.

He struggled under her dead weight and Inspector Simms darted forward to help him get her into a nearby chair.

"I'll get her some cold water," Fee said and she hurried to the back room.

Inspector Franks strode forward, considering the newscaster carefully. He looked at Sam Kerry, who was rubbing her hands, and asked, "Does she faint often?"

"It's the first time that I know of," Sam answered.

He was a burly man with a thick neck and hairy knuckles, but I liked him. I had the feeling that he was the sort of guy you wanted to have at your back in a fight. And I liked how he cared for Elise with such gentle concern. Regardless of the rest of us in the room with them, he seemed only aware of her.

It was clear to me that on his part, there was a lot more going on than a producer to talent relationship. I wondered if Elise had any idea or if she was one of those women who is so accustomed to being treated well because she is pretty that she had no idea that the amount of care and concern he was giving her was above and beyond.

"Why does she think we're here to arrest her?" Franks asked.

I saw the back of Sam's neck turn deep red. And when he swung around, I saw his face was just as flushed. He glared at Franks. "You're not going to, not if I have anything to say about it."

"Well, you don't have anything to say about it, do you?" Franks snapped.

It was clear he was losing his patience. I glanced at Viv and she looked as wide eyed as I felt. Simms cleared his throat and Franks visibly pulled himself together.

Fee came dashing back into the room with a glass of water and a cool cloth. Sam put the cool cloth on the back of Elise's neck and she slowly roused out of her faint. She looked startled to find herself draped in a chair with six people staring down at her.

She clutched Sam's hand and asked, "What happened?"

I glanced at Franks. His eyes were narrowed and I wondered if he was trying to decide how good of an actress Elise was. If she was faking this, I had to give her two thumbs up. She looked genuinely distraught and I felt bad that I had engineered the entire meeting, but if it saved Harrison, I would learn to live with it.

"You fainted, love," Sam said. His voice was gentle and kind. "You've been under a lot of stress and I think it best if we get you to a doctor."

"No!" Elise shook her enviable mane of thick brown hair. "The inspectors are here for a reason; I'd hear it now and be done with it."

Sam shook his head, but Elise sat up and took the cloth off the back of her neck. Fee held out the water to her and Elise smiled her thanks and drank it down. The color came back to her cheeks and she turned her gaze on Inspector Franks.

"I apologize for my behavior. It's been a trying few days," she said. She gestured for him to take the seat across from her.

Inspector Franks took the seat and braced his elbows on his knees. He was still giving her the squinty eye, but I could see her apology had smoothed his ruffled feathers a bit.

"I imagine it has been," Franks said not unkindly.

Sam stood beside Elise's chair and I noticed that Simms mirrored his position. If I didn't know better, I would think

I was watching a live chess match. So far, it seemed Franks had checked her at every move but now it was my turn.

"You know, don't you?" Elise asked me.

I felt the hair on the back of my neck prickle. Sweat dampened my palms as I took a steadying breath.

"About the true nature of your relationship with Mr. Dashavoy?" I asked. I felt Franks turn to look at me in surprise. I'd had a few days to think about Elise and Win and I didn't like what I'd determined. "Yes, I do."

Elise gasped and shot me a hurt look. Yes, my conscience spasmed, but I ignored it. She glanced down at her lap. Her hands were clasped so tightly that her knuckles were white.

"At the party when Win was . . ." I paused. What had he been doing, making a pass? No. His actions had been aggressive and mean; that wasn't a pass which was open to refusal. It was unwelcome attention that had been forced upon my person, which in my book was assault.

I cleared my throat before I continued, "When Win was assaulting me . . ." I had to pause again for the collective gasping. Yes, I imagined speaking so plainly was a bit jarring. I really didn't care. I wasn't going to pretend what had happened was okay. It wasn't. "He was drunk and he spoke about not letting *her* get away with it. That he was tired of being told how to act and how to behave and to smile pretty for the camera. I didn't know who he was talking about until I heard that the two of you were involved."

"So naturally you decided to mention it in front of the inspectors," Elise said.

I shrugged. "My friend is being accused of murder and I know he didn't do it."

"Neither did I," Elise protested. She glanced at Viv, Fee and then me. "You don't believe me."

"If you'd prefer, we can continue this conversation elsewhere," Franks said.

"No," Elise said. "I imagine it will all become public in a matter of hours anyway."

"Your relationship with Winthrop Dashavoy was—" he began but she interrupted.

"False," she said. "The entire thing was a fabrication created by my agent to boost my profile with the press."

"You weren't engaged then?" Simms asked. It was the first time he had addressed Elise directly, and I saw Franks give him a look.

"No," she said.

"And you were not dating?" he asked.

"Not in the traditional sense," she said. She gave us a rueful glance. "Ours was a match made in media heaven. A morning show anchor dating one of the richest men in London; it seemed like such a good idea when my agent pitched it to me."

"What happened?" he asked.

"Win was great in the beginning," she said. "Clever, charming and very photogenic, he really did boost my status at first."

"What happened next?" Franks asked. This time I saw Simms give him a look. I didn't think that I was imagining a tension between the two of them.

"He became increasingly demanding," she said. "He seemed to forget that I was the arm candy that was supposed to bolster his credibility, which was suffering after several business ventures went awry."

"Did he harm you?"

"Fat chance of that!" Sam said. "I never left her alone with him."

Elise gave Sam a tender smile, the sort of smile a girl gives only to her knight in shining armor. This told me more than anything that Elise's relationship with Win had never been more than window dressing.

"No, he didn't harm me, but he was beginning to tarnish my reputation with his behavior, the drinking, the drugs, the public scenes with tawdry girls," she said. "I wanted out. I begged him to end the phony relationship but he refused."

"Why?" Viv asked. "Clearly, it wasn't doing him any good or he would have valued it more."

"I think he liked torturing me," Elise said. "The more upset I got, the more outlandish his behavior became. He was sick and twisted that way."

"What happened at the party?" Franks asked.

Elise and Sam exchanged a glance. It was obvious they were trying to decide if they needed to call for an attorney before they continued talking.

"As I said, we can always do this elsewhere, such as the station, if you'd be more comfortable," Franks said.

"You're quite the pushy git, aren't you?" Sam growled.

"Oy, mind your tone," Franks barked.

"Everyone calm down, yeah?" Fee asked.

"I'm sorry," Elise said. "It's been a very difficult time. My ratings are down and the network has put me on probation."

Her eyes watered up and I glanced away. Now I was beginning to feel the guilt of having her walk into what was essentially an ambush.

"Win was drunk, not a surprise, at the party," she said. "The *Daily Mail* had just published another story about him and I told him I was fed up with it. I told him I was ending the arrangement."

"Then what happened?" Franks asked.

"He told me that if I ended our relationship, he would ruin my career," she said.

"Which is a bloody load of codswallop," Sam said. "He can't touch her. We left the party shortly after, leaving him to wallow in his own stupid, drunken filth."

"Perhaps," Franks agreed. "But there is the small matter that no one knows exactly what time you left."

"We hired a car," Sam said. "Which I already told that one." He paused to point his thumb at Inspector Simms. "Get the receipt from them."

"We're trying," Simms said. His unibrow was lowered over his eyes in a look that I knew meant he was unhappy. "Strangely, they have no record of picking you up at the Carsons."

"But that's impossible," Elise said.

"Impossible or not, it is so," Simms said.

"You're obviously not working hard enough to clear her," Sam said. "Do you like tarnishing her reputation? Do you enjoy the celebrity by association? Tell me, do we have your memoir about the case to look forward to?"

"You are bang out of order!" Simms bellowed. "It is not our job to clear her, it's our job to find a murderer, and if it's you or her or both of you, I'll have no problem putting you in the nick for it!"

His voice boomed and we all jumped. Franks reached up and put his hand on Simms's arm.

"Easy, Simms, it's all in a day's work," he said.

Simms shook him off. "Don't tell me how to run my case."

"It's not your case anymore," Franks said.

The two men stared at each other and I realized that this was probably the source of the tension I had felt between them. Franks coming back to town had adjusted Simms's position so that he was no longer the lead investigator.

"I don't care what the superintendent says, it's still mine," Simms said.

"Listen, this is what happens in high-profile cases," Franks said. "You have no experience leading this sort of media circus, which is why I came back from York to give you backup."

"No one asked you to," Simms said.

"How do you know they didn't ask?" Franks said.

Simms turned away, looking like he wanted to punch something or someone. I hoped Sam Kerry was smart enough not to walk into that.

"Ms. Stanford, Mr. Kerry, even if we do manage to get the record of time from the hired car, we still have one problem," Franks said. "The security camera system at the Carson house suffered a malfunction about ten minutes before Winthrop Dashavoy was murdered. You wouldn't know anything about that, would you?"

Chapter 22

I really thought Elise was going to faint again. Both she and
Sam denied any knowledge of the security camera debacle,
but it seemed weak to me. They were in television; they must
have some technical knowledge. Disabling a security camera system was probably as easy as a sneeze for them.

Franks and Simms dismissed them, and Elise paused
beside me as they were leaving.

"I didn't kill Win," she said.

I didn't know what to say, which was a rare occurrence
for me, so I just nodded.

"I know they're looking at Harrison Wentworth because
of the fight he had with Win," she said. "And I know the
fight was about you."

Again, I nodded. I felt as awkward as a schoolgirl holding up the wall at a dance.

"I'll still run the segment on the morning show," she said. "Even though I am quite certain you set me up."

I could feel my face burn with embarrassment, but I cleared my throat and said, "How Sam feels about you is how I feel about Harrison."

She looked surprised, and I smiled.

"It's obvious that he cares for you very much," I said.

She cast Sam a furtive glance. He was standing with his arms crossed over his chest, looking fierce in the direction of Inspectors Franks and Simms as they talked to Viv and Fee.

Elise smiled. "I care for him very much, too."

"So you understand why I did what I did," I said.

She nodded. Then she surprised me by hugging me. When she had me close, she whispered, "If you want to help your boyfriend, look at Reese Evers."

She stepped back and Sam appeared beside her. Together they left the shop, making a beeline for a waiting sedan with tinted windows.

Now why had she told *me* that and not the police? Reese Evers owned half of one of the most influential moneymaking companies in London. It didn't take a genius to figure out that Elise didn't want to be fingered for tossing Reese's name at the police so she threw it my way instead.

Inspectors Simms and Franks met me by the door.

"All right, Scarlett?" Simms asked.

I nodded. Franks paused while shrugging on his overcoat and hit me with a beady stare.

"Don't feel guilty," he said. "You did the right thing."

"Did I?" I asked.

"Elise has replaced Harrison as our prime suspect," he said. "So yes, you did."

"Harrison is still a person of interest, though?" I asked, wanting clarification.

"Until the case is solved, every person in the city of London is a person of interest," he said. "Including you."

"Wow, and just when I was beginning to feel better," I said.

Franks pushed the door open and a whoosh of cold air blew across my body, making me shiver. I had the feeling there was not enough caulk in the world to stop the cold that was coming.

"Beware, Scarlett," Simms said as he followed his partner. "There is a murderer out there, and if they feel exposed, I doubt they'll hesitate to kill again."

This time I shivered but it wasn't from the cold.

A reasonable person would take to heart the inspector's words and back away from Dashavoy's murder. Well, I am nothing if not unreasonable. I spent the rest of my afternoon going over the guest list that Tuesday Blount had e-mailed me, which had been accompanied by a terse note that pretty much told me to go to hell without actually saying so, because I am stubborn like that.

I was torn between being relieved that Elise was their new primary suspect and guilty because I was the one who had put her there. I just didn't get the killer vibe off her. Yeah, I know, lots of killers are good at hiding their crazy, but I didn't get crazy off her either. And the person who had strangled Winthrop Dashavoy had definitely been crazy or at the very least crazy mad.

This is what kept me poring over the list of guests. There had to be someone whose name would pop out as having had a bad falling-out with Win. My method wasn't very sleuthy. I should have been pounding the pavement, banging on doors, and asking tough questions while chomping on a pipe and wearing a deerstalker cap, but it was cold and windy outside, so I was copying and pasting names from the guest list into an Internet search engine with Win's full name and hoping for a scandal to reveal itself like two pokes to the eyes.

I had worked my way through a third of the list and so far I had nothing. I knew that Nick would probably be able to take a quick scan at the list and immediately tell me who was who and what was what, but I didn't want to intrude on him while he was drilling and filling a patient and I didn't have the patience to wait until he was off work.

While I was doing this, I kept mulling over Elise telling me to look at Reese. Did she think Reese was having an affair with Win like Tuesday had intimated? I supposed anything was possible, but it just seemed such an odd pairing.

Reese was a wealthy widow, who was incredibly well maintained. What would she see in a man so young, who while good-looking was utterly reprehensible? Not to mention the fact that I doubted Reese would have the strength to strangle Win, even if he had taken a shot to the eye and was drunk. It just didn't seem likely.

Maybe what Elise had been trying to tell me was that Reese knew something, or at least Elise suspected that Reese knew something. What had been the relationship between Reese and Win? I had a feeling this was a critical piece of the puzzle and I wondered if Inspectors Simms and Franks had figured it out yet.

Then, of course, I wondered how angry they would be if I asked them about Reese. Simms had been pretty clear in his warning that I should stay away from the case and it was obvious there was some discord between the inspectors about who was in charge of the case.

I had no intention of making myself a target but I knew that owning the hat shop gave me access to people and places that the police didn't have—okay, they had access but I didn't think they were as welcome.

"Scarlett, I am famished," Viv declared. "Can we close early and pick up some take-away?"

"No, what if a customer comes?" I asked. "You can't just change your hours. It takes years to build a customer base—"

"But only seconds to lose it," Viv said. "Yes, Mim bludgeoned that expression into us, although she always closed when she felt like it."

"People were more forgiving back in the day," I said.

"Fine," she said. "If I promise to stay out front with my work and mind the store, will you go get us dinner?"

"That depends," I said. "How far do you expect me to walk? It's cold out there, you know."

"I must have falafel," she said. "You know from Falafel King."

I glanced at the window and felt the cold pressing up against it. It was dark outside and I didn't need much imagination to feel the bitter air in my throat and nose. I would have balked but it was only a quarter of a mile and I was hungry, too. Besides Falafel King really did have the best falafel and it would totally hit the spot.

"Okay, I'll go, but you had better be nice to anyone who comes in," I said.

"You make me sound like I'm a Billy No Mates," Viv said. "Like I don't have any friends or know how to talk to people."

I just stared at her. In the months I had been here I certainly hadn't met any recent friends and she refused to talk about her husband, so yeah, I wasn't sold on her people skills.

"Don't say it," she said. "I'm not discussing him."

I wasn't surprised she knew what I'd been thinking. We'd always understood each other perfectly, and even with this husband she'd wedged between us, we still did. It was a bit of a relief, actually.

I put my purse on the counter while I pulled on my jacket, scarf, gloves and hat. I was still wearing the beanie from the party. I liked the razzle-dazzle of the pearls she had put on it, plus it kept my head warm.

"I'll be back shortly," I said. "Two orders of falafel coming up."

Fee had already left for the day; otherwise I would have picked up an order for her, too.

"Thank you," Viv said. "Don't forget the salad."

"Just make sure you mind the store. No locking the door as soon as I'm out of sight." At her outraged expression, I knew that was exactly what she had planned to do. Channeling Mim's most disapproving expression, I wagged my finger at her and said, "No."

She crossed her arms over her chest and heaved a sigh. I waved to her through the glass as the door shut behind me.

The restaurant wasn't that far away but the night air

was as brisk as I'd feared—that's a lie, it was downright cold—so I hurried my pace, hoping that the exercise would warm me up.

With most of the shops closed or about to close, the street was quiet. I hurried down the uneven sidewalk being careful not to trip. The streetlights on Portobello Road were designed to look old-fashioned but cast much brighter light.

With the old stone buildings all around me, it was easy to pretend I had fallen back in time. Viv and I used to do this to amuse ourselves when we were girls. Being just a few years younger than Prince Will and Prince Harry, we spent an awful lot of our girlhood devoted to daydreaming about our weddings to them.

Because she was older and one hundred percent British, Viv felt that Will was hers, but I argued that since Harry and I are both gingers, our babies would come out with hair like flames, which was just too much. Viv reluctantly agreed, although as the years passed, I think she became more enamored of Harry and his shenanigans. They have the same sort of impulsive streak.

Of course, when we went whole hog into our day-dreams, we were always on our way to a ball at Bucking-ham Palace, wearing big meringue-style gowns and being picked up in a horse-drawn carriage. Yeah, our fantasies might have been influenced by Mim's romance novels, which we devoured as young teens.

Viv always wore a gown of the palest gossamer blue, while I went for pink. Yes, pink, a very pale fragile pink so as not to clash with my hair, but it was always pink. I have mentioned my pink phase, haven't I? Mim, bless her heart, never said a word. She let me wear the boldest shades of pink I could find, as if she had faith that someday I would develop some taste for fashion. I am definitely a work in progress but I like to think I am getting there.

At the corner of Portobello Road and Westbourne Grove, I had to cross the street as the sidewalk was blocked by construction on a storefront. This area was dark as the brick apartments on my right were hemmed in by large thick hedges and a black wrought iron fence. I slowed my pace, since I could feel my heart beating and I was quite warm after the brisk start to my walk.

The brick apartments were set back a bit and I passed a small fenced-in garden, which was looking very barren now. I glanced through the wrought iron. The small dried-up lawn was deserted, not a surprise given the cold. This was exactly the sort of spot where Viv and I would have spun our fairy tales, in fact, we probably did spend more than a few hours in this very one, playing with the kids who lived in the flats above. We would have taken turns, me playing Harry to her princess and her playing Will to mine.

I smiled. I missed the simplicity of those days when life was filled with daydreams of princes, not murderers on the loose. I walked on, feeling the cold catching up to me when I paused. Harrison hadn't been in touch and I wondered if he'd be at the shop when I returned. The desire to see him made me pick up my pace again.

I wasn't sure when exactly I picked up on the fact that someone was following me, but I was very close to the Westway overpass when I got the creepy feeling that some-one was moving up behind me. I walked faster. So did they. I didn't think it was a coincidence.

My heart started to beat faster. While my rational side argued that I was being ridiculous, my instincts were screaming that I was in danger. Instinct won and I broke into a run. The person behind me did, too, and that's when I knew I was in trouble.

Chapter 23

Panic made my heart pound in my ears. I dashed down the sidewalk, clutching my purse, trying to decide if it was heavy enough to use as a weapon. Mostly, though, I was hoping to get to the other side of the underpass, where someone might see that I was in trouble.

I could feel the person gaining on me. He was huffing and puffing and sounded like a big, burly man. I had visions of him stealing my purse then snapping me like a pretzel just because he could.

"*Oy!* Move aside, lady, I'm trying to catch my bus!"

I jerked to the side, and he swerved around me, dashing toward the corner and waving his arm, signaling to the double-decker bus up ahead that was slowly pulling away. He shouted and waved and chased it down, while I collapsed against the brick wall beside me.

Clearly, Simms warning me about the murderer being on the loose had gotten into my head. Boy, did I feel stupid. I trudged on to the restaurant up ahead cheered by its bright green exterior just beyond the dark tunnel of the underpass. I whistled my way there, reminding myself that I was just jumpy from shadows, nothing more.

I checked the time on my phone. I had a half hour until they closed. I ordered for Viv and me and waited while they bagged it up. I hoped it stayed warm on the five-minute walk back, but since Viv had been so insistent on falafel, she had no right to complain if it was cold when I arrived.

Back into the underpass I went. I could smell the food and was tempted to open the bag and just take a nibble, but then the food would get cold and I figured it would be rude to eat without waiting for Viv, tempting as it may be.

The street was quiet. I passed a couple, who looked cozy with his arm about her shoulders, holding her close as they walked in step either home to snuggle or out for an evening on the town. I felt a pang of jealousy, but I forced it aside. I refused to feel sorry for myself because I was single. I liked being single. Really, I did.

Okay, that's another lie. I didn't really like it, but I liked it better than my last relationship, so that was saying something, right? I mean if you have to choose between a no-good, cheating scoundrel and being alone, trust me when I tell you being alone is so much better.

Of course, then there was Harry. If I had to choose between being alone and being with Harry, well, it was becoming increasingly clear to me that I would choose Harry. He was funny, smart, kind and definitely easy on the eyes. A spasm of anxiety gripped my middle. What if someone snapped him up while I was doing my alone thing?

I shook my head. If that happened then Harry clearly wasn't the man for me. Oh, I didn't like the pang of sad that came along with that thought. Maybe I needed to call my mother and beg her to let me out of my no dating promise. She would gloat. Was Harry worth that?

Yes, he was, but what if we didn't work out and I had to listen to my mother's "I knew you couldn't do it" for the rest of my life? This made me think the situation needed careful examination, preferably over a bottle of wine or two with my friends.

Lost in thought, I was surprised when I arrived at the construction site at the corner of Westbourne Grove. I didn't feel like crossing the street. Since there was no traffic, I stepped out onto the road to go around the rickety scaffolding. It was built so that pedestrians could go under it, but it always gave me the willies, like it was just waiting for me to step under it so it could collapse.

I was halfway past when out of the darkness a figure jumped out at me. I started and opened my mouth to scream but no sound came out. The face staring back at me was terrifying with pale skin, arching eyebrows, a smirking mouth with a curved mustache and a long chin patch. It took me a second to realize it was a Guy Fawkes mask just like the one that had been on Winthrop Dashavoy's face at the bonfire party. Then I screamed.

The stranger lunged toward me. I stumbled back into the road. He came after me. A car beeped and swerved, barely missing me. The man ducked back into the shadows.

I took the opportunity to dash across the street. Two of the modern-style red phone booths were on the corner. If I could just get inside one, he wouldn't be able to grab me.

I ran. I heard him right behind me. I dodged to the right and then darted left into the booth. I thought I had fooled him but he was quick. Before I could shut the door, he grabbed the handle of the food bag. I held on until he yanked and then I let go. When he fell backward, I slammed the door shut.

He came at the glass door as if he had every intention of smashing it to get to me. I yelled for help but I doubted anyone could hear me. He was stronger than I was. I could feel my gloves slipping off the door handle as we engaged in a tug-of-war. I didn't know how much longer I could hang on, but I knew for certain that if I let go, I was dead.

He loomed up close to the glass and I could see his eyes moving behind the slits in the mask. The evil smirk was terrifying and I wondered if it was the last thing I'd see before I died.

"What do you want from me?" I cried.

He yanked on the door handle. It almost opened. I yelped and pulled it shut. My muscles were shaking and I didn't think I could hold on much longer.

"Why are you doing this?" I yelled. My frustration dried up any would-be tears and I started to lose my temper. I was terrified and it made me want to hurt him.

"Who are you?" I bellowed. "You're not scaring me!"

He slammed his face up against the glass and I shrieked and reared back. I let go of the door handle and he yanked it open. I screamed as he reached inside to grab me. I tried to evade his hand like a mouse hiding in its cage.

"Scarlett!"

"Oy, you there, get away from her!"

Two male voices, which were now the sweetest sounds I'd ever heard, called from nearby. My attacker punched the side of the booth, barely missing my head, before he darted off down Westbourne Grove.

A pair of arms reached into the phone booth and pulled me out. I was shaking and tears and snot were coursing down my face.

"It's all right, love, I've got you." Nick pulled me up against his chest. The comforting scratch of his dark wool coat brushed my cheek as a sob of relief welled up inside me and came out in a series of pants and hiccups.

"I'm going after him," Andre yelled.

"Be careful," Nick said.

I heard Andre's feet pounding the pavement in the same direction the masked man had taken. I wanted to shout at him not to go. I couldn't bear it if anything happened to him, but I couldn't seem to find my voice.

"It's all right," Nick said. "Andre can handle himself."

I wasn't sure who he was trying to convince, me or him.

"Come here," Nick said. "Let me examine you under the light. He didn't hurt you, did he?"

My face was mashed against his coat. I didn't want to move. I didn't want to be looked over. I just wanted to be absorbed into the fibers of black wool until I was invisible.

"I'm fine," I talked into his jacket.

"What's that?" he asked. "I couldn't quite make it out. It sounded like you need a pint."

That surprised a chuckle out of me and I leaned back and looked at him. He was wearing a silly Fair Isle knit hat with earflaps and a pom on the top. I couldn't believe Andre had agreed to be seen with him looking like that.

Nick's gaze was so kind and caring it almost made me blubber. He ran his hands over my arms and checked me over for wounds and breaks. I could have told him that the only thing broken was my sense of safety on the streets I had walked ever since I was a girl with never a moment of fear until now.

"All right, Scarlett?" he asked.

I nodded. My throat still felt too constricted to get the words out and it was taking everything I had to keep from falling apart and dissolving into a bucket of tears.

"It's a good thing Viv told us what you were about," he said. "We were hoping to meet up with you and grab take-away together."

So it hadn't been happenstance that they found me. Still I felt lucky. I didn't know for sure what my attacker had planned but I didn't think I was overreacting to fear it was bad.

I started to get the trembles and could feel my knees knocking together. I didn't know how much longer I could stand there without running away, screaming into the night. Fortunately, Andre came dashing back to us, forcing me to pull it together.

"He lost me," he said. He was breathing hard and he leaned on the side of the phone booth and lowered his head. He stared up at me and asked, "Was he wearing what I think he was wearing?"

"A Guy Fawkes mask?" I asked. My voice came out unnaturally high. "Yes."

"Gor!" Nick exclaimed. "I didn't see his face. That would have scared me witless."

I nodded. Yeah, I was pretty much there. As if he understood, Andre put his arm around me and pulled me close.

"Call the others," he said to Nick. "Let's take our girl home."

I glanced at the ground where Viv's and my food sat in ruins. Not only had my assailant scared me stupid, he smashed dinner.

Following my line of sight, Andre said, "Your falafel?"

"It was once," I said.

"Don't get in a fizz," he said. "Nick and I will get dinner sorted."

"Viv is going to be so disappointed," I said.

Andre scooped up the crushed bags and tossed them into a nearby garbage can.

"I'm sure she'll forgive you for not fighting harder to save her supper," Andre said. His tone was light and I knew he was trying to jolly me out of my fright. Just having him and Nick here was doing a good job of that.

"Shouldn't we call the police and wait for them here?" I asked.

"No," Andre said. He was very decisive and started walking, leaving me no choice but to go with him. "If they want to come back and see where your dinner went splat, it's on them, but we're getting out of here. If that nutter comes back, I want to be gone."

He didn't have to sell me. We began to hurry back to our section of Portobello Road.

"No, she's all right," Nick said into his phone. "We'll be there in a few minutes."

We were moving so fast, we were there even quicker. We had almost reached the shop when I spotted a man running toward us. My shoulders stiffened at the sight of him but then I recognized the way he moved with a long-legged gait that covered ground fast. Harrison!

I broke away from Nick and Andre. They were my friends and I loved them dearly but there was only one person whose arms could really make me feel safe and that was Harry. I was still several feet away when I launched myself at him. Harrison snatched me close and held me tight with one arm around my back and one cradling the back of my head almost as if he would rock me like I was a fussy child. I would have let him, too.

"Viv called me," he said. "Are you all right? She said you were attacked by a man in a mask."

"I'm fine," I said. But then the vision of the masked face leering at me from the other side of the phone booth glass filled my head and I shivered. Clearly, it was going to take a while for that image to be replaced by happier ones.

Harrison loosened his hold and ran his hands up and down my back in a gesture of comfort. Nick and Andre joined us and I heard them talking about me as if I wasn't there and this was how I knew I was rattled, because I didn't even care.

"Did he harm her?" Harrison asked.

"No!" Andre and Nick said together and then Nick continued, "At least not physically, but he terrified her and that's going to have some long-lasting effects, probably manifesting as nightmares for a while."

"Also, he got away," Andre said. "We need to report this to the police. They need to know what's happening in case he—"

He cut off his words, but I didn't need to hear them. I

knew exactly what he was thinking because I was thinking it, too.

I stepped back from Harrison and looked at them. All three of them were looking at me as if they were afraid I'd shatter. They should know me better than that. I was scared, certainly, but I wasn't a victim and I wasn't going to be one, not if I could help it.

"In case he comes back," I said. I didn't say, although I knew with a chilling certainty that it was true, that it was not a case of *if* but rather *when* he would be back for me.

Chapter 24

They didn't agree with me, but they didn't disagree either.

"Come on, it's been hours since Inspector Franks has heard from me, I'm sure he's missing me desperately by now," I said.

Viv was half in and half out the door as we came up to it. Her hair was disheveled and her face was pale. The end of her nose was red and her eyes were watery.

"I'm sorry, I'm so sorry," she said as she grabbed me in a hug that choked. "I never should have sent you to get dinner. I should have gone myself."

"Viv, it's all right," I said. I squeezed her hard and then stepped back. "Besides if it wasn't me, it would have been you."

"No, it wouldn't," she said. "I don't have your bad luck."

It was true but I thought it tactless of her to point out at that moment.

The men bustled into the shop behind us and Harrison paused to lock the door. We moved out of the front shop area and went straight into the workroom, where Viv set about putting on a pot of tea.

"Sorry about dinner," I said. Amazingly, I was feeling pretty hungry.

"Don't think on it," Nick said. "Andre and I will pop over to our flat, whip something up and bring dinner back here."

"Oh, no, that's too much," I said. "You already saved my life, I think asking for dinner on top of that is being pushy."

"You're not asking," Andre said. "We're offering. Besides it's only going to be sandwiches, nothing fancy, and we'll be back in time to tell the inspector what we saw."

"I don't—" I began but Harrison interrupted me.

"Let them," he said.

He was looking at me as if he expected me to collapse at any moment. There was a part of me that would have liked nothing better, but then there was a part that was so angry, I would have kicked myself repeatedly until I was back on my feet with my fists clenched and ready for battle. Yeah, that would be the really, really angry part.

Fear usually left me in this state. After the shakes and tremors passed, along with the desire to hide under my bed, I got mad, boiling over, whistling like a kettle mad. Oh, wait, that actually was Viv's kettle, no matter, its shrill complaint voiced perfectly how I was feeling.

"All right," I said to Nick and Andre, who were already moving toward the door. "But I'm treating you two to a dinner out on the town. You pick the night."

"Not necessary," Nick said. "But we'll let you."

Viv put the kettle aside to steep while Harrison walked them out. When it was just the two of us, Viv gave me a sharp look.

"Do you know who it was?" she asked.

"No idea," I said.

"Can you tell me exactly what happened? Nick was sketchy on the details beyond his daring rescue," she said.

I smiled. That sounded like Nick. I recounted the story as best as I could. Harrison joined us from the part where I left the Falafel King, so I tried to sound more matter of fact than I felt to keep him from pitying me. It was a silly pride issue on my part, I suppose, but I really don't like to be perceived as weak.

When I got to the part about being trapped in the phone booth with the masked man trying to get in, my voice betrayed me by cracking. I cleared my throat and kept on talking. If Harry and Viv noticed that my voice was raspier, they had the good manners not to point it out.

"Who do you think he was?" Viv asked. "I mean I suppose he could be a stranger who was hired to terrorize you, but why?"

"The mask makes me think it has to do with the case," Harry said. "Given that Win's killer tried to use the same mask to hide Win's identity before he was tossed onto the fire, it makes sense they would try to scare you with the same one."

"Unless it is someone who is using the case to their own advantage and wants us to think that Scarlett's attack is tied to Win's murder, when it could be totally random," Viv said.

"How do you mean?" Harrison frowned.

"What if someone read the papers, learned about the scuffle between you and Win over Scarlett, and decided to use it to commit a thrill murder."

My head was beginning to hurt as it swung between them, trying to keep up with the conversation.

"Like a copy cat killer?" Harrison asked. "But then wouldn't he want to strangle her?"

"Maybe that was his plan," Viv said. "But Nick and Andre messed it up."

"Tea," I croaked. "I need some tea."

"Oh, of course, love," she said. She efficiently poured the tea into the cups after the milk and then added a teaspoon of sugar just the way I like it.

The cup was hot in my hands, almost too hot, but I wrapped my fingers around the china, letting the heat seep into my skin and through my tissue all the way down into my bones.

"There is one thing that no one has considered," I said.

"What's that?" Harry asked.

"We're assuming my attacker was a man," I said. "*He* could very well be a *she*."

"No!" Harry scoffed. "Why would a woman attack you? Women aren't thrill killers, and you have no real connection to Dashavoy."

"Not true," Viv argued. "She was with him right before he lost his life. She could be the reason a woman murdered

Dashavoy. Maybe it was someone involved with Dashavoy who did it in a jealous rage."

"Oh, gag," I said. "I was not with him so much as being pawed by him."

"Maybe, but it's not what really happened that matters, it's how it's perceived from outside that counts," Viv said.

The sound of a fist pounding on the door frame out front made me jump. I glanced at the clock on the wall.

"It's too soon for Nick and Andre," I said.

"That'll be the inspectors then," Harrison said.

"I'll go let them in," Viv offered. She patted my arm as she walked by me. "Drink your tea, love, you'll feel better."

I smiled at her but I was thinking there was nothing in this tea or any other that could make me feel better about what had happened tonight.

"Do you really think it could have been a woman?" Harrison asked.

I thought about it for a moment, trying to remember as much as I could. The person had worn a hooded jacket over their hair, the mask had hidden their face, the height and build were impossible to determine because of the knee length of their coat. These were just bits and pieces of memory. The only thing that was really clear in my mind was the terrifying mask that had leered at me through the glass. I would never forget it or the surge of pure terror it had caused me.

"I don't know," I said. "Yes, no, maybe. The hooded figure was covered up so there really was no way to tell if it was a man or a woman."

"It just doesn't make sense," Harrison said. "What woman would be strong enough to strangle Dashavoy?"

"It could be a woman with help," I said. "Like Elise with Sam Kerry or Tuesday with . . ."

One of Harrison's eyebrows shot up higher on his forehead than the other. "Go on."

"Well, I don't know who would want to help Tuesday," I said.

"She's not a killer," Harrison said. "She may be many unpleasant things but a killer isn't one of them."

"Is that just because you don't want to believe the worst of her?" I asked. "Because you almost married her?"

"Heard about that, did you?" he asked. He looked rueful as opposed to mad so I took that as a good sign that this wasn't too painful for him.

"Just the facts," I said. I didn't want him to think we had gossiped about him, which of course we had.

"Uh-huh." He sounded skeptical. "Here's a question, why would she try to harm you? Why would Tuesday attack you?"

"Because she wants you back and she'll do whatever it takes to get you back, including killing me," I said.

"What?" Inspector Franks asked as he entered the room with Inspector Simms right behind him. "I think you have some explaining to do."

And so I repeated my tale for the second time that evening while Viv made the inspectors tea and put out a plate of chocolate chip Hobnobs. Even with food, my story didn't get any better with an encore performance. Every time I thought of the creepy mask, I got the shakes.

"Clearly, you're a target," Franks said when I finished my story. He looked at Harrison. "And what about Tuesday Blount? We've interviewed her but Scarlett's story gives us a different angle."

"She's not a killer," Harrison said.

I gave him a squinty look.

"She's not," he insisted.

"Are you still carrying a torch for her?" I asked.

"What a lot of tosh," he said. "You know I'm not."

I crossed my arms over my chest and stared at him.

"Who else would try to harm me while wearing a Guy Fawkes mask?" I asked.

"It could be pure coincidence," he said. "Loads of people wear those masks on bonfire night, especially since the movie *V for Vendetta* came out a few years ago. It could be that a robber found one and attacked you while wearing it. It could be pure coincidence."

"If he was out to rob her, why didn't he reach for her purse instead of her falafel?" Viv asked.

"And why chase me into a phone booth?" I asked. "If it was a random attack, wouldn't they have gone after another victim once I was out of bounds?"

"Fine then it is related to Win's murder," Harrison said. "But you have no proof that it was Tuesday."

"And you have no proof that it wasn't," I said.

We were most definitely at an impasse. I couldn't fathom why he was protecting the woman who had broken his heart. Was it just pride? Did he really think that making her out to be a better person than she was made his dating her less unsavory? It did not.

We grew silent, nibbling on cookies and sipping tea. It was all very civilized for a disagreement. It sort of made me want to smash something. I looked at the cup in my hand. It was one of Mim's favorite teacups, a delicate bone china with yellow roses on it. I could never.

There was another knock on the front door, distracting me from my sulks.

"That will be Nick and Andre," I said. "With food."

I don't think it was my imagination that Simms and Franks settled into their seats a bit more deeply.

"They saw the attacker?" Simms asked.

"The back of him," I said. "But maybe they can give you a better description and add their opinion about whether it could have been a woman or not."

I got the feeling the inspectors were happy to stay in our warm workroom for a bit longer. And, of course, there was food involved, and if I knew Nick and Andre, they had prepared more than enough.

"Hot soup! Hot soup!" Nick came dashing into the kitchen holding a large pot with two bright pink flamingo pot holders and his overcoat flapping behind him.

Harrison quickly moved the teapot off the trivet so Nick could put the soup there.

Nick glanced at the officers. "We have company, excellent, I brought plenty."

Both Simms and Franks perked up at this and I couldn't blame them. The smell of the split pea soup, yes, I peeked in the pot, was amazing.

Bowls of soup were passed out while open-faced sandwiches were prepared and plated by Nick and Andre. They described what they had seen upon finding me as they served the food.

"We heard a commotion," Nick said. He looked at me. "Even with the booth door closed I heard you yelling at him."

Harrison's gaze moved to me. I knew he was thinking

that Nick had described the attacker as a man, but I felt as if that were a natural assumption and not an observation, which I would have pointed out but I thought it better that they told the whole story first.

Nick never saw the masked face. Andre did but only briefly when my attacker glanced back over his shoulder to see if Andre was gaining on him. According to Andre, he turned into an alley and disappeared. Simms and Franks grilled him on the precise location of the alley but Andre said he wasn't sure and he would have to go back to be certain.

In seconds, the inspectors were gathering their coats and taking Andre with them. Nick looked less than pleased and decided to join them. We promised to save them soup and sandwiches upon their return.

I noticed both of the inspectors wrapped their sandwiches to take with them and I had a feeling they were at the start of a very long evening. This time I walked them to the front door, letting Viv enjoy her meal.

"Are you sure you don't want me to come with you?" I asked.

Simms gave me a kindly look as if he knew how difficult it was for me to offer to go back to the place that had scared me so much.

"No, you're safer here. Until we know why you were attacked I would prefer you not go anywhere alone."

Well, didn't that give me the warm fuzzies.

"Don't frighten her needlessly, Simms," Franks said. "It could have just been a robbery and not be related to anything at all."

Simms frowned. "All the same, Scarlett, don't take any risks."

"All right," I agreed. My voice cracked and I cleared my throat as if it was just a stray bit of Hobnob making me choke and not the thought of a stranger's gloved hands strangling the life out of me.

"If you remember anything else about your attacker, contact me immediately," Franks said. "We'll be checking the area around the phone booth at Westbourne Grove and then it's back to the station for us."

"I will," I said. "I promise."

Both Nick and Andre gave me quick hugs before they left.

"Don't fret, love, we'll be back in two shakes of a lamb's tail," Nick said as I closed the door behind them.

That made me smile because it sounded like something my mother would say. Then I got sad because after eight months of living in London, I really missed my parents and I knew that Thanksgiving was coming up fast and I was dreading it.

"Lock it!" Inspector Simms pointed toward the door lock with a tap on the glass and I nodded.

I watched as they walked away, the inspectors eating their sandwiches as they went. When they disappeared from view, I was struck by how dark it was outside. The light in the shop made the window glass throw my reflection back at me. I could only stare out into the street if I pressed my face up against the pane and cupped my hands about my face, blocking the glare.

I backed away. I didn't want to look out there. I was afraid my attacker would reappear and cause me more nightmares with his creepy smirking face. Not that I thought more nightmares were possible.

As it was, I was dreading going up to the third floor alone. I loved every inch of this old house but it had been broken into before; I had even been attacked in it before. My homesickness reared its ugly head again. Would it be terribly cowardly of me to buy a ticket on the next plane out of here and go see my parents?

Yes, I knew very well it would be, but I was still tempted. Pumpkin pie, apple cider and crisp autumn leaves crunching underfoot, what wasn't to love about Connecticut in the fall? My parents had recently left New Haven and bought a cottage on the shore in a small town called Briar Creek. I hadn't been to see it yet, but my mother assured me that I would love the quaint little town as it had a very lively library. Suddenly, it seemed like the perfect time to go and see it.

While I was wallowing in my homesickness, Harry entered the shop from the back room.

"All right, Ginger?" he asked.

"No," I said. Lying seemed sort of pointless. I began to pull the shades down over the windows as if I could block out the horrors outside. Funny how a bit of stiff fabric could make me feel safer even if it was an illusion.

"Come here," he said. He walked toward me with his arms open wide and I stepped into them gratefully. At this moment, I would take comfort from anyone who offered but I was especially glad it was Harry.

I pressed my face into his shirtfront and took a deep calming breath. I couldn't help but think how different it was to be held by Harry than mauled by Win. He was dead, murdered, so I supposed it was bad of me to think ill of him, but from what I had learned about him there didn't seem to be a lot to like.

It was small wonder someone had strangled him. As I soaked in the lovely bay rum smell that was Harry, the mean part of me thought maybe it was Win's overpowering cologne that had caused someone to strangle him with his own tie, but then I remembered Win hadn't been wearing a tie.

A cold feeling started on the top of my head; it swept down through my body like I was being slowly encased in ice. Why hadn't I remembered it before? Did it mean what I thought it meant?

I stepped back and looked at Harrison. I must have been wild-eyed because he grasped my upper arms and stared intently at my face.

"What is it, Ginger? Are you all right?" he asked. "You look as if you've seen a ghost."

I stared at him. What if I was wrong? What if it made Harrison more of a suspect? I didn't want to risk that—not until I had more information.

"No, I'm just rattled from before," I lied. I buried my head against his chest and hugged him tight, hoping that my memory proved his innocence and not his guilt.

Chapter 25

Harrison and I rejoined Viv in the workroom. I tried to act normal, whatever that is, but I figured my earlier fright would cover any weirdness I was exhibiting.

I needed to get information out of Harrison but I needed to be subtle or he might catch on and I wasn't sure I was ready to confront that possibility.

When Andre and Nick came back, they reported that there had been no sign of the lunatic in the mask. I felt the tension in my neck ease. I hadn't even realized I was fearful of that.

Andre was sure he had pinpointed the place where my attacker had disappeared, but there was no trace of him, much to Inspectors Simms and Franks's disappointment. They planned to canvas the area again the next day, but it looked as if the person had disappeared into the service entrance of a local pub.

Because no one in the place noticed a masked man, it was assumed that he had taken off his mask before entering. Of course, I still maintained that the attacker could have been a woman, but although they all nodded, I could tell no one was taking me seriously except Viv. I got the feeling the men didn't like thinking of a woman as a cold-blooded killer.

"If my attacker was the same person who killed Dashavoy, do you suppose they were going to strangle me, too?" I asked.

All eyes turned to me and I offered a shaky smile. I couldn't help putting my hand to my throat as the thought of having my airway cut off caused me a flutter of distress.

They all looked at one another as if no one wanted to say it.

"I'd say that's likely," Viv said. She looked grim.

"I suppose it's good that I wasn't wearing a necktie," I said.

"There's a bright side for you," Nick said.

"The tie that Win was wearing was just a regular tie, wasn't it?" I asked Harrison.

He shook his head. "No, actually our ties are specially made for Carson and Evers employees. You get one on your fifth anniversary with the company and are expected to wear it to all of the company functions."

"What a pain in the neck," Nick said. We all looked at him and he shrugged. "It had to be said."

"More like it's the tie that binds," Andre said.

"And gags," Viv added.

We all smiled but I noticed no one laughed. I think they were afraid the joking was too close to home for me at the moment, but on the contrary it made me feel a sense of normalcy like everything was going to be all right, especially now that I had the information I'd been seeking.

"Well, I suppose it's a good thing I didn't *tie one on* before I left," I said.

There was a beat of silence and then Viv giggled, breaking the silence, and the others laughed, actually laughed, at my joke.

Harrison leaned over and took my hand in his and gave it a squeeze and said, "Nothing is going to happen to you, *knot* on my life."

"Oh, ick," Andre protested. "That was terrible, mate."

"I thought it was clever," Harrison said. He glanced around at us, looking put out.

"No, just no," Nick said.

Harrison looked chagrined and then we all laughed. It felt good and cleansing, and I realized that I valued this, this moment in time with these people.

No, they weren't family, except for Viv, of course. They weren't my parents and we had no connection other than enjoying one another's company. But they were my people and I would do anything to keep us safe and together, including risking embarrassment by calling Inspector Franks tomorrow to share my theory with him.

Harrison offered to stay the night on our living room couch. Viv looked to me and I shook my head. Although the offer was tempting, I didn't want to risk spilling my guts about my latest theory. Plus, Harrison was so determined that it wasn't Tuesday, I didn't want to be hampered by his bias.

Hugs were exchanged at the door, and Viv and I locked up after they left. Normally, Viv went upstairs and I checked the lower level one more time before joining her. Tonight, she waited by the stairs while I did my rounds. I appreciated the thought even as it threw me off my game.

There's a wardrobe in the corner of the shop, a large antique carved in exquisite detail with a raven peering down from the top with his wings spread over each door. The detail was so good that his eyes seemed to follow you when you moved about the shop. He had been in that same corner when Mim had opened the shop, and he'd been my only company when I had first arrived from the States as Viv hadn't been here.

I had started talking to him, don't be judgy I was lonely, and I had become rather attached to his beakiness. I had even nicknamed him Ferd the Bird. Normally at night we chatted, but with Viv loitering by the stairs, I was feeling a bit self-conscious.

"You can go ahead," I said.

"You want to say good night to the bird," she said.

I just looked at her.

"Fine, but I'm waiting at the top of the stairs so be quick," she said.

I waited until she was halfway up before I turned back to the shop, making one more visual sweep. Then I glanced at Ferd. I swear he was watching me.

"Good night, Ferd, be on the lookout for bad guys, okay?"

He winked and I knew he understood. Yes, he winked. I know it sounds improbable, which was why I had Viv head up the stairs without me. Certain things, strange things, are best kept to yourself when it might seem to others that you're crazy. For the record, I am not crazy. I swear.

Viv met me at the top of the stairs and we entered our apartment together. Harrison had done a walk-through before he left just to put our minds at ease. Actually, I think it was more to put his mind at ease since he had been quite insistent that he wanted to make sure the upstairs was secure before he left.

Viv slept on the main floor and I was on the one above. I dreaded going up there to my cold, quiet room. It was ridiculous but I was afraid I was going to be seeing that masked face in every shadow. I shivered and Viv slipped her hand through my arm and pulled me close.

"How about we have a sleepover?" she asked.

I squinted at her, not understanding what she meant.

"Go up and get your things and then sleep in Mim's big, old bed with me," she said. "We can giggle and gossip all night if you want."

"Really?" I asked. We hadn't shared a room since we were teenagers and then it wasn't sharing so much as it was running back and forth between each other's room until we either collapsed from exhaustion or Mim yelled at us.

"Yes," she said. "It'll be fun. We'll eat crisps and fizzy drinks and talk about boys."

"Husbands?" I asked.

"Don't push your luck," she said. "I'm letting you stay with me even though you snore."

I gasped. "I do not."

"Oh, yes, you do," she said.

"That was when we were young," I protested. "I've had my tonsils out since then."

She gave me a look that said she didn't believe me not even a little. I looked into the blue eyes that were identical to mine and I felt so full of not just love but also affection for my cousin that I reached out and hugged her hard. She hugged me back just as tightly and for the first time all night I realized how frightened she had been for me. Yeah, mostly, because she had me in a grip that made it hard to breathe.

My specialty in times of great stress or deep emotion is to lighten the mood. It's a coping mechanism from my days in the hospitality industry. When confronted with jet-lagged travelers whose hotel reservation has gone missing and the place is booked to the rafters with a convention of magicians, yeah, it's practically a survival skill.

I turned it on Viv now by breaking out of her hold and giving her a sideways glance.

"He's a male stripper, isn't he?" I asked.

Viv shoved me back a step, but she was grinning instead of looking worried so mission accomplished.

"You're incorrigible."

I shrugged. "Better than a snorer."

She went into her room while I jogged upstairs. Once there, I took a moment to change and wash up and then I called Inspector Franks. I hoped I wasn't waking him, but I really felt that my memory of Win not wearing a tie was important.

He had said that if I remembered anything to call him. Of course, he meant about my attacker but I figured this was significant, too.

He answered on the third ring, more accurately, he barked, "Franks."

"And beans," I said. No, I have no idea what got into me. "Who is this?"

"Sorry," I said. "It was the first thing that popped into my head. It's Scarlett Parker, Inspector Franks."

"Did you remember something?"

I crossed my room and looked out the window. My room looks out over our small patio garden at the back of the house. It was brown and dry now, but Viv kept it full of bird feeders, which I feared made it an all-you-can-eat buffet for the stray cats in the neighborhood. But the birds were quick and I hadn't seen any piles of feathers left behind in a long time, so I took it as a good sign.

"I have remembered something," I said. "But not about my attacker."

"Oh, what then?" he asked. He didn't even try to hide the disappointment in his voice.

"I don't want to say over the phone," I said.

"What?" he snapped. "You have got to be kidding me."

"Sorry, but I'm as serious as a heart attack," I said. "I feel as if someone knows every move I make, and I'm afraid they may even be listening in to my calls."

Franks was quiet for a moment. "Can you come to the station first thing in the morning?"

"I'd rather you meet me at the offices of Carson and Evers," I said. "They open at nine."

More silence.

"It's important," I said. I sensed he was ranking meeting me right up there with an appointment with a dentist's drill.

"All right, nine o'clock," he said. "But it had better be important."

"It is, I swear," I said.

"All right then," he said. "Oh, and Scarlett, I have a constable watching your home tonight just to be on the safe side."

"Thank you," I said. I would have added that it wasn't necessary but it occurred to me that he may have mentioned it just because I feared someone was listening in and maybe it was more for their benefit than mine. Either way, it did make me breathe easier.

"Good night, Inspector," I said.

"Good night, Scarlett," he said.

I ended my call and hurried downstairs to Viv's room. She was already tucked in on her side. The massive bed was big enough for the two of us and two more besides.

"Slumber party!" I yelled and jogged across the room and jumped on the bed. I quickly pulled the bedcovers up, because as everyone knows, bedsheets are magical and keep the monsters out, or at least I hoped so.

Chapter 26

Coffee was my excuse to duck out of the shop and meet the inspector before we opened. Viv was more of a tea in the morning girl, so she just nodded and waved at me with a sleepy yawn. We had stayed up, chatting into the wee hours of the morning.

I had no luck in cracking her about her husband, and we made no progress on our suspects for my attacker or Win's killer, but we did revisit our memories of Mim, which were rich and plentiful and, because it was Mim, odd.

There were so many things I had forgotten, like the way she always put milk in her teacup before pouring in the tea; she felt this was critical. How the Second World War was always referred to by her as The War. Even though she was just a child when it occurred, she still had plenty of stories about it and its aftermath. Oh, and her obsession with the Royal Horticultural Society's Chelsea Flower Show. She attended it every year because she said it gave her great inspiration for her hats, but she also then watched it televised. Yes, they televise a flower show in England as it is that popular.

I have no idea when we stopped talking and passed out. Probably I was in the middle of a sentence and just finished it with a deep breath. I do not snore, no matter what Viv says.

In any case, I found myself hopping onto the tube at Notting Hill Gate on my way to the financial district, where Harrison's office was located, at a much earlier hour than I am used to. I wondered if Harrison would be surprised to see me. I had a feeling the answer was yes, but I had no idea if it was going to be a happy surprise or a gasp of horror.

As I followed the directions to Carson and Evers on my phone, I was the one left gasping. I knew Harrison's offices were in the financial district but I'd had no idea they were in the skyscraper that I thought of as a big beautiful egg.

At forty-one stories tall the Gherkin, as it is called, is one of the most eye-catching buildings in London with light and dark glass spiraling in triangles up its massive sides to meet in a brilliant room at the top. I stood on the walk in front of it, feeling woefully underdressed in my jeans and black Converse sneakers with my thick fleece-lined jacket. Had I known I was coming here, I would have worn a business suit to blend in, but as it was, the best I could hope for was to be taken for a delivery person of some sort, maybe coffee since I still had my paper cup in my hand.

I glanced around the entrance. There was no sign of

Franks. I paced the front and then waited off to the side, not wanting to be seen by anyone who might recognize me until after I was up in the office.

This plan would have been terrific if I hadn't smacked right into Reese Evers coming around the corner. At first, I thought I could bluff and pretend not to know her, but her sharp gaze narrowed on my face. I was sure she knew who I was because of the altercation with Win and because of my past.

Undoubtedly, she had heard my name in the aftermath of the Carsons' party, and let's face it, it wouldn't be hard to do an Internet search of my name and drag up some horrifying pictures. Yes, I had been that hot of a topic less than a year ago.

What I wouldn't give at this moment for one of Viv's floppy hats to hide my face. No such luck.

"Excuse me, you're Harrison's friend Scarlett Parker, aren't you?" she asked.

I sighed and nodded. She looked as polished as she had at the party in the same expensive coat with just dark hose and patent Louboutin pumps showing beneath the hem. I stiffened my shoulders. A fabulous wardrobe did not make her better than me. In the end, it was just clothing and besides I worked with one of the hottest milliners in town. So there.

"Good morning, Mrs. Evers," I said. I didn't think she considered us on a first-name basis.

"What are you doing here?" she asked. One eyebrow was raised higher than the other in an angry expression that made me think she was debating calling security.

I glanced from side to side, hoping Inspector Franks

would make an appearance. No such luck. I checked my phone. I was ten minutes early so I couldn't really fault him.

"Are you here to see Harrison?" she asked.

"Yes," I lied. "He's expecting me."

Now why did I go and say that? Perhaps because I was afraid she was going to have me escorted off the premises.

"Well, I suppose you might as well come in then," she said.

She made it sound like I was holding a gun on her. I made one more visual sweep for the good inspector but I figured he could just get upstairs on his own. I didn't want to risk having Reese run into Harrison and tell him I was here before I was ready for him to know, plus that would really blow my cover, now wouldn't it?

"Oh, right, that'd be great," I said.

Reese led the way through the revolving glass doors and over to security. I had to be formally admitted as a guest since the building is not open to the public. Reese then led the way to one of the elevator banks. I didn't get much of a chance to gawk at the reception area as she was moving very quickly. My impressions were of floor-to-ceiling glass with large steel triangles shaping and holding it all together.

From my brief glance at the directory in the lobby, I noted that the offices for Carson and Evers took up floors thirty-one through thirty-three. Reese hit the button for floor thirty-three and I went along with it, hoping that it was the floor where I would find Harrison because suddenly I felt like I was deep in the ocean and my water wings had deflated.

We were the only two people in the plush elevator. I

wasn't sure if I should try to engage Reese in conversation or not, something told me not, but then, when else would I have the opportunity? I braced myself against her stern frowny face and asked the question I had been dying to know the answer to, good manners and talk of the weather be damned.

"Were you in a relationship with Win?" I asked.

She reeled back as if I'd slapped her.

"I . . . what . . . how . . ." she stammered and I interrupted before she hurt herself.

"I'm sorry," I said. I meant it. She looked again as if she was going to cry and that hadn't been my intention. "You seemed quite distraught at the bonfire when his body was found."

She wilted against the wall of the elevator as the floors whooshed by, and I felt sorry for poking at her pain. Sometimes I can be a truly hideous person.

"Don't be," she said. "I made a spectacle of myself, which I'm sure Win would have found very entertaining and equally unseemly."

I said nothing but wished the elevator would go faster so I could leave the stench of my bad manners behind and not be stuck in here, where it lingered like a bad smell.

"I cared for him," she said in a small voice. "He knew and he toyed with me. We were never involved, not my choice, but as it turns out, it is better for me that we weren't. The police would no doubt have found the pathetic older woman in love with a younger man angle impossible to resist."

Oh, this just got worse and worse, didn't it?

"It was seeing him strangled in my tie that did me in," she said.

My head snapped in her direction right as the doors opened on the thirty-third floor. "What did you say?"

"It was my necktie that he was killed with," she said. Her voice was small and sad. I had no patience for it.

"Yes, I got that, but what do you mean *your* tie? It belonged to you?" I asked.

She stepped out in the swank lobby, which was furnished very modern in hues of black and gray with brushed steel accents. The black floor shone to such a high gloss it looked like water and for a moment I thought I would plunge into its bottomless depths, but no. It wasn't even slippery.

"Good morning, Amanda," Reese said as she walked past the front desk, where a middle-aged brunette sat.

"Good morning, Mrs. Evers," Amanda said. She glanced at me but didn't acknowledge my presence. I blamed the jeans.

Reese kept going and I hurried after her. The elevator had opened at one end of the large circular floor and I could see staircases, which led to the offices below. It was a very open design. Breathtaking views of the city of London were visible through the floor-to-ceiling glass windows, and I wanted to press my face up against them and soak it in, but Reese had a destination in mind and I had to follow.

It occurred to me that when Harrison had said he had a corner office, he meant that he had a rounded office. Still it must have been better real estate than Win's for Win to be so mean about it.

"This is Harrison's office," Reese said. She stopped beside a closed glass door. It was a large space filled with bookshelves on the wall behind the desk, which was situated so that the view of the city was to his right.

"It looks like he isn't in yet," Reese said.

I was struck by this side of Harrison I had never seen. There was something intimate about seeing his work space without him here and the desire to snoop just about killed me. Not that I was looking for anything in particular, just a glimpse into his working life without him underfoot to distract me.

"You can wait in my office," Reese said. She did not sound very welcoming. Still, I needed an explanation about the tie.

"You were talking about the tie," I said. I took a sip of my now cold coffee, trying for a nonchalant look that I do not think I pulled off.

"They're all my ties," she said.

She took off her coat and hung it up in a narrow closet built into the same set of wood bookshelves that I'd seen in Harrison's office. She gestured for me to have a seat as she took the seat across from me.

"I don't understand."

"They're mine because I designed them, you see."

"Oh, I didn't know," I said.

"When an associate reaches their fifth anniversary with the company, they are given one of the Carson and Evers ties," she said. I must have looked confused because she continued, "I was an art major before I went into finance." She paused to give me a small smile. "I hadn't realized that being an art major required a vow of poverty, so I decided to get an advanced degree in business. Designing the neckties let me blow the dust off of my old art skills, which my husband encouraged."

I saw a portrait of a white-haired man in a suit on the shelf behind her desk. I had no doubt this was Mr. Evers.

"I saw Harrison's tie on the night of the bonfire," I said. She was mellowing while talking about her neckties, so I thought a little praise might not be out of order. "The intricately woven initials C and E make a fabulous pattern in the silk."

She tipped her head to the side and considered me. "Thank you. I designed the pattern that the initials make, and then I hired a designer from Robert Talbott to commission the silk and then to create a sevenfold tie out of the fabric."

"Sevenfold?"

"Cheap ties have a lining sewn into them, but a sevenfold tie is created by folding one piece of fabric seven times to give it heft and an incomparable drape," she said.

I felt like I should be taking notes to share this with Viv. I'd had no idea the world of tie making was so complex.

"Have you given out many five-year ties?" I asked.

"Less than a dozen," Reese said. Her eyes narrowed. "Why?"

"Just curious," I lied. "One more question, is each tie designed specifically for the wearer?"

"No," she said. "They are identical, well, except for the numbering. My husband, God rest his soul, felt that if a person left our employ to go to another firm, they had to turn in their tie, sort of like turning in their keys to the office. He even wrote it into their contract, so when each tie is made, it has a tiny number stitched on the underside. When a person leaves, we take their office keys, their parking pass, and their tie."

"Have many people left?" I asked.

"No one so far," she said.

My heart started to hammer in my chest. This could be a clue. Where, oh where, was Inspector Franks?

"My husband was buried with his tie," Reese said. She looked a little weepy, but I had no time for that. Harsh but true.

"Is there any way you can tell me the number of Win's necktie?" I asked.

Reese pulled a tissue from the box on the shelf behind her. She dabbed her eyes and then slowly lifted her head to look at me.

"I'm sure it's in his personnel file," she said. "But why? The police must have his tie in their evidence room, marked as exhibit A."

I stared at her. Did I trust this woman? She had admitted that she had unrequited feelings for Win. She could very well be his killer. I glanced at her. Maybe it was just a gut instinct or a desperate hope, but I didn't think she had anything to do with Win's death.

"When did you see Win at the bonfire?" I asked.

"I didn't," she said. "Not until . . . his body was found."

"When I saw him earlier that evening . . ." I paused. There wasn't much point in bringing up the scuffle, so I didn't mention it. I cleared my throat and continued, "He wasn't wearing a tie."

Her eyes went wide. "But they're required at company functions."

"Win didn't strike me as someone who was hampered by the rules," I said.

"Harrison—" she began but I interrupted her.

"Was wearing his tie all night," I said.

"I know," she said. "He's always very good about the business. You know I tried to suspend him?"

I nodded.

"I was wrong," she said. "He's a good man. Despite the issues between him and Win, I know Harrison would never have harmed Win."

"But someone did," I said. "And they used one of your ties to do it."

She nodded. She looked pale and a fine sheen of sweat had broken out on her skin.

"Are you all right, Reese?" I asked.

"No," she said. "You know what this means, don't you? One of our own killed him."

Chapter 27

"That's sort of what I figured," I said. "How can I get a list of the ties issued with their numbers?"

"We'll need to go to personnel," she said. She rose from her desk. She looked a bit wobbly, and I understood but we really didn't have time to cater to it. Inspector Franks would be here soon and I wanted to have the information for him.

Reese drew in a deep breath and turned to me and said, "All right then, follow me."

We went back into the hallway that lapped the inner offices like a racetrack. It was brighter now as the sun had risen higher and was streaming in through the windows on the east side. We passed several offices and then Reese pushed through a door marked *Personnel*.

A young woman sat at a desk that overlooked the files.

I figured this was some sort of punishment. All those windows and she got stuck in the room with a view of files. She must have made someone mad.

"Can I help you, Mrs. Evers?" she asked.

Reese forced her lips into a smile that could only be called one because her lips curved up. There was nothing happy or reassuring about the look.

"No, thank you, Rene, I just need to grab some paperwork for the new girl." She paused to gesture to me. Rene looked appalled at my jeans but had the grace not to say anything.

I gave her a tiny finger wave and a superior look. She'd undoubtedly be on the phone to all of the other employees, trying to find out who I was, as soon as the door closed behind us.

"Wait, on second thought, would you mind terribly fetching me a glass of water?" Reese asked.

Rene looked irritated in a "that's not my job" sort of way, but she was obviously hesitant to balk to the boss.

"I wouldn't ask, but I have such a headache starting, and Mary"—she paused to gesture to me—"doesn't know where the watercooler is."

Reassured that this was an emergency and not an abuse of power, Rene gave her an understanding smile. "Of course, I'll be right back."

We waited while she left, closing the door behind her.

"Mary?" I asked.

"Scarlett is too unusual of a name. I didn't want to have to explain what we're doing," Reese said.

"What are we doing?" I asked.

"Pulling Win's personnel file," she said.

"Don't you have all of this stuff online?" I asked.

She strode over to the file cabinet and used the key she had taken from her desk to unlock it. These weren't your nineteen fifties postwar steel cabinets, oh no, these things were some exotic wood that slid out with a delicate whoosh of air. Very slick. Very expensive.

"We do," she said. "But if I access them online, then I have to sign in and anyone else in the company can see that I am searching Win's file."

"Including the killer," I said.

She looked pained. "Let's just say it's better to do this the old-fashioned way."

Reese pulled out the second drawer down and began flipping through the folders. She paused, studied the folders more closely and flipped through them again.

"Something's wrong," she said. "His file isn't here."

We stared at each other for a moment and then the office door began to open. Reese slammed the file shut and snatched a paper off the top of the cabinet.

"So you'll want to have these filled out and returned to me as soon as possible," Reese said.

Rene caught the last half of the sentence, which Reese ended by thrusting the paper into my hands. She then smiled at Rene and took the paper cup of water from her.

"Thank you so much," she said.

"No trouble," Rene said and she resumed her seat at her desk. A glance at her computer monitor showed a complicated spreadsheet, so unless it was one of those quick-the-boss-is-coming fake spreadsheets, she appeared to be doing rather complicated work.

Reese guzzled the water with an unladylike gusto that

made me like her just a little. She crushed the cup in her hand and tossed it into the recycle bin.

"Feeling better?" I asked. I was going for solicitous but somehow I think sarcastic came out.

Reese nodded. Then she turned to Rene and said, "Tell me, has anyone been in to use the files recently?" Rene looked at her in surprise and Reese added, "I'm just wondering if we should do away with the old hard copies."

"Oh, well, Mr. Wentworth was in here a few days ago," she said.

Reese looked at me. I glared back. I was quite certain Harrison had a good reason for looking at the files. Really, I did.

"And Mr. Carson gave a file to the inspector, the older one with the mustache," Rene said.

"Inspector Franks," I said.

"That's right," she said. "Why? Was there a problem?"

"Oh, no," Reese said. "Like I said I was just wondering if they still got any use, and it looks like they do. If you'll excuse us, we'll leave you to it."

"All right," Rene said. She gave us a cheery wave, which I returned even though I felt like I was leaving her a prisoner in the windowless room.

Outside I was again trailing behind Reese. I wondered if Inspector Franks had shown up and was waiting for me downstairs. I wondered if I should call him. I wondered if Harrison was here yet, and if so, what was he going to say when he saw me? Yes, there was a lot of wondering happening but not a lot of doing, mostly because I was afraid to take my eyes off Reese.

My internal caution alarm was clanging and I thought

it might be advised to eyeball the viable exits. I had really admired the egg-shaped building from the outside, but now that I was in it, I wasn't so sure. How did one get out of here in case of an emergency? Or was I just panicking? Yeah, that felt about right.

"I'm going to have to go into the human resources portal," Reese said.

She sat at her desk and clicked away at her keyboard. I chose to pace the length of her office and back. It was a large office. I wondered if that helped the executives think bigger thoughts. Maybe if everyone had spacious offices, they'd all think bigger.

Nervousness was making it hard for me to focus. Who had access to the files? Rene, obviously, but she didn't seem to have an ulterior motive. Still, I figured I'd better check.

"What's Rene's story?" I asked Reese. "She wasn't involved with Win, was she?"

"No," Reese said. "She's new, fresh out of university and happily engaged. She spends more time planning her wedding than she does working."

So the spreadsheet had most likely been a decoy, which made me feel better. It would have been appalling for someone so much younger than me to have a grasp of such a complicated form.

"Who else has access to the files in that room?" I asked.

"Only the senior staff members," Reese said. She didn't look up from her computer. "Tyler, Harrison, Tuesday, Steve, Anne, and of course, Win would have had access as well."

"Who are Steve and Anne?" I asked.

"Two other associates," she said. "They've both just reached their five-year anniversary."

"Tuesday and Anne, did they get neckties, too?" I asked.

"Silk scarves," Reese said. "Do stop prattling, I can't look at this and converse at the same time."

Duly chastised, I resumed pacing. I checked the time on my phone. There was a text from Inspector Franks: Where are you?

I quickly texted back that I was on the thirty-third floor.

I waited but there was no immediate reply.

"I found it," Reese said. She glanced at the small printer in the corner behind her desk. "The invoice for his tie is in his file and it lists the number stitched on it. I'm printing a copy of it."

"Excellent," I said. "Now if the police find that this number is different than the number on the tie he was strangled with, it could lead us to the killer."

Reese moved to stand beside the printer. I noticed her hand was shaking as she pulled the invoice out of it. "I hate to think that it was one of our own."

She moved back behind her desk and glanced at her computer screen. "That's strange."

"What?" I asked.

"Win's file, the file I was just in, was wiped clean," she said. She leaned over to examine the screen more closely and began clicking her mouse. "And I've been locked out."

"Who could do that?" I asked.

"I think you'd better take this paper and go," she said. Her voice trembled and the raw fear made the hair on the back of my neck prickle.

She held the sheet out to me. I started across the room to take it when her office door banged open.

"Reese, Rene tells me you have a new hire . . . what's this?" Tyler Carson stood in the doorway, looking perplexed. He stared at me. "You?"

"Hi," I said.

I gave him a tiny wave as I reached out to take the paper. He was too quick for me, however, and snatched it out of Reese's hand before I could. He glanced at the paper and then at Reese.

"Explain," he said. He sounded angry and I saw Reese flinch. Then she shook her head and blew out a breath.

"I know," she said. "Everything."

She shifted her feet, almost in a fighter's stance. This got my attention. Pale and tight lipped, Reese looked frightened and enraged all at the same time. Emotion was pouring off her in waves and my inner sense of caution was now clanging like a five-alarm fire bell. Something awful was about to happen.

"That sounds very dramatic," Tyler said. He gave her a confused half smile. "Why don't we discuss this in private?"

"No, I know what you did," she said. Her voice was low and growly, sounding more angry than scared now as if her courage had just needed a few minutes to build itself up.

Tyler heaved a put-upon sigh. "We've been over this and over this. I don't know what you think you know . . ."

"Win wasn't wearing his tie at the party," Reese said.

"Pah!" Tyler scoffed. "Of course he was, it's mandatory."

Reese pointed to me. "She says he wasn't."

Tyler turned and looked at me. His gaze was sympathetic and kind as if he felt my tension and was pained by it. I felt myself relax. Tyler was such a nice man. He took

243

the care of his company seriously; I knew he wouldn't let someone get away with murdering one of his staff.

"You were mistaken, weren't you, Scarlett?" he asked. "You were overwrought at the party, which was quite understandable given Win's boorish behavior."

I nodded. *Huh?* I shook my head.

"No, I was up close and personal with his shirtfront," I said. I looked at Reese, who was shaking her head at me. "Not on purpose. It just sort of happened."

Now she was shaking her head more frantically, which made me feel terrible given that she had just admitted to pining for a relationship with Win that he had denied her and here I was talking about his awkward pass at me.

"I'm sure it was because he was drunk and because he hated Harrison," I said. I glanced back at Tyler. "But you're wrong. I am quite certain he wasn't wearing a tie."

"That is quite unfortunate," Tyler said. Then he lunged at me.

Chapter 28

Taken by surprise, I jumped back out of instinct, which was a good thing because Reese hurled a solid glass paperweight at Tyler, popping him in the ribs with a sickening thunk.

He dropped the invoice as he grabbed his side with an *"Oomph!"*

"Grab the paper!" Reese yelled.

I snatched the sheet off the ground. Dancing back just before Tyler caught me with a kick in the head. He staggered forward as I dashed for the door.

"Run, Scarlett, ru—" Reese's voice was cut off with a sickening crunch.

I had no doubt if I went back, Tyler would get the paper, the last bit of evidence that Win was strangled with—and I knew this was no longer a wild guess—Tyler's necktie. I had to hope Reese could fend for herself and I had to keep going.

Now I was damn thankful for my jeans and Converse sneakers. Had I worn a power suit and heels, I never could have bolted out of Reese's office as fast as I did. There is a message there but I had no time to ponder it. Probably it was that normal people in suits don't have to run for their lives, but that's just a theory.

I glanced up at the ceiling and saw a sign that showed a white stick figure running on a green background with an arrow pointing. I assumed this meant *go this way*. I did.

The elevator was out as it would be too easy for Tyler to catch me while I was waiting for it and if he got in with me, he could strangle the life out of me before we hit the twentieth floor. It was going to have to be the stairs. I scanned the ceiling looking for more of the green signs with the little running man on them.

I was lapping the offices in the center of the floor, trying to read the doors as I flew past. I heard a shout behind me and I knew it was Tyler. He was gaining on me. I stumbled. Not helpful but terror makes me a tad uncoordinated.

Finally a severe-looking gray door tucked into the wall showed a picture of a stick figure and an arrow pointing down. I pushed through it, wondering if an alarm would sound. I heard nothing.

I debated going upstairs to throw him off then I could get out on a random floor and take the elevator down. But stairs are not my friend. Even at home, going up the two flights of steps, a total of twenty-four, yes, I counted, and my thighs burned and I was sucking wind by the time I got to the landing in front of my bedroom. It was just embarrassing.

So up was out for the thigh burning but also, what if

the doors were locked from the stairwell side, not allowing me in? I could be trapped with a killer below me and no way out. On that note, I hit the steps running.

I had just cleared the second landing when I heard the door slam open and Tyler was running down after me.

"Scarlett, give me that paper," he yelled.

If I had any doubt about its significance, he had just cleared that up. I grabbed at the door on the landing. It was locked, so I had made a good call there. I ignored Tyler and kept going. I couldn't be distracted. I had to make time, thirty-one floors to go. I could do this. I just prayed he was in worse shape than I was.

Five more flights and I was sucking wind hard. Snot and tears were leaking from my face and I was sweating like I had just run a 10K. My knees were wobbly and my ankles felt crunched. Every muscle in my legs felt wrecked. I kept going.

I glanced up to see where he was. My heart sank. Where there had been a two-story gap between us, we were now at one and he looked like he was gaining on me. I poured the speed on, my feet flying over the steps, my hand skimming the cold steel rail as I put distance between us. I could outrun him. I decided to try and jump down the last few steps to increase the distance. Big mistake.

I did not stick the landing. My ankle turned and my leg went all noodly under me. I fell in a heap. Then I heard a noise that caused my blood to freeze into cubes in my veins; judging by how light-headed I went, the cubes caused my circulatory system to shut down. When Tyler's laughter echoed in the stairwell, I almost passed out.

Instead, I grabbed the handrail and hauled myself up. I

grunted with the effort. The pain in my ankle turned my fear tears into serious pain tears. I hauled myself up anyway.

"Scarlett, seriously stop," Tyler said. "At this point, you're just making a spectacle of yourself."

He had stopped running and was now standing on the landing above me, doubled over trying to catch his breath. I took great pleasure in the fact that he was winded. What can I say? When death is imminent, you take victories where you can.

I pulled out my phone and opened an app.

"Who are you calling?" he asked. "The police?"

I ignored him. I turned my back to him and snapped a quick picture of the invoice then I sent it to the first three people in my contacts, Harrison, Viv and Fee. Someone had to get this, but I didn't have time to tell them where I was. Darn it. I stuffed the invoice into my phone case, hoping it would be safe there.

"What if I am?" I asked. I held the phone to my ear, pretending to call while the message sent with its attachment.

"I'd say that's unfortunate," he said.

"You got that right," I said. He was at the top of the steps just a short staircase away from me. "They're going to bust you for the murder of Winthrop Dashavoy. You strangled him with your necktie and I have the proof."

"Proof? Don't be ridiculous," he said.

"If it's not proof, why are you so determined to get it back?" I asked. "And while we're at it, why did you kill Win?"

"I didn't—" he began but I cut him off. He was a sociopath, he was never going to admit to his crime, but I was pretty sure I had it figured.

"Your wife is a lot younger than you," I said. "It must be hard keeping a beautiful woman like Ava faithful to you, probably keeping her doped up to her eyeballs helps. Is that what Win did for you? You kept him employed so long as he kept your wife 'medicated'?"

It was a long shot, but I was betting I was right. His face went eight different shades of angry red, leaving it mottled and rashy looking.

"You can't prove anything," he said.

"Maybe," I said. "But when I visited your wife the other day she certainly had a lot to say about Win."

He didn't hide his surprise fast enough. I saw the widening of his eyes and I knew I'd struck a nerve.

"That's right," I said. "Your wife knows what you did, too. And she's willing to tell the police and you will be arrested."

I might have overplayed my hand here. Tyler laughed. It was chilling. Then he looked at me with eyes I had once thought were kind but now saw as calculating and cruel.

"I sincerely doubt that," he said.

"Really, why?" I asked. I didn't really care. I was in full-on stall mode now, trying to weigh my increasingly limited options.

"My dear," he said. "Who do you think I have on my payroll?"

That got my attention. I looked at him and saw his Cheshire cat smile.

"Who?" I asked. My voice was barely a whisper but it echoed in the cement walls.

"Your dear Inspector Franks, of course," he said. "Why else do you think he came all the way from his vacation

249

in York if not to clean up this little spot of trouble I've found myself in?"

I gripped the handrail so tightly my knuckles went white. "You're lying."

"No, I'm not," he said. "And you're wrong about me keeping my wife drugged. She came to me damaged, addicted to pills, but she hid it so well for so long, and then, I found out about her condition and discovered who her supplier was. It was Win. I begged him to stop, but he laughed and said his plan was to steal both my wife and my business and there was nothing I could do to stop him.

"Then he showed up at our annual bonfire party not wearing his tie," Carson said. "He knew it was mandatory. I told him to wear mine. He refused and taunted me about the day that he would own my company and burn all of the neckties. I was so angry. He gave me no choice."

"Choice? You're a murderer," I said.

"No, I'm not," he said. "Don't you see? I had to silence him just like I tried to silence you that night on Portobello Road."

Oh, my god! Carson was the man in the mask who had chased me. I felt sick and dizzy. The stairwell spun and I started to see spots. I was afraid I was going to faint.

Carson shook his head at me and resumed walking toward me. I had no doubt that this time he would kill me for sure. I had nothing to lose. I thrust my phone into my coat pocket and threw my leg over the handrail. I slid out of reach just as he lunged for me.

The turns were the worst part. They were very tight and I got my leg stuck the first time and barely got it out before I broke my shinbone. By the second level I had figured it out. Slide backward and kick the legs out at the turns. The heat from the metal on the fabric of my jeans was searing but I kept going, knowing that it was the only way I could outdistance him.

Carson yelled after me and I saw him pick up his pace on the steps but he didn't try to ride the rail like I was. A few more turns and I was starting to get dizzy. If I fell off the rail, I was a dead woman.

By the fifth turn I had left Carson several flights behind and I had to close my eyes for fear that I would throw up. It was a losing battle. A whiff of smoke caught my attention and I glanced behind me to see a man standing on the landing, smoking. Behind him the door was propped open just a crack.

He saw me and his eyes went wide and the cigarette fell out of his mouth and onto the smartphone he'd been looking at.

I grabbed the rail, chafing my hands as I braked to a stop. Carson's steps were ringing out upstairs. The man on the landing was shaking the burning cigarette off his phone. I swung my leg over the rail and ran at him, ignoring the searing pain in my ankle.

"Inside!" I barked. "Inside now!"

He stared stupidly at me until I ran past him toward the door. I grabbed him by the arm and pulled him with me as I yanked open the door and dragged him inside after me, closing the door behind us.

"Does the door lock?" I asked.

He stared at me, not speaking. It appeared I had shocked him into a stupor. I had no time for that either.

"Does the door lock?" I yelled.

The man blinked at me and then glanced at the room beyond me. I turned and noticed that all of the sound in the room had stopped. The office of cubicles filled the room and every person had popped up out of their designated box like meerkats on sentry duty.

A fist slammed against the door and I jumped. The door rattled on its hinges. Carson was banging on it and yelling, "Open the door, Scarlett. Open the door. You can't win this."

"Do not open that door!" I yelled at the man, who had also jumped at the sound of Carson's fist. "The man on the other side is a killer. He will kill you all."

Perhaps I was overdramatizing but I couldn't risk any weakness in the ranks.

A woman at the desk closest to me, with an enormous knot of black hair on her head, cleared her throat and asked, "Do you want me to call the police?"

"Yes, do it now," I said. "Please."

She gave me a quick nod and ducked back down into her cubby. The banging on the door stopped, and the man who'd been smoking looked at me.

"Do not open the door," I said. "He's probably still out there, waiting."

The man nodded, looking scared. He was young, looking to be just out of university. He had a thick mop of black hair and his face was aesthetically unshaven. I had read this was a new look that ad campaigns were using to make men look more virile. Whatever.

"What's your name?" I asked.

"Adi," he said. "I'm just an intern here. Ah, man, I burnt my phone."

"It's okay, Adi, you're doing fine," I said. "Can you tell me what floor I'm on?"

"You're on the eighteenth floor," he said.

"And what office is this?" I asked. I made my voice seem very matter-of-fact when inside I was having a complete freak-out.

It worked. He swallowed and blew out a breath and his voice was calmer when he spoke, "It's Quantum Calculations, it's an accounting firm."

"Okay, can you lead me out of here?" I asked.

He nodded. "Yeah, I can do that."

We passed the girl in the cubicle who was on the phone, and I paused to say, "Tell them that a killer is in the stairwell. His name is Tyler Carson."

I heard the collective gasp emitted from the group. So they knew him. This could go badly for me.

"I have the proof that he killed Winthrop Dashavoy," I said. "I must get it to the authorities, and I need your help."

Adi looked at me then at the door. "Tyler Carson, one of the richest men in England, are you sure?"

"Positive," I said. "He was afraid Win was planning to take over his company just like he'd taken his wife."

There was a moment of silence while the room absorbed this information. Adi studied me closely and then nodded.

"All right then," he said. He turned and looked at the people in the room. "I saw him, I saw him trying to catch her. Whatever you do, do not let him in."

A buzz of conversation began, and two men came forward. They positioned themselves on either side of the door and crossed their arms.

I wanted to weep with relief. Maybe I was going to survive this after all.

"He'll be stuck in the stairwell unless he can get someone to let him out. The lower sixteen floors are a Swiss insurance company, so I don't know how lucky he'll get," Adi said. "You can beat him by taking the elevator, but let's hide that hair of yours."

Adi was taller than me by six inches and he was moving fast. I had to pump my wobbly legs to keep up. He snatched a hooded coat off a coatrack and tossed it to me.

"Put that on with the hood up," he said.

He hit the elevator button while I put the larger coat on over my own. I pulled up the hood, covering my red hair.

"That should work," he said. He adjusted the hood a bit before he was satisfied.

The elevator arrived with the pleasant *ping* of an electronic bell. It was empty. I wasn't sure if that was good or bad. He went to step inside with me, but I shook my head.

"No, stay here," I said. "It's too dangerous."

The doors started to close.

"But—" he began to argue but I cut him off.

"I'll return your coat," I said.

He looked like he was going to jump in with me, but the doors shut. I felt both relieved and disappointed. The coward in me would have liked the company but I couldn't bear it if he was harmed because of me.

The elevator glided down the floors. I remembered that Mim had been very excited about the Gherkin, which was completed a few years before she died. She loved that it was the tenth tallest building in the city, and that its elevators moved at a clip of six meters per second. I couldn't believe these ridiculous thoughts were flitting through my mind, then again, anything to keep the panic at bay.

I glanced up. Surely I should have reached the lobby by now. It felt as if the elevator were crawling. I wondered if Carson had managed to sneak out of the stairwell. Would he be waiting for me? The elevator stopped on the eleventh floor. Three people got on. No one even glanced at me as they stayed on the other side of the compartment, chatting about the upcoming weather forecast for the weekend.

At first, I was annoyed. Why are you stopping my getaway elevator and then talking about inanities? But then I realized that they would make an excellent cover for me to hide behind when we reached the lobby.

When the car stopped, I gestured for them to go first and then I followed, sticking close to their heels as if I were a part of their group.

It worked for about ten steps, but as we came around the corner of the elevator bank, a hand grabbed my arm, stopping me.

I balled my right hand into a fist. If it was Tyler, I was going to drop him with a sucker punch. Okay, I was talking myself up, since the only thing I'd ever punched was a pillow.

"Ginger, what are you doing here? What was that message about? Hey, whoa!"

Luckily, Harrison ducked just before my fist would have connected with his nose. I put so much weight behind it, it spun me around, pushing the hood off my hair while I fought to keep my balance. He caught me about the waist and then frowned.

"Whose coat is this? It's enormous on you," he said.

"Harrison!" I cried. I hugged him hard and fast and then started running for the door. "No time!"

The front of the Gherkin has two massive revolving glass doors. I hit the one on the right with Harrison jumping right in behind me. As it began to turn, I saw Inspector Franks coming in the other. We saw each other at the same time, and in a nanosecond, I knew it was true. Everything Tyler Carson had told me about the inspector was true.

"Ginger, what is going on?" Harrison asked.

I looked at him in panic. Then I started trying to push the door to go faster.

"Franks is bad," I said. "He's a bad cop! Carson murdered Win, I have the proof, Reese might be dead, and we have to get the hell out of here!"

Harrison stared at me and then saw Franks. He didn't hesitate but shoved the door with all his strength. As soon as the sweet rush of November air hit us, he grabbed my hand and we bolted. We were running flat out, past businessmen and women in suits and shiny shoes, racing down St Mary Axe toward Leadenhall Street.

I looked over my shoulder once and saw Inspector Franks with two constables running beside him. They were gaining on us.

"Where are we going?" I shouted at Harrison.

"Aldgate," he said. He glanced back. "If we make it. Run, Ginger, run!"

Chapter 29

We didn't make it. A black sedan hopped the curb and screeched to a halt in front of us. The passenger door was shoved open and I glanced inside to see Inspector Simms looking at us.

"Get in!" he cried.

Harrison looked at me and I shrugged. Could we trust Simms? I had no idea.

"I know about Franks. I know he's—" Simms stopped talking as if he couldn't bear to say it out loud. He looked angry and sad at the same time.

It was a leap of faith but just because Franks had let me down didn't mean Simms would, too. There was no place else to go and Franks was almost upon us.

I climbed into the front seat and Harrison took the back. I had barely shut the door and was just reaching for the seat belt when Simms hit the gas. We shot out onto the street, narrowly missing a couple of pedestrians.

"Slow down, man, you're going to get us killed," Harrison said.

"I can't. The two PCs with Franks left their cars out front. They'll be on us in seconds," Simms said.

I glanced out the rear window, and sure enough, Franks and his two henchmen were running for their cars.

"What about Tyler Carson?" I asked. "I left him in the stairwell."

"Franks's men got him out before we could nab him," Simms said. "This is why I need to get you to safety."

"How did you know where I was?" I asked.

"Reese Evers called me and told me everything," he said.

"Is she all right?" I asked.

"Carson tied her up, but he must have been in a hurry, because she got free and called us," Simms said. "She has a nasty head injury, but she'll be okay. Luckily, I was on duty and not Franks and took the call."

"I'm trying to keep up, really I am," Harrison said. "But I'm lost. Could someone please tell me what the bloody hell is happening?"

Simms gestured for me to do it.

I turned in my seat so I was facing Simms and could see Harrison. Then I started with the memory of Win not wearing a tie, my time with Reese, and ended with Tyler's confession on the stairwell. Both men were silent, not asking questions, just listening.

When I got to the part about Franks, they both looked pained. "And that's when I ran into you," I said to Harry and then turned to Simms and added, "And then you appeared. I don't think I'm overstating that you saved our lives."

Simms nodded. "I've been tailing Franks. Him coming back from York the way he did just felt . . . wrong."

"I can't believe it," Harrison said. "I liked him, really liked him."

"There might still be an explanation," I said. "Maybe he's deep undercover, trying to out Carson."

Simms shook his head. "I'd have known if he was."

The traffic slowed to a crawl and I saw Harrison look out the back window as if he expected Carson or Franks to rise up in the window like Godzilla or King Kong.

"I think we're safe now," I said. "They can't catch us and I still have the invoice, plus I sent you and Viv copies of it."

"You sent one to Viv?" Harrison asked. He scrambled with his phone, pressed the front of it and held it to his ear. He checked the time on his wristwatch and then made eye contact with Simms in the rearview mirror.

"She's not answering," he said.

"That's it then," Simms said. He fired up the siren on the car, forcing the traffic out of our way.

"What is it?" I asked. "What's going on?"

They exchanged a glance as if trying to figure out what to say, infuriating, and then Harry said, "Viv isn't answering the shop phone. She should be open for business by now."

"Oh, god, Viv!" I cried. "She's in danger, isn't she? Just because I sent that stupid text."

"I seriously doubt they're after her for that," Harrison said. "There's no way for them to know about it, but they do know that Viv is important to you, so—"

Hysteria bubbled up in me like a geyser, only the stuff that came out was a flood of tears, snot and a whole lot of panic.

I looked at Simms and yelled, "Step on it!"

As soon as the car in front of us moved over, he floored it, zipping through the traffic in a way that would have made me vomit if I hadn't been singularly focused on getting to Viv.

The dash through London was a start-and-stop affair as we alternately crawled and raced, paused and pushed, shoving our little car to the max as we darted around corners and forced our way to Notting Hill and Portobello Road.

My heart was in my throat as Simms drove by the shop and parked three buildings down at the curb across the street. A sick feeling twisted in my gut as I noted that the window shades were still drawn as if the shop had never opened. I glanced back at Harrison and he had the same tight look on his face.

I went to open the door and Simms held me back.

"Wait," he said.

"But she could be in trouble," I argued.

"And if you go racing in there, it could get worse," he said.

I stared at him. Did I trust him to have the knowledge and experience to get my cousin to safety? He had just discovered that his mentor and partner was bad. Could he do this?

He must have read my doubts because his gaze was steady and he said, "Trust me."

I nodded. "What do we do?"

"We're going to park here," he said. "Then we're going to

get out of the car and walk across the street as if we're headed to the pub. Then we'll slip into the alley and work our way to the back of the shop, where you can let us in, right?"

"Right," I said. I wanted to run, I wanted to hurry, but Simms was very clear that if anyone was watching we had to look like regular neighborhood folks going about their business. I put the hood up on my borrowed jacket so that my hair didn't draw any attention.

"On three?" Harrison asked. "One, two, three."

We all popped out of the car and I noticed that both men turned their collars up and hunkered down into their coats. I didn't know if it was from the cold or to hide their faces. I didn't much care. I just wanted to get to Viv.

We crossed the street with a chilly November wind at our backs. I felt like it was urging us to hurry, which unsettled me even more.

We passed the pub and circled around the large brick building into the alley in back. It appeared empty; only one garage door was open but no one was there. We moved past several more buildings until we reached the back gate of our small patio garden.

Viv's bird feeders brought in flocks of birds and when we arrived they all scattered with some indignant chirps and mad flapping of wings. I swear the ingrates waited for her in the morning and they started singing about breakfast an hour before she woke up. A glance over the wall and it looked as if she hadn't even been out there today.

I reached up to unlatch the gate and lead the way in, but Harrison stopped me.

"Let me go first," he said. I started to argue but he held up his hand. "It makes sense that I'm here as the business manager. If there's a problem, I can bluff that I'm just here to do the books."

"He's right," Simms said. "If you go in and Carson is already here, he'll have no reason to keep either of you alive."

"Except he doesn't know that you have the invoice now," I said. "When I tell him that—"

"He really won't have a reason to let you live," Harrison said.

Shivers rippled down my spine. Still, I felt like I should be the one to go in and save Viv. She was my cousin and I had gotten her into this mess.

"At least connect your phone to mine so we have an idea of what is going on," I said.

Simms nodded and Harrison called my cell phone and I answered it, leaving the phones connected so we could eavesdrop on him while he went into the house. Harrison put his phone in his front pocket, out of sight but easily able to pick up sound.

He reached over and squeezed my hand before he unlatched the gate and entered the patio. I was too short to see over the back wall and Simms stayed hunkered down so he wouldn't be seen. The only way we could tell what was happening was if Harrison told us on his way inside. It was maddening.

I heard him unlatch the back door. He didn't call out a greeting, which told me Viv and Fee weren't in the workroom in the back. My heart sank into my feet. This was bad, really bad.

Simms was listening intently to my phone. I wondered if his training taught him to listen for other sounds, and if so, was he hearing good noise or bad?

I wanted to ask him, but I didn't want to miss any sounds coming from my phone by talking over them. A tense few minutes, okay probably seconds, passed with no noise. I checked my phone to see if it was working. Our phones were still connected.

I bounced on the balls of my feet trying to channel my anxiety. What was taking so long? Why wasn't Harrison saying anything?

Thud! Oomph! Then I heard a low voice say, "Run."

The sounds that came out of my phone weren't voices. It sounded like someone just got clobbered and let out a groan. I didn't think, I acted. My hand shot up and unlatched the gate and I was pushing my way into the garden. Simms grabbed my arm, but I ripped myself free.

"Scarlett, you have no idea what's going on in there," he whispered.

"I know, but that's my cousin and my future boyfriend in there," I hissed. "I have to go."

He stared into my eyes, which were probably looking a bit deranged. Then he held out his hand and said, "Give me the phone."

I slapped it into his hand and shut the gate. He caught it before it slammed but I really didn't care who heard me coming. These were my people and this was my place and I would do anything to protect them both.

Chapter 30

I paused at the back door. I had no idea what I would find. Had both Vivian and Harrison been strangled like Win? I couldn't bear it. I steeled myself for whatever horror awaited.

I opened the door and stepped inside to find the workroom—empty. I'm not going to lie that was a bit of a letdown. I had been gearing up to kick some booty and here I was standing in an empty room. I listened for sounds from the shop; there was nothing.

How could this be? It was almost midday, Viv was supposed to have opened the shop hours ago. How could it look like it had never been opened? Even if Carson or Franks had beaten us here, would they really have pulled the shades to make the shop look closed?

My heart was thudding hard in my chest. I crept through

the workroom. I heard nothing, not the muted sound of voices, or whimpers of fear and pain, or even the sound of a body being dragged. Yes, I have a dark side.

At the doorway, I hunkered low and peered around the doorjamb. The store was dark. I could see the hat stands in the shadows holding up Viv's creations as if an audience of heads were watching the unfolding drama. Clearly, my dark side was getting downright creepy.

I stepped into the room, aiming for the door which led upstairs. It was closed, which I thought was odd because why wouldn't whoever raided our shop and house just leave the door open? I should have thought it through.

The lights in the shop snapped on and I blinked against the sudden brightness.

"Come in, Scarlett, we've been waiting for you," Tyler Carson said.

He was standing in one of our seating areas and on the blue chair in front of him was Viv, tied up and gagged with some of her own velvet ribbons. Sprawled on the floor at her feet was Harrison, and he was unconscious.

"You have been quite the busy little bee, making trouble for me," Tyler said.

I often hear people say that redheads are crazy, prone to temper, you know, all the old clichés that can't be attributed to the color of hair really. And yet, when I saw two of the people I care for most in the world at the mercy of a man that I knew to be capable of murder, well, I went a little loco.

One minute I was blinking against the light and the next thing I knew I had launched myself claws fully extended right at Tyler at top speed and full force. I planned to give him a good thrashing, as they say.

Unprepared, Tyler went down hard, taking a display of Viv's new caps with him. I landed on him hard with an unintentional elbow to his sternum, which looked like it hurt him pretty badly. Yay me.

"Stay away from my friends!" I shouted in his face. I am a much better yeller than a fighter.

Carson tried to shove me off, but I clung like a burr hoping that Simms would charge in and help me, but it wasn't Simms who lifted me off Carson and planted his foot on him, pinning him to the ground. It was Harrison.

"Ginger, you are amazing!" Harry hugged me tight and I returned it in full, I was so relieved that he was upright and not, well, dead.

"You're making a mistake, Harrison," Tyler said.

"No, you did," Harrison said. "You were my mentor. I had nothing but the highest regard for you and look at you now. A broken man, a killer, what did you think you were going to do? Kill us all?"

"No," Tyler protested. "I swear. I just needed the evidence. Let me up, I promise you, I would never have harmed you."

"The knot on my head begs to differ," Harrison said. "And the ribbons cutting into my friend's skin prove otherwise."

"You have to listen to me," Tyler said. He began to thrash and Harry put more weight on him holding him down.

"Ah, but you see, I don't," Harrison said. Then he punched Tyler right in the temple, knocking him out. His shoulders relaxed and I realized how angry Harry had been.

"Help Viv," he said. "I've got him."

"Simms has my phone," I said. "Call him."

On wobbly knees, I hurried around the couch and began to work on untying Viv while Harrison took his phone out of his jacket to let Simms know what was happening.

"Are you all right?" I asked as I worked on the knots, knowing full well that she couldn't answer me but asking anyway. "I'm so sorry, Viv."

"Not your fault," she said as I loosened the tie from her mouth. "Ouch!"

"Sorry," I said. Her long hair was caught in the tie. I dropped the ribbon and hugged Viv close. "Thank goodness you're all right. I was so afraid!"

"I'm fine." She hugged me back. "And now that I know you're safe, I'm even better."

"Your husband is a politician, isn't he?" I asked.

Viv barked out a laugh. "Oh, Scarlett, you're trying to get me when I'm vulnerable, aren't you?"

"Is it working?" I asked.

"No," she said.

"Why not?" I cried. I pulled her to her feet. "If you had been killed I wouldn't even have been able to contact him. Viv, you have to tell me who he is."

She began to cry and I put my arm around her shoulders to comfort her. "Come on, sweetie, it can't be that bad."

"Oh, but it is," she said. "His name is William Graham and, oh bother, he's an insurance man in France!"

This last bit was said on a wail. I can honestly say of all the things I had expected, that was not it.

"So he's employed!" I said. Always looking on the bright side, that's me. "Yes, but *ew*," she said. "Insurance!

It's so boring. He might as well be a telemarketer or a used car salesman."

"Viv, seriously, that's incredibly shallow of you."

"No, it's a compatibility issue. I'm a creative type," she protested. "We have nothing in common and we'd never get on in the long run. Don't you see? That's why I left him. We're doomed."

"Girls, I appreciate the moment, really, but—" Harrison began but I interrupted him.

"Not necessarily, Viv," I said. "Opposites attract for a reason, maybe the two of you would balance each other."

Viv shook her head, not just a little bit but in a frantic motion back and forth.

"Do you really feel that strongly about it?" I asked. "It seems to me you're not really giving it a chance."

"No, Franks," she croaked. My stomach fell into my feet. I knew what she meant with just one word. I turned to look over my shoulder and there he was.

Inspector Franks stood in the doorway to upstairs. When Harrison would have charged forward and thrown a punch, Franks held up a very large knife. I recognized it from our kitchen; since neither Viv nor I cooked, it looked wonderfully sharp and terrifyingly lethal.

"Back up," Franks said.

We stumbled backward. Harrison moved in front of me and Viv, obviously trying to shield us.

"How could you fall in league with Carson?" I asked Franks. My sense of betrayal was acute. I had thought Franks and I had a sort of bond over his liking country music from the States and me being from the States. "How could you?"

He cringed and I knew I'd made a direct hit. There was weariness in the sagging flesh around Franks's eyes that made me realize he was tired, exhausted in fact. I had no sympathy. None. He had chosen his path and now he had to live with it.

"Just give me the invoice," he said. "Everything else can be managed, no one will be harmed, but I have to have that invoice."

"Why?" Harrison barked. "Because Tyler is lining your pockets with gold?"

Franks shook his head. A look of raw pain flashed across his face. This was personal. The only reason Franks would have helped Tyler cover his crime was for personal reasons, and for Franks, personal meant family.

And then I remembered that the very first night I had met Ava Carson, she had told me her father liked country music. I had thought little of it at the time, but now . . .

"Oh, wow, she's your daughter, isn't she?" I said. "Ava Carson is your daughter."

I heard both Viv and Harrison gasp and Franks nodded. I didn't think it was possible but he looked even wearier than before; it was as if he was aging right before my eyes.

"She was such a beautiful girl," he said. He looked rueful. "She takes after her mother that way. She left us for the high life, said we were too low class for her, then she married *him*. He kept us away from her, never allowed us to visit or make contact. Then he called, he needed help, he promised he'd give us our daughter back. My wife . . . I . . ."

Franks broke down, and I couldn't help it. I felt my eyes fill up with tears for the man who had been trying to get his daughter back. Then I remembered that getting his daughter back had almost cost me and my friends our lives. My tears dried up.

"It's too late," I said. "You can't save Tyler from what he's done."

"But—" Franks protested.

"Simms has the invoice," I said.

Franks dropped the knife as his knees gave out and he caught himself on the edge of a chair. Harrison jumped forward and snatched up the knife from the floor. Just then the back door slammed open and Simms arrived with several constables.

I watched as Franks and Simms faced off. Franks looked distraught.

"I'm sorry," he said.

Simms jerked his head toward the door. "We'll discuss it at the station. Where's Carson?"

"Behind the couch," Harrison said. "He's having a bit of a lie-in."

Simms's unibrow rose up and he gestured for his men to go and gather Carson.

"I'll need you lot to come to the station and give your statements," he said to us. Then he turned to me. "I'll need the evidence."

"You already have it," I said. "It's in the back of my phone case."

"Brilliant," he said. He took my phone out of his pocket and took the invoice out of the back. As he glanced at it, I could see his heart grow heavy. I could tell that just as Harrison was struggling to accept Tyler's betrayal, Simms was doing the same with Franks.

"I'll drive us in," Harrison said. "As soon as we've all calmed down."

Two constables trudged back into the workroom, carrying a very groggy Carson between them. We stood witness as Simms made a formal arrest of Tyler Carson for the murder of Winthrop Dashavoy.

There were more police cars and officers outside. It didn't take long for Carson and Franks to be put into separate cars and whisked away.

The three of us stood staring stupidly after them. I don't know if it was the aftermath of the horrific morning, or the relief of finally getting the truth about Viv's husband, but I suddenly felt the need to get my British on to restore my nerves.

"Spot of tea, anyone?" I asked. I didn't wait for the others but headed straight for the kettle.

Chapter 31

It was the fourth Thursday of November. I was lying on my bed, thinking about pumpkin pie and feeling pathetically homesick. I turned on my tablet and looked for a live feed of the Macy's Thanksgiving Day Parade, but of course, due to the time change the city of New York was still asleep, which bummed me out even more.

It had been a little over two weeks since Simms had arrested Carson. Harrison and Reese were trying to salvage the business, but it looked like it was going to be an uphill battle. It is hard to trust your money to a company where the CEO murders his staff.

Harrison seemed up to the challenge, and I had no doubt that he could do anything he set his mind to. However, the hours he was putting in, and with that awful Tuesday Blount, were a bit worrisome. I had seen him only once since we had given our statements at the station following Carson's arrest, and he had looked exhausted all the way down to his shoes.

This was another reason I was not feeling up to the day. I was afraid I was losing Harrison to his work and his life with Tuesday. She had said I wasn't cutthroat enough to survive in Harry's world. Maybe she was right.

The two women who had been in the shop a few weeks ago, Carol Landers and Mary Tavistock, had called me twice to tell me that Lucas Martin, their friend who ran an art school in Paris, was very interested in having Viv come and teach. One part of me loved this idea as it was an excuse to go to Paris, but another part of me was too tired to even think on it. I wondered if Viv would care if I had a mental health day.

A knock on my door roused me enough to grumble, "Come in."

Viv stood in the doorway, looking terrific in a blue cashmere sweater dress and knee-high black suede boots. It was much dressier than we usually looked for the workday.

"Are you being a layabout?" she asked. "Come on, time to get up and face the day."

"I'm calling in sick today," I said. "I have a fever or a rash or something and it might be contagious. I'd steer clear if I were you."

"What you have is an advanced case of homesickness," she said. I looked at her in surprise. "What? You didn't really think you were hiding it that well, did you?"

"I did try," I protested.

"I know," she said. She looked very sympathetic, which

did help but not enough to make me get out of bed. "Let's go shopping; that will perk you up."

So that explained the pretty dress and boots. She wanted to shop. It was tempting but no.

"I can't," I said. "I'm too weak."

"Well, now I am worried," she said.

I refused to be moved by her concern. I pulled the covers over my head and burrowed deep like a badger.

"Fine," she said. "I'll bring you some tea and toast, all right?"

"Coffee," I corrected her. "And a muffin, thank you."

I didn't remove the covers until she left. I went back to my tablet, looking for something, anything that would fill the gaping hole in my chest. I wasn't sure how much time passed. I played several rounds of solitaire and read the *Daily Mail* online, trying to distract myself or numb my brain, hard to say which.

Once my parents were up and about in Connecticut, I supposed I could video chat with them, but it wasn't the same and I was afraid it would only make me feel worse.

I felt my throat tighten. I shut off my tablet, knowing there was nothing that would help. I figured I might as well wallow. The tears were just brimming my lower eyelids when there was a knock on my door again. Viv with coffee, well, that was something.

I took a second to pull down on my lower lids, which made the tears recede, and then I coughed and called out, "Come in."

The door pushed open but it wasn't Viv who stood there but Harrison.

"Ah!" I cried and yanked the covers up over my head.

"Good morning, Ginger," he said. "Or should I say afternoon?"

"Go away!" I cried. I was not at my most hospitable before coffee or a hairbrush.

"Viv said you're feeling under the weather," he said.

He sounded as if he was getting closer. I poked my face out from under the blanket.

"Do you always enter a woman's bedroom when she specifically tells you to go away?" I asked.

He smiled at me and I felt like maybe I needed to lie down. How can one man's smile do that to a girl? Then I noticed the cup and bag in his hand.

"Yes, I do," he said. "Especially when I've been demoted to delivery person, I believe you requested coffee and a muffin."

I shoved one hand out of my blanket and took the coffee. "Thank you," I said. "You can just leave the muffin on the desk on your way out."

His eyebrows lifted. "Are you giving me the bum's rush?"

"No, I'm merely encouraging you to go on with your day," I said. He was in a suit. It was obvious he had business to attend and I didn't want to hold him up.

"Too bad," he said. He took a long flat rectangular case out from under his arm and dropped it on the bed. I glanced from it to him as he made himself at home on the foot of my bed.

"Present?" I asked.

"Backgammon," he said.

"I don't know how to play," I protested.

"I'll teach you," he said.

I eyed him warily. Shouldn't he be at work? He still

looked tired. Maybe he needed a break from the chaos that had consumed him since his boss had been arrested.

"All right," I said. "Can I at least clean up?"

He cocked his head to the side as he studied me. "No, I like you this way."

Yeah, that was probably one of the nicest things a man has ever said to me. I let the bedcovers fall off my head and ran my fingers through my hair in an attempt to smooth it.

He watched me with amused eyes and I realized I wasn't even embarrassed to be seen in my thermal top and flannel pajamas. I would have been mortified if it had been anyone else, but Harry had seen me in my pajamas before and I realized that even though we weren't dating we shared the sort of intimate knowledge about each other that only a true friend knows, such as how you look in your pajamas or when you're asleep, what your favorite cocktail is or how you like your steak cooked, or what sort of things make you laugh or make you low.

"You're here because I'm homesick, aren't you?" I asked.

"Viv might have mentioned it," he said. "But also, I thought you'd like an update on Inspector Franks."

"Oh, I would," I said. "I still have a lot of mixed feelings about him."

"DI Simms said there is an internal investigation pending to see if Inspector Franks actually impeded the case or not," he said. "In the meantime, he is not under arrest. And on a happier note, he and his wife have reunited with their daughter, Ava. She is being treated for her drug addiction and the three of them are planning to leave London to go and live in York, assuming Franks is cleared."

"I know he made a bad call in his attempt to help Carson," I said. "But I can't really fault him given the circumstances."

"Carson could have killed you, first in the phone booth and then in the stairwell. I can't forgive Franks for endangering you like that, not even if I understand his concern for his daughter," Harrison said. His jaw was clenching and I could see he was angry, so I decided to change the subject.

"So you think you can school me in backgammon, do you?" I asked.

The grin he sent me was pure joy. "Oh, I know I can."

He wiped up the board with me in the first game, but I rolled several doubles in the next and trounced him.

"How is that possible?" he asked, bewildered. "Were you fibbing? Are you really a backgammon shark in disguise?"

"Let's play a tiebreaker and see," I said. It had been sheer dumb luck on my part but there was no need for him to know that.

"I have a better idea," he said. "Why don't you get dressed and I'll take you out for an early dinner."

I glanced at the clock. It was past three. Where had the day gone? But then, I knew. I'd spent it laughing with Harry and had forgotten all about my homesickness. I waited for it to kick in again with the realization but it didn't. I was okay, still missing my folks, of course, but okay.

"All right," I said. "Give me five, er, twenty minutes."

Harry packed up the board and left my room. He was in a suit so I wanted to look equally presentable. I snagged a heather green sweater tunic, a long plaid skirt and my brown boots and dashed into the bathroom across the hall to do a quick overhaul. I was back in fifteen minutes, mostly because I realized I was starving, always a motivator.

Harry was sitting on the top steps, tapping on his phone. He looked up with a smile when I burst out of the bathroom door. His dark wavy hair hung over his forehead and his bright green eyes sparkled at me.

"You look lovely, Ginger," he said.

My heart did that ridiculous fluttery thing and I felt my face grow warm. "Thanks, Harry, you're not so bad yourself."

He led the way down the stairs, and I felt my nose twitch. Something smelled amazing, more than amazing, something smelled like a turkey roasting. I shook my head. I must have Thanksgiving on the brain if I could pull that smell out of my mind, either that or I was so hungry I was starting to hallucinate.

We walked through the doorway into our flat and I stopped short with a gasp. Standing in the middle of our flat, wearing a Native American headdress and a Pilgrim's traveling hat, were my mom and dad.

"Happy Thanksgiving, pet," my mom said and she opened her arms wide. I didn't hesitate. I ran right into her hug.

"Happy Thanksgiving, princess," my dad said and he wrapped his arms around both of us.

I cried big, hiccuppy, gulping sobs of ridiculously happy tears as I clung to my parents in a hold that I'm sure mooshed their middles although they were too polite to say so.

"How did you . . . why didn't you tell me . . . what are you doing here?" I babbled.

Mom handed me a tissue. "Viv and your friends arranged it all as a surprise."

"You did?" I whirled around to find Viv standing with Fee, Nick, Andre and Harrison.

"Happy Thanksgiving, Cuz," Viv said. She hugged me tight and I was sure I was going to puddle up all over again.

"But how?"

"Andre picked them up from the airport yesterday and they spent the night at their place," Viv said. "You and I were supposed to be out shopping while Nick cooked the turkey this morning, but you ruined that so I had to call in Harrison to babysit you and make sure you didn't leave your room."

"You were alone with her in her room?" my dad asked Harrison. He looked very stern.

"Playing backgammon, sir," Harrison said. "I swear."

My dad laughed and clapped him on the shoulder. "Just joking, son, but good answer."

"Andre, you picked up my parents, and Nick, you made the turkey," I said. I felt myself bubble up again as I hugged them.

"And I made sure we had the right cranberry sauce from a can," Fee said. She blew an orange curl out of her eyes as she proudly held up a can of jellied cranberry sauce.

I'm not quite sure why but that gesture did me in and I blubbered as I hugged her, too. There was nothing pretty about it. I was sure my nose and eyes were red as the tears coursed down my cheeks. This was what it meant to be truly loved, and I felt it all the way down deep.

"Thank you all so very much," I croaked. My throat was tight and the words hurt on their way out, but it was okay because I was enfolded in a group hug that quite simply meant the world to me and let me know that I was truly home.

Nick outdid himself with the turkey and the trimmings. After the meal, we sat in the sitting room and talked and laughed and joked until my parents, still jet-lagged, called it a night. Nick and Andre followed shortly thereafter, taking Fee home with them.

Harrison stayed and helped Viv and me clean up. There was so much I wanted to say to him, but I didn't know where to start. I think he understood because when I walked him to the door, he hugged me and didn't let go. We just stood there, wrapped around each other as if imprinting the moment on our hearts and minds.

"I like your parents," he said.

"They like you, too," I said. I could tell because my mother gave him seconds of pie, and my father called him "son." He never did that.

I felt him relax as he stepped back. "Well, that's a good thing because I expect they'll be seeing a lot of me in the future."

Then he kissed me, swift and sweet and full of promise. I found myself grinning when I locked the door behind him. As I checked the shop, I could feel Ferd the Bird watching me.

"Don't look so smug," I chastised him. "I'm still not dating him."

Ferd didn't look like he believed me, and honestly, I wasn't sure I believed myself.

When I arrived upstairs, Viv was sitting at the kitchen counter, picking at the last of the pumpkin pie.

"Harry get off all right?" she asked.

I was momentarily shocked but then remembered that the Brits use "get off" where we use "take off," making it an entertaining question at the very least.

"Yeah," I said, trying not to smile. "Say, I wanted to ask you about something."

"Let's hear it then," she said. She handed me a fork and I stabbed a bit of crust.

"There's an art school in Paris that is interested in having you come and teach a class in millinery—" I began but she cut me off.

"No," she said. "Absolutely, not."

"What? Why?" I protested. "I really want to go to Paris. It's been ages and this could be so much fun."

"Then you teach the class," she said. She rose from her seat and tossed her fork into the sink.

I frowned at her. The Viv I used to know would never have passed up an opportunity to visit the City of Light. Something was wrong. And then it hit me.

"Your husband is in Paris, isn't he?"

"Shh!" She shushed me as if my parents could hear on the floor above us.

"That's it, isn't it?" I asked.

"The last I knew that's where he was," she said. She looked miserable.

"Viv, you can't go on like this," I said. "You have to resolve this situation once and for all."

"I don't know what to do," she said. "I don't know what to say to him. Things were left very badly between us."

"Please," I said, holding up one hand. "I am the queen of the bad breakup. I will guide you in fixing this mess."

"Promise?" she asked. She looked so hopeful that I knew the situation had been weighing on her more than I had realized. I nodded and she reached across the counter and hugged me tight.

"Paris, here we come," I said.

Be on the lookout for more Hat Shop Mysteries
from Jenn McKinlay.
In the meantime, keep reading for a special
preview of her next Cupcake Bakery Mystery . . .

VANILLA BEANED

Coming April 2016 from Berkley Prime Crime!

"Viva Las Vegas!" Tate Harper sang at top volume. Then he did some sort of shimmy shake thing that Melanie Cooper was sure was supposed to look like a suave, swivelly hipped Elvis but more resembled a person suffering electrocution.

"Viva, Viva Las Vegas!" Angie DeLaura slid across the bakery floor, bumping hips with Tate while they sang together.

Mel was behind the counter loading the display case with vanilla cupcakes and ignoring them, well, trying to ignore them. Her two best friends in the whole wide world were making complete jackasses out of themselves, so it was pretty hard to remain indifferent.

"What? Now we're offering cupcakes and a show?" Marty Zelaznik asked. He'd entered from the kitchen and stood beside Mel while he tied on his apron.

Marty was the main counter person for Fairy Tale Cupcakes, the bakery that Mel owned with Tate and Angie. He was a bald, shriveled-up prune of a man, but the older ladies loved to baby him and he had a special charm with the young ones as well. To Mel, he was as integral to the success of the bakery as the flour in her cupcakes.

"They're a little overexcited about our upcoming road trip," Mel said.

"So you're really going?" Marty asked. He kept his voice low as if he didn't want Tate and Angie to hear him, although Mel was sure there was no way they could over the racket they were making.

"Yup," Mel said.

"You know you don't have to if you don't want to," Marty said.

"Yes, I do," Mel said. She put the last cupcake in the display and closed the back of the case. "We are three equal partners in this venture, and they want to franchise."

She tried to keep her voice neutral but she couldn't help it if the word "franchise" came out sounding more like "black death."

"So what if they do?" Marty asked. "You're the master chef; I think that gives you extra say."

Mel reached over and squeezed his hand. "It'll be o—"

Whatever she'd been about to say was interrupted by the front door being yanked open with an enthusiasm that did not ring of joy.

"Vegas? As in Las Vegas? Oh, hell, no!"

Tate and Angie stopped singing and their sick dance moves stumbled to a halt.

"Liv!" Marty goggled at the woman on the other side

of the shop. "What are you doing here? You know we have an agreement. Neither of us sets foot in the other one's bakery."

"Oh, sugar lips, relax," Olivia said.

Marty's bald head turned an embarrassed shade of fire-engine red at the endearment and his bushy eyebrows rose so high he almost had a hairline.

He opened his mouth to speak but Mel got there first, mostly so that Angie would not feel behooved to tackle the other woman, who happened to own a rival bakery, to the ground and drag her out by her feet.

"How can I help you, Olivia?" Mel asked.

Olivia's gray corkscrew curls popped out of the topknot on her head as she strode forward.

"I saw a social media update that somebody is opening a franchise in Vegas, is this true?" Olivia demanded.

She stood across the display case from Mel in her blue chef's coat looking like she wanted some dough to knead, or more accurately some butt to kick. Mel glanced at Marty, Olivia's sort of boyfriend, and he gave her a sheep-ish shrug.

"What if it is?" Angie asked.

She turned and strode toward Olivia, looking like she was getting ready to do some damage. To Olivia's credit, she didn't even flinch, which was saying something since the two of them had rumbled before.

Tate deftly slid in between Angie and Olivia and looped his arm around Angie's shoulders, anchoring her to his side. He met Mel's gaze over Angie's head and gave her a bug-eyed look that she interpreted to mean he wanted her to take the discussion elsewhere.

Right, because Olivia was about as easy to move as a mountain. Feeling cranky about the Vegas sitch, Mel opted to go on the offensive instead.

"Maybe we are. What's it to you?"

Tate's eyes almost popped out of his head while Marty clapped his hands onto his bald head as if he had just witnessed a car crash and had no idea what to do.

"I'll tell you what's it to me, Princess," Olivia snarled. "With a tasty knuckle sandwich."

She began to roll up her sleeves. Mel stepped around the counter. She was feeling just ornery enough to welcome a scuffle. She and Olivia started to circle each other like two boxers squaring off in a ring.

"I can serve up a pretty mean five across the lip when I want to," Mel said. She hoped she was the only one who heard the lack of confidence in her voice. Truth to be told, when upset, she was more of a snacker than a fighter.

"Code Blue," Tate said to Marty.

"What?" Marty squawked.

"Code Blue!" Tate yelled. The veins in his neck began to pop and Mel wondered how much pressure he was exerting to keep Angie in place. "We talked about this; this is a Code Blue situation."

"I can't remember what Code Blue means!" Marty cried.

"Think!" Tate growled.

Marty's face puckered up with the effort. Then he broke into a smile. "Oh, yeah!"

With a smooth move the likes of which were seen only in Fred Astaire movies, he vaulted over the counter by swinging his legs up and over the side, dropping to his feet right in front of Olivia.

She looked surprised and then went to move him aside, but Marty wasn't having it.

"No, Liv," Marty said. "We need to talk."

Olivia made a face like she'd just tasted something sour.

"You just don't want me to pound your boss into the tile," she said. She sounded put out about the whole thing and Mel felt behooved to protest.

"Who says you're going to pound me? I could take you with one hand tied behind my back," Mel said. She lifted her right arm and flexed her muscle; it sagged and she hastily put her arm down.

"This thing between you and me," Marty said. He pointed from her to him and back. "We need to make it official."

Olivia blinked. Her mouth trembled and her eyes got watery with tears. "Oh, Martin, I don't know what to say."

"That's right," he said. He puffed out his chest as if he was quite proud of himself for coming to this place in life. "I think it's time you became my official girlfriend."

Olivia's face fell. "What?"

"That's right," he said. "I want to make you my main squeeze."

Olivia plopped her hands on her hips and glared. "What does that mean? I get a dresser drawer in your bedroom of my own now? Is that the elevated status you're offering me?"

"I thought you'd be happy," he said. "You're always asking me where this is going. I figured we could make our coupleness official-like."

"Official-like? We've been dating for over six months. I thought I already was your girlfriend," she said.

"Oh," Marty said. He cast Tate a worried look, who helped him out with a shrug.

"Martin Zelaznik, you're about as romantic as a case of beer," Olivia snapped.

"Hey, a microbrew can be very romantic!" Marty argued.

"To a knuckle-dragging Neanderthal," Olivia shouted.

"She has a point," Angie said. "Six months is a long time for a woman to go undefined."

"True that," Mel said. "You really can't string a girl along like that."

Marty looked outraged. "What? You're on her side now?"

Mel and Angie exchanged a look of understanding with Olivia. Then they nodded.

"Well, if that don't beat all," Marty exploded. He glowered at Olivia. "Fine, if you're looking for more from me then spell it out. What do you want exactly?"

"Living together," Olivia said. "If we're a couple, then I want that crinkled-up old face to be the first thing I see every morning and the last thing I see before I go to sleep."

"Is she even listening to herself speak?" Tate asked Angie.

"Shh," Angie hissed.

"But . . . but . . . but . . ." Marty stammered.

"I'm giving you one week to decide," Olivia said. "If you choose not to live together then we're done, finished, as in, *Hit the road, Jack, and don't you come back no more, no more, no more, no more.*"

Mel glanced at Marty while Olivia sang the rest of her

ultimatum. He looked like he'd been smacked upside the head with a rolling pin.

Olivia turned and strode to the door. "Oh, and Princess, I hope your Las Vegas franchise blows up in your face but thanks for having my back with him."

Olivia jerked her thumb at Marty and Mel nodded. She wasn't sure if she and Olivia had just bonded or not. She suspected not since Olivia was still cursing the possible franchise.

The door shut behind her and they all turned to look at Marty, who slid into one of the dining booths like he was a melting ice cream cone.

"Live together?" he asked. "As in cohabit?"

Tate sat across from him and leaned across the table to pat his arm. "You okay?"

"This is all your fault," Marty said. He pointed a bony finger at Tate like he wanted to stick it right in his eye.

"My fault?" Tate asked. "How do you figure?"

"Code Blue," Marty said. "You had to call Code Blue."

"There was going to be a smack-down," Tate said. "We agreed that if that ever happened, you would step up and distract Olivia with relationship stuff."

"Really?" Angie pushed Tate farther into the booth and sat down beside him. "When did you two pumpkin heads come up with that plan?"

"About the time Marty and Olivia started their thing," Tate said. "I knew there would come a day when she would barge in here and start something. This was our agreed-upon plan to, er, redirect her ire."

"Well, that sure worked out, now didn't it?" Marty asked.

His sarcasm was thick enough to frost cupcakes with. "Now what am I going to do?"

"Looks like you have to make a decision," Mel said. She sat beside him and patted his shoulder.

"Aw, man," Marty whined.

"Look, it could be worse," Angie said. "She could be pressuring you to get married."

Marty gave her a flat stare.

"Or not," Angie added before glancing away.

"One week," Marty moaned. "How am I supposed to figure out the rest of my life in one week?"

"It'll be okay," Tate assured him. "We'll be in Vegas, so you'll have the whole place to yourself, plenty of time to think things through."

"I've got a better idea," Marty said. "How about I go to Vegas and you stay here."

"You know I would absolutely take you up on that if it weren't for the whole franchising thing," Tate said. Mel thought it spoke well of him that he managed to look so earnest. "We're going to be so bored what with meetings with the lawyers and the person wanting to buy in and looking at real estate. Really, it's going to be a total snooze fest. Right, girls?"

"Right," Angie said. She kicked Mel under the table and Mel added, "Ouch . . . right."

One look at Marty's narrowed gaze and Mel knew he didn't believe them, not even a little.

From *New York Times* bestselling author
Jenn McKinlay

❧ ❧

HAT SHOP MYSTERIES
CLOCHE AND DAGGER
DEATH OF A MAD HATTER
AT THE DROP OF A HAT
COPY CAP MURDER

❧ ❧

PRAISE FOR THE HAT SHOP MYSTERIES

"A delicious romp through my favorite part of
London with a delightful new heroine."
—Deborah Crombie, *New York Times* bestselling author

"Fancy hats and British aristocrats make this
my sort of delicious cozy read."
—Rhys Bowen, *New York Times* bestselling author

jennmckinlay.com
facebook.com/jennmckinlay
facebook.com/TheCrimeSceneBooks
penguin.com

M1600AS0915